HORSE SENSE

HORSE SENSE

Karin Bundesen Baltzell
and
Georgianne Nienaber

Authors Choice Press
New York Lincoln Shanghai

Horse Sense

Authors Choice Press
an imprint of iUniverse, Inc.

iUniverse books may be ordered through booksellers or by contacting:

iUniverse
2021 Pine Lake Road, Suite 100
Lincoln, NE 68512
www.iuniverse.com
1-800-Authors (1-800-288-4677)

Horse Sense is a work of fiction, but it was inspired by actual events. Some locations, events, and organizations contained in this novel exist, but are used fictitiously. All other plots, themes, dates, events, locations, organizations, persons, names, and characters contained in this material are products of the authors' imaginations. Any resemblance to any locations, organizations, persons, or characters, real or fictional, living or deceased, is entirely coincidental and unintentional.

Quote by Charles de Kunffy copyright by Dressage Today.
Used with permission.

ISBN-13: 978-0-595-38299-6
ISBN-10: 0-595-38299-1

Printed in the United States of America

For Prince Charming who started it all.

The improvement of the horse is its own reward.

—Charles de Kunffy

ACKNOWLEDGMENTS

The authors wish to thank their families. They supported, in every sense of the word, this project. They cajoled, prodded, read endless copies of the book, and made suggestions of every sort, from start to finish. We wouldn't have done this without them.

In addition, we would like to note our appreciation to Dr. James Collins of the University of Minnesota Veterinary School. He gave us the Royal Tour, and helped us solve the mystery, all for the joy of doing it and helping two people he didn't even know!

Frank Dosal arranged a tour of the Federal Building, which gave us insight and first-hand information beyond the ordinary. We couldn't have had the intimate knowledge of the inner workings of the Federal Building, rules, and regulations had he not "gotten us in the door."

The authors are indebted to Donna Danorovich-Meyer, Elizabeth Rufenach, Kathy Blake, Nancy Smith and Laura Rosecrance. Sarah Nienaber worked behind the scenes with Web design and cover graphics, and was the inspiration for one of the characters in the book.

All of the above would have been to no avail had not Robin Netherton, Editor Extraordinaire, bailed out our bacon.

Special thanks to horse lovers everywhere, who are trying to help horses and make life better for them. They cannot speak for themselves.

PROLOGUE

▼

Tremor snorted as the electric fan kicked in, circulating the heat that collected in the barn's rafters. Usually the black stallion was oblivious to the whirring and soft swish of the fan blades, even in the middle of the night. The only other barn sounds were the shifting hooves and soft rustlings of the mares rearranging the hay in their mangers. Something had unnerved the magnificent horse, setting in motion ancient instincts of wariness and flight.

At seventeen-plus hands, he could see to the far end of the barn aisle. Nothing. He sniffed, ears forward, then back, noting nothing more than the usual barn odors of urine, sweet manure, leather, and oils. He snorted again and went back to picking through the stems of hay that had fallen to the mat on his stall floor. The Dutch Warmblood mare across the aisle shifted in her box, jingling the bells that her owner had tied to her stall door.

Tremor was aptly named. The horse had shocked the classical European dressage community when his true abilities became evident. It was unthinkable that a thoroughbred off the track could ever compete with the European masters—even if he was the grandson of Seattle Slew, descendant of Bold Ruler, with the blood of kings coursing through his powerful heart. A savvy amateur trainer had noticed his performance form, and the big black had rocketed through the FEI international dressage levels, surviving accusations of steroid use and competition fixing. No other horse could do the extensions and suspensions as perfectly as he.

World-class trainers had shaken their heads in disbelief. His lineage had produced the perfect horse, in the body of a thoroughbred, no less. The combination of Tremor's marvelous genes and a willing and brave heart went on to take the Olympic gold for Team USA. Now, two years later, the semen of the retired racehorse was worth $100,000 a session. Serious breeders hoped that his offspring would not only share his spectacular obsidian color, but that the perfect diamond star would be the kiss of the gods on the foreheads of his progeny. Of course, this meant nothing to the stallion. His world was the dressage ring and his ample stall. There were times when he longed for the herd. Not in a conscious way, of course. It was more of a longing for companionship. He looked forward to the stream of visitors that would line the paddock fence at his turnouts, the constant parade of veterinarians, and the curious who would stop by his stall to look, but not touch. Stallions as a rule were not to be approached, but Tremor truly enjoyed his human contacts. Humans could offer him nothing more than the herd; nevertheless, they were the only source of touching he had. The sure hands of his groom on his face and especially around his ears pleased him even more than the steady hands of his riders, and he had carried the best riders in the world. Grooming offered some comfort and relief from his longing.

The stallion snorted again. Someone was there. He sensed it first, seconds before the shadow played on the mare's stall door. His stomach wasn't telling him it was feeding time, and other early-morning intrusions had meant it was time to be loaded into the van. His liquid eyes focused into the darkness as the figure approached his stall. Tremor shifted toward the grate in his door, eager to embrace the companionship that was surely to be offered.

The door slid open and he nickered softly. A treat. Gloved hands offered him a sugar cube, which he chomped politely, yet with some hesitation. He was trying to decipher the smell, but it didn't matter; the hands were gentle. They started to play around his ears and he felt content.

The furtive human worked quickly putting a saline-soaked sponge on the stallion's right ear, with an alligator clip holding the sponge firmly in place. Without the sponge the clip might leave a mark. Unacceptable. No traces could be left behind.

Tremor shook his head lightly at the new sensation, but it wasn't unpleasant, so he waited patiently for the carrot he smelled in the coat pocket. The hands continued moving downward from his ear, past his throat, and lingered at his jugular groove. A sharp slap on his breast caused him to startle, but he immediately calmed as the hands worked over his ribs and to his flank.

The hands lifted his tail, his only flaw, really. Thoroughbreds never seemed to have the perfect long flowing tails of the warmbloods, yet in his racing days, Tremor's tail was like a banner trailing behind him. He felt something being attached to the skin around his anus. Again, that was nothing unusual, since he had his temperature taken often. He nuzzled the silent one, hoping for the carrot or a stroke on his face.

Nothing. No pat, no murmur of encouragement as the person brushed past him and out of the stall. A general uneasiness began to creep through the stallion's consciousness, increasing his rate of breathing. Sensing danger, Tremor turned to look at his flank. The mare across the aisle was responding to Tremor's anxiety. The feeling of alarm spread swiftly as the instinct of the herd pulsated throughout the building. The mares began to rock back and forth in their stalls.

All movements seemed to be in slow motion compared to the emotional energy that was flowing through the barn, as the horses became one entity in their anxiety. The gloved hands took the ends of the wires attached to the stallion and jammed them into the electrical outlet on the nearby support beam.

The whites of the mare's eyes were the last thing Tremor saw before his majestic black body crumpled into a heap on the sawdust. Hearing no whinny or warning snort, the mare returned to her water bucket and took a long drink. She restlessly knocked against the wooden sides of her box and pawed the ground.

A muffled curse floated through the barn as the shadow form slipped in Tremor's fresh excrement, a macabre signature of death by electrocution. The wires were retrieved and coiled, and the sponges went into the pocket with the carrot. The shadow played along the wall and vanished into the deep night as the sound of partying came from the main house.

CHAPTER 1

▼

The sleek Gulfstream looked puny next to the other jumbo jets. From it two passengers emerged and were immediately clutched by the bitter wind. Huddling deep into their coats, as if the fabric could really protect them, they scurried toward shelter. The wind pushed them sideways as its icy fingers tried to grip anything loose. They pressed forward, heads bent.

Carlos was the first into the terminal, and he was aware that John was shivering.

"Quite a change of pace from Patagonia, eh, old buddy?"

John looked at Carlos, crossed his eyes, and said, "What a genius. I bet you could even be an investigator for a living! You sure do know how to detect the most subtle clues!"

The old friends laughed, thumped each other on the back, and made their way to customs with their carry-on bags. Once their passports were examined and stamped, they turned to each other again for the briefest of goodbyes. That was easy to do. They had been friends since the sixth grade, and they saw each other often. One was short and rotund, the other tall and athletic. But there was an ease between the two of them bred from long years of sharing lives and travels.

"Hasta la vista, my wily friend!" said the smaller, balding, man.

"And you, too, Minnesota-boy. Thanks again for the plane ride back, and the hospitality. Tell your dear Iris hello for me!" And with that, Carlos swirled out into the terminal, leaving John to make his own way to the ticket desks, where he needed to arrange for the next trip he and his wife Iris were planning.

The airport was busy for this early in the day, and Carlos found himself dodging people and luggage. There seemed to be lines everywhere. He looked over the tops of heads, many still in snug hats, and tried to see where there were open spots to move. It was at times like these that he did not mind being well over six feet. His height, along with his muscular build and Latin features, always gathered stares. At least, he thought that was why people looked at him askance. Women would have said it was because he was drop-dead gorgeous. His dancing, piercing eyes seemed especially to catch their attention.

The crowding was the worst part about re-entry from his time in Patagonia. It shattered the peace he had gained from the wilds. Carlos began to deep-breathe. He was glad he had eaten the last of the Argentine fruit while he was on the plane. He would have hated to have had to throw it out at the insistence of some stolid customs agent.

As he found his way to the Caribou Coffee stand, he thought that of all the places he had traveled, Patagonia was truly one of the most stunning. He was pleased that he had just spent a month there with dear friends. Yet though he loved Patagonia, he recognized its irony. With the beauty always came the beast. There was so much poverty, and so much wealth.

But then, his job was to deal with people who had money, or who wanted to get it through insurance collections. People with money, lots of money, were constantly looking for ways of spending it, and then of increasing the value of what they'd bought. A favorite money dump was horses. Not just ordinary horses, but horses that also provided excitement, training, and challenge. And Carlos was the man who in the end saw to the exchange of money—or not.

It was his job to go to the rough places. However, he had never gotten used to the choice of so many wealthy people to pay enormous sums of money to be inconvenienced. And Patagonia definitely could be considered inconvenient. But then, some of the wealthiest acquired their funds by nefarious means and wanted to be someplace remote. Someplace very difficult to get to. Someplace an insurance investigator like Carlos would never go to check up on their claims. Someplace like Patagonia.

Carlos Dega was not known to be an ordinary insurance investigator. He looked into horse claims. That was all he did. It involved plenty of travel. What he liked most about his job was that he often was given the most difficult cases, after the regular investigators had given up or were ready to cash in million-dollar portfolios. The challenge made his blood race and his mind quicken. He'd gained admirers in his field for his tenaciousness at going after the kernel in the mystery, and solving it. He'd gained enemies as well.

He was good at what he did…the best, as a matter of fact, and he knew it. Some people interpreted his confidence as arrogance. He never felt that. But at times it grated on those he worked for. At his best he was passionate. At his worst, he was fierce.

Horses were more than a commodity to him. Yes, the best show horses represented serious investments, but investing in a living creature was not the same as purchasing a ten-year CD. Horse investing was much more complicated and sometimes much more sinister. Life and death could be too easily manipulated for financial advantage.

Carlos knew this was his personal soapbox. As far as he was concerned, horses were the most abused and mistreated animals in America. Impossible obstacle courses taxed the animals' endurance and cardiovascular systems, often pushing the animals to the brink of serious injury and beyond. So often owners viewed the animal as an article of commerce or a showpiece. When the merchandise failed, the owner's investment also failed, unless events led to an insurance payoff or tremendous stud fees.

As he worked his way toward the taxis, Carlos heard his pager beep. He didn't remember turning the damn thing on, and he wished he hadn't when he saw the phone number and message crawling across the readout. Susan Lindstrom, Assistant U.S. Attorney in the Minneapolis Federal Courthouse. "Urgent…important case. Please call immediately. 612-545-5800."

The thought of an urgent case made his stomach turn. He hated injustice. He might have a chance to help make things right, at least for one animal.

Still, Carlos had spent time with Susan before. He felt unsettled about how they had parted ways. She had a special charisma, and a way of making him feel…he couldn't put his finger on it…he'd have to work on what it was she did to him.

He managed to wind his way through the endless airport construction, into the skyway, and back down to the street, and then ran across to the cab area. He had to wait in line. He tried to keep the deep breathing going and let his shoulders come down from his ears. Determined to maintain the peace of the South, he distanced himself from the traffic noises.

He counted about twelve people in line ahead of him. Then he glanced at the person getting into the next cab—a smallish woman dressed in black. Her shoulder pack had the Olympic emblem embroidered on the side. With her head ducked down, she popped into the cab. He noticed a trim ankle being pulled inside. The door slammed, and she was gone.

Carlos trembled. He bit his lip. It couldn't be Kate. He was just in a reverie. Kate was…where now? In Spain? In Brazil working with the polo ponies? It would be too much of a coincidence for her to be coming home now, at the same moment he was.

He realized his hands were wet with sweat, despite the cold. There were several places where his soul was still tortured, and Kate fit one of those slots. He had loved her truly once, and hadn't recovered from her rejection of him. It had been a lot of long years since he had trusted women. Since Kate, actually.

He had tuned out the noise so effectively he didn't hear the horn honking next to him. The cab driver had the passenger window rolled down.

"Hey, buddy. You want a cab, or what? You're next in line."

"Oh. Yeah. Thanks." He jerked on the handle and folded his lean frame into the seat.

"Forty-seventh and Abbot."

"Is that near the Linden Hills area?"

"Yeah, closer to that than Fiftieth and France in Edina, but more like halfway between the two."

"Great bakeries in that neighborhood. Lots of great bakeries," the driver said.

"Which is your favorite?" Carlos never tired of looking for little locally owned bakeries, especially if there was a coffee shop with the real stuff in it, home-roasted.

The cab driver was local. White-bread type. Probably some Scandinavian derivative. Carlos could only guess what he would choose. It took quite a while for him to answer.

"Turtle."

"Hummm?" Carlos's mind had wandered to the phone call he had to make. He didn't want to answer the beeper page Susan had sent. He had decided that he would go home, check the silk fern, have a good workout, and then face the call.

"Turtle. You know, Turtle Bakery. Linden Hills. Not far from you. I love that place."

Carlos could not think of a Minnesota cab driver as being a cabbie. That might be so in New York, Chicago, L.A. or Atlanta, but not Minneapolis. Life was a bit more straightlaced here, more reserved, and therefore it assumed a more proper demeanor. "Oh, yeah. Me too."

"You know, I was hoping you lived further out, like maybe Elk River."

"Why?"

"I had to wait two and a half hours to get this fare, you know, in line at the airport. Now, if I go back there, it will be another two-and-a-half-hour wait in line with the other drivers till my next fare. Can you imagine the taxes we drivers pay? The license for the airport is sky-high. Not to kid ya about the sky part." He chuckled at his own pun. "I mean to tell ya, it's rough. I can hardly clear my expenses every day with these airport fares."

Carlos didn't know if that was a rush to get a better tip, but he let it blow over him. He had other things to think about. He kept nodding and "mmmm"-ing as the cab pulled off Highway 62 onto France Avenue. Not too far to his house. He couldn't really think of it as home. Leaving John and Iris' estancia felt like leaving home. He realized he was going through a culture shock. A big one.

A few minutes later he was paying the cab driver and wishing him well in the airport queue. The slate-gray sky was typical for this time of year. He looked up. Carlos often thought Minnesotans spent half the day, when there was sunlight, looking up to savor it. The other half of the day they spent looking up to see what the sky was going to do, when and if a storm was coming or going. It was a habit bred of long years of working around the weather. He tried not to let it rule his life, or his workouts, but it did. To think he had begun to take the weather for granted while down South made him shake his head at himself.

The house was spotless, just as he had left it. He liked order. It lent serenity to the mind. He kicked the door and let it stand open to the February air. A little freshness would do nicely—at least for a few moments. Here, a few moments in the cold could seem like a long time.

The elusive Minnesota winter light bathed his living room. He loved the leather chairs, oriental rugs, and deep matching sofas that surrounded the fireplace. These were rooms that he felt reflected his sense of order and stability. His office, his private bastion, was painted a deep red, and the walls were filled with pictures of horses. Some of the photos were of him in dressage uniform standing next to the horse. Each picture held a memory for him, as they represented cases he had solved or horses he had ridden.

He checked the fridge to see what he had left for himself. Living alone did not have the surprises bestowed upon those who lived with others. He found four bottles of St. Pauli Girl, some apples that were past their prime, and a few frozen $1.99 dinners. The six jars of dill pickles merited consideration. He reached in and grabbed a large cold one, and sucked on the pickle juice as he contemplated what he would do.

He decided to take time to stretch his limbs, mind, and soul a bit and go for a run. His run would be delicious. He knew enough to enjoy it, as he didn't know when he would get another. If Susan's phone call meant what he thought, he would be busy, even though he didn't want to work just yet. He felt good, despite the hours of flying. He was rested in both body and spirit. Patagonia always did that to him.

Carlos found his heavy sweats, wind gear, Gore-Tex running shoes, and stocking cap. He warmed up by stretching, jogged in place to get his body heat revved, and then raced out the door to do his ten-mile loop around Lake Harriet, Lake Calhoun, and Lake of the Isles. Even in the early afternoon, the paths around the lakes were crowded. People were exercising their dogs, talking with friends, walking, jogging, and pushing baby strollers. Carlos never tired of seeing the great mix of abilities, skin colors, and sports. In the spring there would be rollerbladers and bikers, once the ice, snow, and grit were cleared from the pathways.

He was right. He enjoyed his run in the crisp air enormously. The miles seemed to have no bearing on his mind, as he mulled over some of the horse cases he had been involved with and heard about during his career.

Carlos had seen so much in his investigations. Some of the cases he could prove, the rest were shadow thoughts, a sickening knowledge that ate at him. The methods of killing were many and unspeakably evil. He never ceased to be shocked by what humans would do to animals, especially horses. He'd seen legs smashed with crowbars, burnings, and injections of salmonella. Ping-Pong balls in the nostrils effectively cut off the airways, but the idiot who thought of that torture forgot to remove them, an easy win for the insurance company Carlos was working for at the time.

One asshole of an owner tied a piece of sheet-metal to the back of his race-horse and turned him out in an electrical storm, all because the horse had had a few lackluster races. As fate would have it, the lightning missed the horse and hit the guy's house instead. The fire department responding noticed the sheet metal, which had been left attached to the horse in the confusion.

What really got to Carlos was that there was nothing illegal about killing your own horse unless outright cruelty or insurance fraud could be proved. His job was to focus on the fraud. Everyone who even had the barest notion about killing their animal, or anyone else's animal, should be sent to jail on charges too numerous to mention—at least that was his feeling. Then Carlos corrected himself. It was more than a feeling. It was his mission. He advocated for horses. Represented them, really, much as a lawyer might

He rounded the curve of Lake Harriet and adjusted his breathing. He looked at his watch. He had a good pace going. The serotonin was kicking in, but it didn't seem to take the edge off the memories of his cases. It was usually like this before he started a new case. His mind was trying to find relationships.

Killing horses for money had been a dirty little secret in the industry for years before Susan Lindstrom and some nameless little snitch brought national attention to a few of the indiscretions of the show-horse world. But there was so much more. The scams involved owners, veterinarians, trainers, top Olympic riders, gigolos, and hit men. The whole mess made many politicians' escapades look like a cakewalk.

This horse stuff rarely got the juicy media coverage. It wasn't sexy enough…although there was plenty of sex to go around, too. Lonely heiresses had con men consistently preying on their desolation and vulnerability. Oh, there were a couple of stories about the heiress who disappeared from the New York theater district while on holiday. She was worth millions, and her body was never found, at least according to the official report. Someone dug up a corpse in a county forest preserve outside of Cincinnati. The medical examiner said it wasn't the heiress. When the dental records were requested, none could be found. The records finally turned up, and when they exhumed the body for a second time, the head was missing. It was anyone's guess at this point whether it was her or not. But it certainly looked suspicious. Of course, any corpse without a head would look suspicious. And then, there were no traceable fingerprints. Heiresses are not prone to be fingerprinted.

Carlos remembered his peripheral involvement in that case. The heiress, who knew nothing about horses, had purchased a string of worthless racing stock at the urging of her gigolo boyfriend. The boyfriend was a suspect for a while in the murder investigation, but that went nowhere. No one could figure a motive…although there sure was plenty of opportunity. Carlos was in charge of the disposition of the horses, since he was often called upon to do appraisals. At least this time the animals were still alive. Too many times the "investment" was dead and he had to figure out whether the "accident" was phony or not. As far as Carlos was concerned, a horse killing was murder…even if the feds couldn't, or wouldn't, use that label. He knew, and he would continue to work to make horse murderers take responsibility for their actions.

Carlos mentally shook himself. This run should be for him. It was for The Zen of the Mind where all else faded from "his little gray cells," as Hercule Poirot would say. He suspected that soon he would be taking another hard, up-close-and personal look at the horse industry. It was his job, but something about all those previous cases racing around in his head made him feel uneasy. Maybe he felt this nervousness because there were too many unresolved murders—both horse and human. And he was an idealist. He wanted to solve them all and bring every lowlife to justice.

He felt invigorated from the run, and was grateful there were plowed walks and trails. No telling when the next storm would come to make running outside much more difficult. While he was cooling down, he called Susan. Better face it now. He dialed her direct, private number. Either she was at her desk, or she wasn't.

She was in. He couldn't say he was pleased. He'd take another month off if he could.

"Carlos?" she said when she heard his voice. "Is that really you?"

"Yeah, sure." Before he'd even finished the words he could have kicked himself. That was pure and simple Minnesota talk. Yeah, sure—tinged with a Spanish softness.

"You don't sound like yourself. What's with all the heavy breathing?"

"Just got back from a run."

"How far did you run?"

"Oh, you know, the usual around the lakes. Made some good time, too."

Susan let out a little sigh. "For a guy almost forty, you're in great shape."

"Careful, now. My age is a sacred thing. I have two whole years before I hit those big numbers."

Susan laughed. She heard Carlos say, "Susan, I gotta tell you, I am not glad to hear from you."

She was disappointed to hear that, but tried not to let it show. "I know, Big Guy, but come up and see me as soon as you can. There's a new case, and you're the only one who can help me with it. We've got some things we need to discuss, and I don't want to talk about it over the phone."

"That makes sense. By the way, how secure is your office?"

"We're talking Minnesota here! People are too nice to breach security. Besides, this place is built like Fort Knox. You know it's a new building. New security. Top of the line. No one is going to be in my office that I don't invite."

Inexplicably, he was irritated. "No, Susan, that's not true. Remember last year when the city offices in St. Paul were bugged, and it was all over the front pages of the Star Tribune? No one knows who did it or why. I need to remind you, we are dealing with some nasty people here, not your typical Minnesota Nice."

"Just come in. Stop the lectures."

"Yeah. Sure. Be there in about a half an hour." Damn! He'd said it again. He was Minnesotan straight through his Hispanic skin. Through and through. He figured Minnesota lurked in his bone marrow.

CHAPTER 2

▼

Susan Lindstrom turned off the speakerphone, looked under the phone for a bug, shook her head, and stretched as she stood up to look out the window. She wouldn't know a bug if it bit her. She smiled wryly at her own pun.

The view left a lot to be desired. Although the Federal Building was a dream for everyone who used it, the new building did not come with a new view. Looking at that maze of concrete where people parked their cars didn't do much to relax her mind. Next to the car park was a pink building that housed Lefty's Lounge. It was somewhat funky, and when she worked late at night she saw some very interesting people enter and leave. But her favorite line of focus was the old Milwaukee Railroad clock tower. It brought back memories of train rides as a child, and of an era that seemed to have more time, at least for her.

She felt slightly annoyed at Carlos, but even more upset with herself for playing into his paranoia. He always brought out intensity in her, and now was no exception. She knew of no one who felt lukewarm about Carlos; either they were very cold or passionately enthusiastic about him. Susan felt the term "hot" worked for her.

She didn't get to be a top name in the U.S. Attorney's office by allowing fear or paranoia to enter the equation. Barely thirty-five and standing just less than five feet four, she had red hair that was a perfect complement to her, fiery personality, which was especially visible in the courtroom. Judges, defenders, law clerks, and other prosecutors respected her courtroom delivery and her dedication to her clients. Her legendary work ethic included marathon eighteen-hour days. The steady clip-clip of her spiked heels on the marble hallways of the Federal Courthouse was her signature.

This case was taxing even her well-known abilities. Someone was murdering horses, but no one in the horse world was talking. This frustrated her. Susan knew someone had to know something, but her usual informants were not forthcoming, and she could get no leads strong enough to follow.

She had seen the bodies piled up in the freezers at the University of Minnesota Veterinary Hospital, and heard about more at equine clinics in New Jersey, Texas, Illinois, New York, Rhode Island, and L.A. Follow the money to the enclaves of the rich and horsy set, and you'll always find a dead horse or two, she thought.

Susan knew of magnificent show horses that had insurance policies and medical care better than her own. These horses started at $100,000, and the owners had every reason to take good care of their investments, or so they claimed.

She knew this recent horse death was the tip of some great iceberg. Somewhere there was a much larger, hidden picture. Carlos had more experience with this sort of thing, and she wanted him to help her discover solutions that could be lurking behind the demise of a great animal. Convincing him to help her was going to be tricky. Susan knew. He had been hard to coax into aiding her the last time. He didn't need the money, so the usual dangling carrot did nothing for him. Susan had learned that Carlos received big percentage payments when he saved his insurance contractors huge dollars. He was a shrewd stock market investor as well. It amounted to his being independently wealthy.

Carlos had never confided in her, but she knew more about him than she probably should. A few computer checks here, some newspaper clippings there, and the pieces of Carlos's life had begun to fall into place. She trusted him, but her researching skills were always itching to be used. And, as an attorney, she couldn't help but feel that more information would yield more advantage. Personally, she wanted to know more about the tall, lean man who was rarely flummoxed in a horse death case. He wasn't so lucky in relationships with human females, and Susan could see why. Too silent. Women liked to talk. But given his tendency toward silence, he made a good listener. There was a calm around him most of the time that could give a woman an anchor in a storm.

Carlos knew the show-horse world better than anyone. He could be so helpful in this case. There had been rumors that he had been through something horrid. Susan wasn't sure what had happened. Maybe some day he'd tell her.

Hell, she detested the shady horse world she was investigating. She had told her sister she'd be crazy to let her niece ride anywhere in the Minneapolis area. Of course, that was an overstatement, because there were some nice stables, but she only acknowledged that grudgingly to herself. And then there were the horses. They could capture a heart in a second, if people let themselves be open to them.

Which brought her back to this case. She knew this latest death had to fit into the whole picture, and she needed Carlos before the evidence disappeared. A horse death didn't leave you with a body for any appreciable time. The freezers couldn't hold a carcass of twelve to fifteen hundred pounds for very long before it was sent to the rendering plant. People liked to get their money's worth from their investments, or cut their losses and collect insurance. Those dealing with horses were always moving on.

Susan was one of the first federal prosecutors to put two and two together when the 1986 tax reform act eliminated sport horses as depreciable assets. It didn't take a rocket scientist to notice that an awful lot of horses started dying from unusual causes after that. These were so common that even innocent accidents had the aura of suspicion about them. Just this year at the World Dressage Finals in Palm Beach, there was an accidental short in the wiring under the footing in the arena. Two horses suffered seizures and fell before it was discovered. It turned out the whole episode was due to the carelessness of an electrician, but the episode made her files anyway.

This horse thing was an unbelievable cottage industry. Dressage, especially, was a concept that took her a long time to grasp. An esoteric, ancient form of riding that emphasized unseen communication between horse and rider, the sport didn't exactly capture her imagination or that of the public. Susan got more interested in the sport when the career of the most famous racehorse in the world, Tremor, took an unexpected turn, and the animal won the gold medal in dressage at the Olympics. Susan learned then that it was difficult for a racehorse to switch professions, as it were, from racing to dressage. She was still trying to figure out the warmblood vs. hotblood issue. She knew changing from racing to dressage had something to do with this blood issue.

Tremor's image was immediately and heavily syndicated after the Olympic win. Maya, Susan's eleven-year-old niece, was the proud owner of a Beanie Baby image of the big thoroughbred, not to mention a Breyer horse model that was almost impossible to obtain. The fact that Maya was so smitten scared Susan. She wished there was some way she could shield her from the terrible news.

Susan's horse investigations almost always led her down paths she would rather not travel. There were barns filled with pedophiles and worse, but no one wanted to hear about it. Even the movie industry was buying into the shiny horse fable. Cinemas were showing films that just perpetuated the romantic myth about horses. Susan preferred to think of it as the wacko horse world, populated by charlatan healers at best and pond scum at the worst.

But, again, she was overreacting. She had met some wonderful horsy folks, Carlos being one of them. And there were many owners and managers of barns dotted throughout Minnesota and Wisconsin who were delightful. And although she hated to admit it to herself, she loved the horses. It was her anger at those using horses as an industry that colored her view and slanted her usual objective eye.

Susan knew her weakness was her tendency to overreact. But with her red hair and fiery energy, she was not the slightest bit inclined to moderate her reactions. She got where she was, thank you very much, due to them.

CHAPTER 3

▼

Susan was happy to see Carlos. It had been a while. She noticed he was more gaunt than he'd been the last time they met. He was still muscular, with great shape and tone, but somehow there was a greater edge to his spareness, and she felt sad for him. There had been talk of his "troubles," but she had not actually seen him since the heart-wrenching event. Because of what had happened to him, she hated the whole horse world even more. Not the horses, but the milieu in which they were forced to live as show animals. Carlos had helped her realize there were undesirable people in the world doing unspeakable things to horses, and sometimes doing awful things to people as well. People she cared about.

All business, Susan didn't let on she had a soft spot for Carlos. She looked up from her desk, checked her wristwatch, and asked, "Trouble finding a parking place?"

"With three ramps within three blocks? I don't think so. Nice to see you, too, Susan. Guess we can skip the chit-chat then, huh?"

"Sorry, Carlos, I didn't mean to sound abrupt. You know I'm glad to see you."

"For the work I do, or for my quintessential being?" He raised his left eyebrow and there was a hint of a smile playing around the edges of his full lips.

"First a lecture, then the philosophizing. Now I know why you're the man for this job." Carlos loved watching Susan laugh. All that red hair pleased him when her humor and dander were up.

"Well, what of this new job, this new case?" He started to sit, and then thought better of it. "I have an idea. Let's go outside."

"Carlos, you know this is February in Minnesota. Are you thinking a stroll through the skyways?"

"Actually, I was thinking of going to the Caribou Coffee shop down the street. Grab a steaming brew, chat, be less formal. I was, indeed, thinking of going outside. You know, the Great Outdoors? You city folks think of going to the skyways that connect all the buildings downtown as being outside?"

Susan brushed the jab aside. "Is this more of your paranoid stuff?" She fired the question from slightly tight lips while crossing her arms over her chest.

A nice chest, Carlos noted.

"You may not realize it, Susan, but I've been flying a long time from far away. I am tired, not pleased to have to jump into work again, and don't need you to be the consummate lawyer and have you cross-examine me. Are you coming with me, or not?" He knew he sounded tough, and didn't mean too. This was one of the things he and Susan had done in the past—get edgy.

She gathered her coat in her arms, found her all-purpose boots, and snatched up her wallet. "I'm with you. Let's go."

They came out of the building, turned right, walked over a block, and then turned south on Nicollet Mall. There were shops, small businesses, restaurants, and bookstores. It was a friendly street, and several people waved at Susan as she went past. She loved this part of the city. There was such a mix of architecture and faces, and she liked the amalgam of different businesses. It wasn't all steel, glass, and stone here. This was her neighborhood.

A few blocks later they turned into the Caribou Coffee shop and were immediately assaulted with the smell of powerful brew. It forced Carlos to comment, even though their walk had been taken in silence.

"Now, this is an intimate spot for a private chat." He looked at her and let his eyes wander over her ears and neck when he said the word "intimate." "Remember that, Susan. The best place to hide, or, in our case, conduct private business, is out in the open, with lots of people around. It makes it harder for listeners to pick up on a single conversation."

She was still piqued with him, still disbelieving that anyone would go to all that trouble, to hear what they were saying. She let it pass with a pleasant nod. She didn't notice that Carlos was toying with her slightly.

"Tall cappuccino, decaf, skinny, please," was her only reply. It was directed toward the pimply-faced guy behind the counter, who looked like he should still be in high school, and maybe was. Carlos was elaborate with neither his order nor his words. "Black regular."

The kid shouted to someone behind the next counter. They moved over and waited for their order. When they found a small round table that didn't wobble too much, they took off their coats and warmed their hands around the familiar cups with the caribou deer leaping across the imagined turquoise meadow.

"So, Susan. Now I am ready. Tell me the news and why you called upon me, freshly back from my Argentine paradise. Your call said urgent. If a horse has died, these things usually are. Who has died now?"

That was one thing Susan always appreciated about Carlos. He said "who," not "what." Horses were people to Carlos, and that made him seem, somehow, just a bit more vulnerable and human. She was hoping that would make him more open to her. Sometimes their edginess with each other confused her.

"Oh, Carlos. He is such a beauty. Was. Seventeen hands high. Volcanic black. He was out to stud, and getting very high fees. One night he was put to bed by his groom, and the next morning, yesterday, he was down in his stall. Deader than dead. He was in his prime. Nothing else was more disturbing than to see the distraught groom in the photos taken at the scene by the local vet." She sighed. "He's at the U of M, of course. They're the only facility with a cooler big enough for a guy that size."

Troubled eyes followed her mouth as she spoke. "And the name?"

"Well, we know the owners were absentee. I assume they are important folks in the horse circle. There is actually a consortium that owned him. I can get you the list of names."

"Yeah. That would be good. But I really wanted to know the name of the horse."

"Tremor." He let his breath out slowly, looked out the window, and blinked hard into the light coming in from the window. He focused out for a long time.

Susan let him have his space.

"We should go together to see him," Carlos said.

"I was afraid you were going to ask me to do that. I don't think I can."

"Right. I'll go. If I think I need you, I'll page you." He stood up abruptly, ran his fingers through his thick, rather long black hair, and took a deep breath.

Seeing his hair made Susan stop in the midst of picking up her empty coffee cup. It shone from sheer health, and the nape of his proud neck was circled with a few wavy curls that had escaped his combing. She liked seeing his hair longer. It made him appear more warm and carefree. His hair was almost like the majestic mane on the now fallen stallion.

Carlos turned and raised an eyebrow toward her.

They threw their cups into the trash. As Minnesotans, they prided themselves on being tidy. They walked onto the street and felt the humidity in the air. More snow would come tonight. As they rounded the corner by the Courthouse, Carlos said goodbye with a small wave from the brim of his cap. Susan smiled one of those wan, lukewarm, I'm-thinking of-something-else smiles, and turned to cross at the corner. Neither of them saw a dark figure in a navy down parka and stocking cap follow Susan across the street.

CHAPTER 4

▼

Carlos slid easily into the black leather bucket seats of the red Dodge Ram pickup. Leather seats weren't the best choice for Minnesota winters, but the smell and feel of the leather reminded him of the saddle. While waiting for the engine to warm up, he opened the file folder Susan had given him in the coffee shop.

He wasn't prepared for his response to the photos. The sight of the magnificent black lying in his own excrement caused Carlos to gasp involuntarily. The bitter cold air seared his lungs, making him cough. As an insurance investigator, he had seen more gruesome photos, such as those of the show jumper in Florida that had its front legs cracked by a crowbar in a botched scam. The horse had bolted from its trailer and into the path of a semi on Alligator Alley. Tremor's death, however, was personal, and a hundred times more devastating. The fact that Tremor had been stabled at Grande Glade would make this job even harder for Carlos. There were too many ties to the past. Too many secrets. Too many lies. Somehow, he really didn't want to know the answers about this death, but he owed it to Tremor. He had known that horse, had felt his warm breath, scratched him between his ears, and looked into his eyes. Tremor would be counting on him, somehow. Carlos jammed the gears of the big truck into reverse, squealed his tires as he jerked into forward, and sped much too fast down the ramp.

Grande Glade was the showpiece of the Twin Cities horsy set. Its miles of white PVC fencing that never needed paint contrasted sharply with the peeling cedar fences of the struggling facilities that surrounded the metro area. There were dozens of barns from Forest Lake to Delano, but none were as pretty or expensive as Grande Glade. Room, board, and training were significantly overpriced there compared to the competition, but the rich divorcees and widows who subsidized the show-horse world seemed to think that the more they paid for a service, the better it had to be. Basic rules of supply and demand had nothing to do with the economics of owning a fancy show horse. There were cheaper and better facilities around, but it was Grand Glade's impression of wealth that attracted even more money. And money meant power. Grande Glade could throw its weight around.

Grande Glade boasted the anchorwoman from Channel Seven, the governor's wife, various strata of Mary Kay ladies, as well as several heiresses as showpiece boarders and clientele. And children. Lots of wannabe Olympic hopefuls came here, wanting to "be somebody."

But most of all, Grande Glade had Sasha Podsky—the magnet that held the facility together, attracting even more money and faux prestige. Podsky had a Svengali-like appeal to the women who spread money like manure at his facility. Carlos had run background checks on Podsky before, always to come up against the same problem. There was no background. There was no doubt that Podsky knew how to train a horse. He got results in the show ring. But too often his efforts produced "problem" horses. Classical trainers complained that Podsky would cruelly crank show horses into position, using whips and spurs and neglecting the basics. This gave Podsky's clients instant winning results at the expense of the horses, which quickly soured on the whole process. Horses worked this way developed behavior quirks and mean streaks. Podsky would then sell the problem horses and find his ladies new ones, making commissions coming and going while at the same time charging exorbitant training fees. It was quite the scheme. And Podsky ran it well.

Podsky's collaborator in all of this was his somewhat dimwitted and adoring wife, Raja. She supported Sasha's extravagant tastes in clothes and food with her significant inheritance and by running a holistic center, which was loosely affiliated with the show barn. Raja spent her days roaming the barn and lounge areas, spouting New Age platitudes and extolling the soulful virtues of her philandering husband to his hangers-on. Carlos never could figure out whether Raja knew how many clients Podsky was sleeping with or whether she even cared. It amazed Carlos how many of their clients referred to Sasha and Raja as "nice people." Folks in Minnesota sure could be easily fooled.

It especially grated on Carlos that Podsky's name was similar to that of the revered Colonel Alois Podhajsky of the Spanish Riding School in Vienna. A syllable's difference in the surname was sure to create confusion that Podsky would be reluctant to dispel. Podsky made all kinds of claims to a fabulously successful past on the CDI show circuit, but Carlos had never been able to track down the results. Interesting how Podsky remembered all the events, but no newspaper, magazine, or bureau for horse events could even come up with his name on a computer search. Either he lied well, or his past had been expunged.

Podsky claimed he had worked the Florida circuit while in his thirties. Some thought that he had been involved in insurance scams. It was common knowledge that Podsky was mentioned in many horse-world rumors. However, he was always in the background, never a recognizable principal player. Mysterious barn fires, shootings, and dozens of horse deaths surrounded, yet were never directly connected to, several brothers in Florida for whom Podsky had worked. Carlos had read all the files and several true crime novels related to those particular cases. When one of the brothers was indicted, Podsky quietly left his employment and took his family to Minnesota. Land was cheap in the woods up north thirty years ago. He built his own barn and began to develop his reputation.

Podsky's daughter, Kate, named by Raja for Katherine Hepburn, was Podsky's last chance to realize his own failed international dreams. Even more than investigating this case, Carlos dreaded having to deal with Kate. He had heard that she was working with polo ponies on the world circuit. He hoped she was still there, or anywhere but here. His looked down at his hands and saw they were trembling slightly. Had he seen her at the airport? And if so, what was she doing coming home? She seemed to hate her father and barely tolerate her mother. On the other hand, Kate was beautiful. When she decided to please, she could wrap a man around her finger in ten seconds or less. There was a time when he was willingly within her circle of enchantment. Maybe she had come home to work her spells on someone. Or maybe he was only imagining that she was in Minnesota.

CHAPTER 5

▼

As Carlos pulled up to Grande Glade, he looked for a parking spot in the sun. Winter was long in Minnesota, and he wanted to maximize the short days by keeping as much warmth in his bones as he could. He also wanted to take a moment to compose himself. Closing his eyes, he took a few long deep breaths. Years of meditation and breathing training took over his autonomic nervous system, and each inhalation and slow exhalation brought a sense of calm to the internal raggedness. Now he was ready to face the artificial people of the glitziest stable in Minnesota. It was a shame that so many who used this place didn't appreciate its natural beauty. All they saw was the glamour, the who's-who of the horse world.

The wind was slicing as he walked toward the stable. His mirrored sunglasses kept his eyes from tearing in the bright light. They also would hide where he was gazing and how he was feeling. Sunglasses were an occupational asset. He detoured to hang on the rail of the outdoor practice ring and watch the horses against the wooded horizon. Several hardy souls were out in the mid-afternoon light, giving their horses, and themselves, a much-needed dose of outdoors. February offered hope of spring on days like this, although everyone knew the reality that would be several more months of winter weather. Natives of this state were experts at fooling themselves about the weather. People at this stable were experts at fooling themselves about lots of other things as well.

The horses were frisky, and the young girls, who had to be about twelve years old, were having fun with their training exercises. Carlos let his eyes wander to the beauty of the estate. The main house was a throwback to the Eastern tradition, with an English manor-style home and separate barns and stables. The barns and stables were brick-fronted. Lots of money had been spent purely for aesthetics. The guest house had a large pool in front of it. Pools were a luxury in this part of the country; they were empty too much of the year. The pool he was looking at had a few frozen logs in the bottom to absorb the expansion of the ice and keep the cement from heaving.

He could see the main house with its matching brick exterior and white French doors overlooking the paddock, so that rich owners could sit on the porch in nice weather and have a drink while fawning over Podsky. In the winter, they could sit in the burgundy leather chairs by the fireplace and look out through the glass doors, feeling fine and important. The slightly rolling lawns undulated down to a small lake on the edge of the woods that were filled with great oaks, birch, and poplar.

Riding trails wound throughout those woods, but they were never shared with the community. They were strictly private territories for the "swells" of Grande Glade. As he gazed toward the woods, Carlos noticed a lone rider coming out of the trees. He made a mental note of that. This was not the normal time to take a ride through the woods. Weather could change in a hurry, and horses could get spooked or slip on the icy trails. The wind could play tricks on the ear and cause misjudgments. Why would someone be taking that chance today?

"Excuse me, sir?" came a voice from Carlos's left. He turned.

"Yes?"

"I've noticed you standing here for a while. Do you belong?"

"Now it's my turn to say 'Excuse me. What does that mean, exactly?'"

"I meant, do you belong here? I've never seen you before, and we don't like to have strangers hanging around."

"And who might you be? Someone with authority, I hope?"

"I'm not sure you could say that, but I am here a lot, and I have a horse here that I ride." She said this rather breathlessly. She had a sweet shy smile, and stood all of four foot nine inches. She was sweaty, which was going some in this wind and temperature.

"You're quite sure of yourself for your age—what, twelve years old?"

"Hmmm. Not quite. Almost twelve."

"Well, perhaps you can tell me where I can find Mr. Podsky, then. You are right; strangers lurking around could be a problem. Maybe you shouldn't even be talking to a stranger. That could be dangerous for you."

"Oh." She looked as startled as a deer caught in headlights. As she began to back away, she pointed into the barn. "He's there someplace, talking to the governor's wife. Can't miss them. They're having a fight." And she was gone around the corner before Carlos could say thanks.

When Carlos gingerly pushed open the great doors, he thought he might see Podsky, perhaps even with the governor's wife. Instead, the barn aisles were empty. He wandered around, but it seemed quite deserted. He went to the lounge area, always a refuge for people waiting, or those who wanted to look into the show ring while enjoying their comfort. In other words, a place to keep everyone with money happy, or have a conversation with some degree of privacy, if such a thing existed in a barn.

Carlos kicked the snow and dirt from his boots just before entering. Years of habituation around show barns had made the action an unconscious gesture. His frame filled the doorway, and he took off his sunglasses, letting his eyes adjust to the dim light coming from the fireplace at the far end of the room. The smell of the wood smoke was comforting, but he was careful not to let down his guard. It wasn't good for business to get too comfortable, even though the leather furnishings and six-panel walls were seductive.

Finding himself alone in the lounge, Carlos watched the current lesson in the indoor dressage arena. Twenty feet of glass wall gave him an unobstructed view of the proceedings. Podsky was strutting about in tight black breeches and highly polished boots; his white turtleneck accentuated his aristocratic look. Carlos noted that Podsky was wearing spurs, which seemed an unnecessary pretension in the lesson situation. A flick of a switch on the wall next to the window let Carlos listen to the lesson.

"Yah…that's good…push, push…keep her light."

A young girl, perhaps sixteen or seventeen, was riding a beautiful white Egyptian Arab. Carlos smiled at the partnership between the girl and her mount. They were doing perfect lateral work, solid second level. She had nothing to be ashamed of; they were a good team. Podsky's rantings were a distraction from the beauty of the moment.

Until recently, the United States Dressage Federation's Region IV, of which Minnesota was a member, was considered to be the backwater of dressage competition. The region included states west of the Mississippi and east of the Rockies, which traditionally had been the home of Western riders. Gradually, money was changing all of that, but the real action on the circuit continued to be in Florida in the winter and the East Coast during the summer. California was trying to become a competition center on its own, but reality dictated that old money and horses were synonymous, and the oldest money could be found only on the eastern seaboard. Of course, the most prestigious international competitions and breeding farms were generally still considered to be in Europe, home of even older money and the true aristocracy.

Carlos loved watching the dressage horse work. It reminded him of the compulsory figures of ice skating. It was the technical, formal part of skating that was difficult for most skaters, yet that, when combined with the artistic, made it possible to achieve eminence. It was the same with horses, and they, too, had to do the figures. Combined with that extra little something—flair—a horse could really be something. A horse could be worth a great deal, too, if all factors combined toward greatness.

The little Arab and her rider completed a lovely halfpass across the arena as Carlos pondered why someone like Podsky would be languishing for so long in Region IV. He obviously had a lot of money in the facility, an easy eight million, but why stay here? True, he had a ready supply of racehorses off the track at Canterbury Downs that he could train and broker, but that wouldn't seem to be enough to keep him in the so-called dustbin of the dressage world.

In a way, Carlos was surprised that Podsky would be spending time training an Arab, of all things. There must be some money in it, or he wouldn't bother. Technically, any horse was suitable for the discipline of dressage, but the real money was in warmbloods these days. Arabs and thoroughbreds were considered too hot-blooded for the sport.

The Eastern European influence on the sport was almost a stranglehold. Years of cross-breeding had combined the genes of cold-blooded draft horses with the hotbloods. The goal was to get a horse that was forward and animated, yet calm enough to be invisibly controlled by the rider.

One thing Carlos liked about dressage was this tension in the horse. It took skill to work with a horse to get it moving into all the forms required, and just as much skill to keep the horse calm, while remaining relaxed oneself. It was a manner of walking the edge, and being at one with the horse at the same time.

The French doors leading to the office area opened, distracting Carlos from the action in the arena. A blond woman, with hair a little too long for her age, which Carlos immediately guessed to be close to forty, emerged from the office. Her riding attire was much too tight to offer any comfort in the saddle, but since her breeches looked as if she had never sat in a saddle in them, tightness was probably not a problem. Serious riders were usually pretty dirty once they left the barn. This woman was a picture of fashion rather than function. She looked vaguely familiar.

The imposing sight of Carlos caught her off guard. She brushed her left eye with one hand while straightening her hair with the other.

"May I help you?"

The question was more of a challenge than an offer of assistance. Her challenge registered with Carlos. This woman was not easily intimidated. She didn't introduce herself. Fine. He wouldn't either.

"I'm here to speak with Sasha Podsky."

"Is it important? He is tied up with a lesson right now."

Let the games begin, Carlos thought. Should he tip his hand and let her know why he was here, or not? It might be interesting to see her reaction. He didn't know who she was, but she wasn't Raja Podsky. He had known Raja when she had been called Bernice. Raja was short, unattractively plump, and overly solicitous. This woman was a polar opposite to Raja, and evidently a new player in the world of horses. How serious a player, Carlos couldn't judge. He shifted into his unfocused gaze, which gave him a better sense of his surroundings and the person he was eye-dueling. That gaze always unnerved those who did not know him. This woman held her ground, but there was beginning to be a look of distress about her. There was something about her eyes. That was all he could read. Maybe he would chance it anyway.

"It's an insurance matter, just routine."

Did her face fall for just an instant, or was he looking for something that wasn't there?

"Well, please don't interrupt his lesson. My daughter is getting ready to show and needs the concentration."

"I can wait."

With that challenge established, the woman left and got in her car. Carlos turned his attention back to the tutelage taking place in the arena and decided to wait for Podsky to finish before entering the barn area. He didn't want to push his hand or his authority too far just yet. Better to act casual about the whole affair.

The woman's BMW screeched out of the parking area, spewing a shower of gravel against the windowpane. Carlos' attention shifted to the window in time to glimpse the woman having an animated conversation on her cell phone as she sped away. A second, identical BMW remained parked outside—the daughter's, no doubt.

Carlos wondered if the little rich girl noticed or even cared that her mother was not staying for the lesson's conclusion. His chest tightened as he thought of his own father working two jobs to support Carlos's riding career. The world of Grande Glade was a universe away from those days. But perhaps he was being unfair. Privilege did not necessarily coincide with a lack of horsemanship. The woman's daughter was connected with her horse, judging by the flawless execution of the dressage patterns under Podsky's tutelage. An Arab was a "cheap" mount for dressage, and not very easy to ride in the amount of collection necessary to get high scores in the show ring. This girl had a bond with the animal that went far beyond a desire for a "made" horse.

Carlos's focus returned to the events that had unfolded since his arrival at Grande Glade. It struck him as more than a bit odd that in less than ten minutes, two different people had tried to discourage him from staying. How in the world did they ever get business, being so closed and unfriendly? Some of the smaller barns were filled with people who were warm and open, and they always made sure strangers didn't stay strangers for long.

As Podsky kept the lesson going, Carlos looked around the lounge. He wanted more than anything to sit by the fire and read a magazine, one of the many horse and equipment types that were lying around, all new and shiny. Two of his favorites, Dressage Today and Chronicle of the Horse, were within reach. It wasn't that many years ago that Dressage Today had done a feature on him, but it seemed like an eternity had passed since then. So much had happened that he would rather forget. His gaze returned to the room. He could see how it could seduce unsuspecting people into relaxing so that they would be open to taking any advice given. There was an air of authority, as well as deep luxurious comfort, projected here.

Carlos was about to go back into the barn proper to have another look when the lesson ended. Instead, he walked into the show ring and noticed the horse getting distracted, too easily distracted, Carlos thought. Podsky stiffened imperceptibly, and Carlos tipped his hat without taking it off.

"Sasha." This time the nose was elevated slightly in response to Carlos's greeting. He'd be damned if he would call him Mr. Podsky like the stable hands.

"Yes. Of course. I am Mr. Podsky."

"Good for you." He knew it wouldn't help him get any information by being cutting, but he didn't think he was going to get much from this interview anyway. It was, at most, a formality.

"I beg your pardon?"

All business, Carlos went to the heart of the matter. "I'm here about Tremor. I've been asked to look into his untimely death. I need to do several things, and that includes interviewing his groom, seeing his stall and tack, and talking to people in your barn, or anyone who might be connected to the horse in any way. I'd like to do that now, with whomever is available, and then set up appointments with those who are not here."

"Oh, yes. Terrible thing. Terrible thing. I don't understand why all the questions, however. Yet, I do want to help."

Carlos figured he wanted to help about as much as he wanted to stuff a rattler into a mesh bag. Carlos knew that Podsky abhorred publicity. His polished image was a shiny lure, which he used to troll the wealthy suburbs of the Twin Cities for horsy wannabes. He would continue to make sure his precious image was protected—at all costs. Bad publicity would do him no good, at this point especially.

"I'd like to start with you, Sasha."

"And, do you have a card?" It grated. Their paths had crossed in so many ways, over so many years, that Podsky's pretense of not recognizing him was as ludicrous as it was insulting. Still, Carlos went on with the charade. "Of course." Sasha took the card and didn't look at it.

"Let's step into your nice cozy lounge, shall we?" Now Podsky was irritated, but he covered it well. He was supposed to give the orders around here, and no one really crossed him in any way, or took the lead in conversations. Why Podsky put on airs griped Carlos. He was a virtual unknown outside of Region IV, in spite of his nebulous past glory days. And anyone in the horse world knew that Region IV was the last region in which people wanted their horses to compete.

Neither could Carlos figure out why women were drawn to Podsky. The man was well built for sixty, but he had a curiously ugly face, with slightly tipped eyes that lent him an almost ancient oriental air. He sported a wispy beard, but no mustache. In general, his facial features didn't seem to go together. Carlos smiled to himself at the mental image of Susan's niece, Maya, playing with a Mr. Potato Head.

"Do you find something amusing, Mr. Dega?"

"'Carlos' will do, Sasha."

Good, Carlos thought. Best to keep Podsky off guard. Perhaps he could irritate him enough to unleash one of his famous temper tantrums. The last time he and Podsky had squared off was when Carlos interrupted a lesson to claim his horse and take him home. Podsky had actually abandoned his student in the arena in order to challenge Carlos's right to remove the animal from the barn. Carlos had kept his back to him then, knowing that if he had spun around to face him they would have come to blows. It was time to meet again.

With an oily smile, Podsky opened a cabinet beneath a small wet bar set in a corner of the room.

"Carlos, certainly then. May I offer you a drink?"

"Water would be fine."

"Water it is, then."

Podsky walked over to the microphone next to the viewing area.

"She seems to be cooled out, Cassie. Have Britt hose her down, and put her away."

Carlos thought the instruction was an unnecessary distraction. Was Podsky looking for time to compose himself? It seemed the right time to strike—while Carlos was still calm and Podsky shaken.

"What can you tell me about Tremor?"

Podsky settled into the overstuffed leather sofa and motioned Carlos to the facing chair.

"There isn't much to tell. Tremor took sick so suddenly that no one even suspected it. I gather it was a terrible case of colic during the night. It happened quickly."

"Were you on the premises at the time?"

"I very seldom leave. There was a region awards banquet that night, and we were entertaining at the main house until quite late in the evening."

"Did anyone go to visit Tremor during that time? Perhaps someone noticed that he was in distress. Colic usually manifests itself with early symptoms."

"All of the guests were free to roam the estate. Tremor was a magnificent animal. I'm sure that some of the guests visited his stall. The only rule we have is there is to be no flash photography in the barn. I'm sure you can understand why."

Carlos was sure that the no-photography rule had something to do with the fact that Tremor's image was highly marketable. Magazines would pay handsomely for candid shots of him in his surroundings.

"Yes, I do understand. Now, do you recall anyone mentioning anything unusual about the horse or his surroundings?"

Podsky was irritated again.

"Certainly, Mr. Dega, anything unusual would have been looked into immediately. Tremor was a valuable asset to this facility. It was an honor to have him stabled here."

"Carlos, remember, Sasha?"

"As you wish."

Carlos tried another route. "What about his groom?"

"Another reason we would have noticed a usual case of colic. Her name is Britt…Ewing, I believe. You will have to ask my wife, Raja. She takes care of the help. In any case, her quarters are above the barn. A stairway leads from her apartment to the barn area. She is the first thing Tremor sees in the morning and the last thing he sees at night. Or saw…"

Carlos made another mental note. It piqued his curiosity that Podsky claimed not to know the groom's last name. The groom attending to a breeding stallion was arguably the second most important part of the operation, next to the stallion's viability as a breeder. It was a well-known story in horse circles that the groom of Tremor's grandfather, Seattle Slew, risked his job to attend to the transfer of the horse to another facility, leading the stallion into the trailer despite orders not to assist. Such was the bond between groom and horse. Breeding stallions especially were dependent upon consistent human contact, and their groom was a large part of that consistency. Podsky was compulsive about details and wanted to know everything that happened in his kingdom. He would certainly know the name of Tremor's groom. Maybe it was part of the game that Podsky was playing with Carlos.

It seemed something was not being said. Podsky's vagueness looked feigned. Carlos would speak with Raja about the groom. He glanced at his notepad, more for effect than anything else. He had all of the particulars memorized. He was beginning, as well, to have more questions than answers.

"I see that there were actually three owners, a consortium of sorts."

"A two-million-dollar investment generally requires a consortium, Carlos." It clearly grated on Podsky to call this intrusive, prying man by his first name. He wanted to keep the distance and keep him in his place. "His stud fees proved Tremor to be a good investment."

"Do you recall what those fees were?"

"I believe this year he was standing at $100,000 with a guaranteed live foal."

Carlos made another mental note. At that rate his stud fees would be worth millions in a very short time. This horse was certainly worth more to his owners alive than dead. He was insured for only two million. The owners couldn't be very happy, although they would recoup their initial investment, minus stabling and training costs. He might be able to wrap this case up quickly and put it all behind him. This place made his skin crawl, and he couldn't wait to get out of here.

"I'll take a look at the barn, particularly Tremor's stall," Carlos said.

"Go right ahead." Trying to maintain his control, he gave Carlos permission, although Carlos had not asked for it. "I believe you know the way. I have some phone calls I would like to make. Tremor's nameplate is still on the stall. He was in the last stall at the far end from the lounge here. I believe all of his tack is in the tack room."

"Good. One other thing before I leave you to your work. The names of the investors? I have Cindi Moreno, Fiona Andersson, and Randolph Decker listed as having insurable interests in the horse." Carlos punctuated his remarks by stabbing his pen over each name as he said it.

"You would know more than I about that. Often, the owners of high-priced horses have nothing more to do with them than an investor does with his stock portfolio. In this case, I am acquainted with Mrs. Andersson and Ms. Moreno. In fact, they are both upper-level riders on the circuit. Mrs. Andersson stables other horses here. She is the governor's wife, and Ms. Moreno is in television. Quite lovely assets for the facility, actually." Podsky couldn't help posturing. "You know what I mean. However, the name Randolph Decker is new to me. I don't believe I've ever met him. If your company tells you that those three have insurable interests, I would know nothing else."

That explanation seemed plausible to Carlos. Too often, horses were business investments, and there was no emotional attachment to the animal by the owner. He would have to interview the owners later. Right now, he wanted to see Tremor's stall and check out the breeding facility.

He looked around suddenly, as if he would see something new, and asked Podsky, "Did you use a phantom or a jump mare for Tremor?"

Carlos noticed that Podsky's mouth twitched faintly at the question.

"Of course we would use a phantom. Tremor was much too valuable to risk his hind legs or back by allowing him to mount a mare in heat. A phantom was sufficient. It was easy to train him to mount the table."

This answer, too, was entirely plausible. An artificial vagina was used frequently with valuable stallions, especially ones that were skittish or didn't travel well. This process avoided behavioral problems that might occur when a stallion was asked to mount a broodmare. The breeding table made access to semen easy. Then it could be collected for transporting to broodmares. Phantoms eliminated the cost of actually transporting the horse. Some stallions even preferred it to an actual mare.

Podsky continued, "It was also cost-effective from our management standpoint. We don't make mares ready for collection. You know that can be quite time-consuming and have other problems associated with it. We use a nearby facility. The same place prepares and transports Tremor's frozen semen. We run a simple, clean operation here, Mr. Dega."

With that statement, the Russian Monarch of Grande Glade rose from his chair and turned on his heel as if marching in a parade. He literally high-stepped out of the room into the riding rink.

Carlos shook his head and left the lounge the way he had come. The stable had the usual comforting ambiance. He found the proper stall. He was about to unlatch the door when he heard muffled sobs. Looking around, he saw no one. He called softly, "Hello?"

He heard sniffling and the rustle of sawdust. All of a sudden a head popped up in Tremor's stall. "Hello?" he questioned again. "Excuse me. I don't mean to interrupt."

"No, no, it's all right. I'm sorry. I was just trying to say my goodbyes to Tremor and clean up his stall so we can put another horse in here, and, well, it just got to be too much, and I fell apart."

"You must be Britt. I'm sorry for your loss," Carlos intoned.

"Yes, well...you seem to be the only one." She looked up and dried her cheeks with the back of her hands. Sawdust was sticking in her hair and all over her pants. She wore sorel boots and an old orange down vest. Carlos thought her to be about twenty, give or take a year or two.

"Perhaps the others here don't understand how close you become to a great animal like Tremor when you are the groom. So many think that if you clean up and do all the dirty work, you don't like the job or the horse. But, of course, they would be wrong, wouldn't they?"

At his words, her face softened, and tears welled up in her eyes again.

"Oh, here I go again. I am so sorry." She wiped her nose on her sleeve. It looked like this wasn't the first time she had done it.

Carlos wished he were the kind of man who always carried a fresh hankie in his back pocket. He wasn't. He wanted to offer some comfort or solace. Instead, he stuck his hand out and introduced himself. "Carlos Dega. Call me Carlos, please. I'm here to investigate Tremor's death."

"Investigate? What do you mean?"

"Are you surprised?"

"Well, umm, well...do you mean you think I had something to do with his death?"

Trying to be soothing, Carlos looked at her with sad eyes, and said, "How hard for you now! I don't know what really happened to Tremor yet, but I mean to find out. There hasn't been a moment that I've thought you had, or would want to have, anything to do with his death."

"Whew." He heard her ragged breath go out as if she had been holding it for a very long time. She took the elastic out of her long blond messed hair, shook her head back and forth, and pulled it all back into a ponytail. It was not unattractive. She had beautiful clear skin, gray eyes, and gorgeous long dark lashes that grew that way all by themselves. He didn't mind just looking at her while she adjusted to this information. He could see her changing gears in her mind. "Well, then, what can I do for you?"

She seemed to say "well" a lot. Maybe it was her youth. Maybe she just thought in "wells." Maybe it was kind of cute.

"Thanks for asking. Several things would be helpful. First of all, I want you to let me just look around alone. I need to get a feel for this place. Secondly, do you think there is anything out of place, or missing, or not as it should be?

"And the third thing I would like is your opinion of the people who had contact with Tremor. That means contact in any way, big or small."

Britt was quick, both in step and mind. She was already moving out of the stall and going toward the tack room. "I'll meet you in the tack room, Mr. Dega. I'll look around while you do what you need to do here." As she made her way down the hall, Carlos shouted, "Carlos. Call me Carlos."

Britt had done a thorough job on the stall. Fresh sawdust left the air pine-scented, and the tongue-and-groove walls of the stall had been wiped down with some kind of oil soap. The automatic waterer was antiseptically clean. All in all, the stall was more than ready for its new tenant. Except, of course, for the outside wall, which had been boarded over with plywood. That must have been where they removed Tremor's body. Otherwise, whatever personal feelings he harbored for Podsky, Carlos had to admit that he ran a topnotch facility.

The stall was big. Pacing it off, Carlos figured it was about twenty by twenty, give or take a foot. The ceilings were high for a barn area. Usually height was kept to a minimum in northern climates to maximize heat retention in the winter months. Obviously, heating costs were of no concern here. Aesthetics were. Fans high in the rafters circulated the heat downward from the huge ventilation ducts that snaked through the post-and-beam facility.

Podsky had thought of every convenience. Brass-plated electrical outlets were strategically placed on every support beam. Carlos allowed himself to reflect on the past for a moment. When he rode Julio for Costa Rica, there were no such conveniences as electrical outlets for clippers and vacuums. He smiled as he thought of the look in Julio's eyes as he would try to approach him with the tools for the body clipping. They had had several "discussions," as his father would have said about that procedure.

Carlos stepped out of the stall and ran his hand over the brass nameplate that claimed the space for Tremor. Reaching into his pocket, he found his Swiss Army knife and carefully unscrewed the four corners of the oak block that held the plate. This belonged to Britt, but he thought she would never presume to take it on her own.

Everything was as it should be. There were no horses in the barn at this time of day; they were all in individual turnouts. Podsky's student was in the grooming stall at the far end of the aisle tending to the little Arab. Everything was spotless. Britt had performed her duties well. Carlos wondered if she had any other help during the day. It was a tremendous job, but most grooms and stable help who loved the animals were fastidious as well as hard working. He would make a point to compliment her later on her work.

Carlos noted a door to an outdoor stairway—no doubt the one Podsky had mentioned that led to the loft where Britt lived. He could see why Podsky said she was the first person Tremor saw in the morning and the last human contact he had at night. The horse would have had a clear view of the stairway entrance through the bars of his stall door. Horses, he knew, thrived on this kind of bonding. The object of their affection was viewed more as a familiar member of the herd than anything else. Before they entered a major competition, Carlos would always sleep on a cot outside Julio's stall. It brought comfort to both of them. If only he had slept there every night…Carlos banished the thought. Regrets too late would only cloud his thinking. He needed to concentrate on the problem at hand, not one of the past.

"Carlos, dear! Is that you? How nice to see you!"

Carlos adjusted his gaze to the far end of the aisle. The sound of the little-girl voice was gratingly familiar. He knew who it was without having to look.

"Bernice, Sasha didn't tell me you were here today."

"It's Raja, now, remember dear?"

Carlos remembered all right. He had first made her acquaintance when he was a migrant stableboy and she was called Bernice Mischke. Carlos's first glimpse of Bernice was when she was one of Podsky's riding students at a training facility near Ocala, Florida. Although he was only a boy at the time, Carlos knew enough of the ways of men and women to know that poor, pudgy Bernice didn't stand much of a chance in the competition for Podsky's affection, which she so clearly desired. All that changed rapidly when circumstances revealed that Bernice was the sole heir of a forgotten Polish prince, whose fortune was recovered along with priceless artwork when a former Nazi revealed the location of the stolen cache to an insurance investigator for Lloyd's of London. Her newfound wealth and position ignited a latent passion in her poor Russian teacher. It soon became obvious to the young Carlos that money could buy much more than material items. Bernice bought a husband and a new life. Podsky managed to get himself a guaranteed meal ticket and a new country to boot. And eventually, Bernice acquired a new name, too, after she discovered her gift for New Age prattle.

"Raja, then, it will be, Bernice, though try to ignore me if I have a few slips of the tongue. Sasha and I just had a conversation."

"You did, dear? Whatever about?" The constantly open excited eyes created by her plastic surgeon got even wider, if that was possible without having her eyelids crawl over her forehead.

"You must know, B—…Raja. Surely you are not as unaware as you and Sasha claim."

"Why, whatever do you mean?" The wide eyes again, or still; Carlos couldn't decide which. "Are you referring to our tragic experience a few days ago?"

It was all he could do not to roll his eyes at her. "If you are talking about Tremor's death, yes, then we are both discussing the same thing. Why don't we talk about this someplace more private, Raja."

"Oh, I couldn't possibly, dear. I have a group waiting for me right now that want me to read their auras." With that, she blew him an air kiss and fluttered off down the aisle.

CHAPTER 6

▼

The fatigue of the journey was beginning to set in, and he was weary of this whole place. It brought back deep unpleasant memories that drained him emotionally, and the owners were still as impossible to deal with as ever. Carlos decided he would have a final talk with Britt, and then go home and hibernate.

The tack room smelled wonderful. Britt was putting the last of Tremor's tack into a box. She turned as Carlos entered, even though he was fairly certain he had made no noise. She was intuitive, as well as observant. He liked that. "Here is all I could gather from Tremor. I thought that maybe you would want to look at it before I give it to the owners. It just breaks my heart to see his gear."

Carlos thought she might cry again. His eyes examined hers, but all he saw was a greater depth than he would expect from a young woman. "You've taken wonderful care of his things, Britt. His stall is immaculate. His tack looks well oiled. I think you've done a great job, from what I've seen. It shows that you cared a great deal for this horse."

"You're kind."

"No, Britt, I am not kind. But I am observant. What I am telling you are facts, and you did well by this horse, and his owners. Your work reflects well on this stable, too. Now, would you be up to answering some questions?"

"Well…" she sighed—a deep long sigh as she looked in the box. "I'll do my best, but do feel free to ask me again some other time. I'm rather a mess right now."

"Britt, do you keep a journal or a daily log of your horse care, or the horses' workouts, or anything?"

"I, well, have my personal journal. You know, just for me with my very private self. Sometimes I talk about the horses, but I don't think anything you might use. I mean, well, I could look later if you like, but I don't see…"

"Do what you can, Britt. Look it up later, and give me a call. Here's my card in case you find anything. I would appreciate it."

"Yeah. Sure." The Minnesotan's familiar reply.

"What about the owners? Can you tell me anything about them?"

"There really isn't too much to tell. They don't show up often—didn't show up often—to deal with Tremor. I see Mrs. Andersson around the stable for her daughter's training and events, but she didn't come to see Tremor much at all, even when it would have been so easy to do so. I always found that a bit strange. And then, there is Ms. Moreno, but, you know, she is so famous and all, and doesn't get out to the stable. She doesn't ride or anything. I've only seen her once, when she came out to see that Tremor had arrived here from California safely—when they bought him."

"Is that typical of your owners? I mean, of any of the other horses you have under your care?"

"Well…" Carlos had just about decided that Britt said "well" so much to give herself time to think. "I have only one other horse right now that I groom. They wanted Tremor well cared for. And I also rode him on training rides, you know. So, I don't exactly know what is typical. It's just that…" her voice died out and she stopped.

"What, Britt?"

"With a horse that fine, and sweet, I would think they would want to be here a lot. He was one of the best I've ever been with, a real beauty in so many ways. And then, when he died, I would have thought they would have wanted to come, to see him, or to know more about the way it was when he died. Instead, Mr. Podsky borrowed a forklift, and ripped a hole in the wall, and just hauled him out of here like so much manure. And it all seemed slow. I would have thought that Mr. Podsky would have…I don't know, just gotten to it sooner, or something. Oh, I don't know. I guess I'm just rambling here. I was disturbed."

"One last question. Anything unusual the night he died? Any noises you could hear in your quarters? Anything out of place?" His tone was hopeful.

"It's really weird how I never think about those things, you know? I mean, until something dreadful happens, even the unusual thing seems kind of normal, or at least, at the time, something might not stand out to be unusual. It's later, when I give it thought in the context of the whole story, that something might stand out for me. Do you find that so, Carlos?"

"Give it your best thoughts, Britt. Yes. Later things take on a different hue, and stand out in funny ways. Anything little could be of utmost value to me. You have my card. Call me at any time of night or day. I'll get back to you after I've had some time to go through some more information."

"Yeah. Sure."

He left her as she lifted the box with Tremor's grooming supplies. The outside wind and air were just what he needed. Nothing like Minnesota fresh air to clear the senses. Carlos was thinking of how Podsky had said both Fiona Andersson and Cindi Moreno were excellent riders. Yet Britt said Cindi never came to ride. Interesting. Why would Podsky deliberately lead Carlos to believe Cindi was frequently at the stable to ride when she obviously wasn't? He pulled on his hat and gloves and headed for the truck. With his head tucked down into his collar, he didn't see the small figure move quickly into the shadow of the trees. His thoughts and vision were on going home and shaking this sense of dread he felt creeping around him like a black cloak. He shivered, and it wasn't entirely from the cold.

CHAPTER 7

▼

Susan checked her watch while waiting for her elevator to stop at the fifteenth floor. It was almost five. The meeting with Carlos had taken longer than she expected. Most of the other federal workers had left the building by 4:30. The doors opened, and she waved at the guard as she breezed past him toward the ladies' restroom. A little cold water on her face would feel good—maybe wake her up for the long evening ahead.

As she looked up from the sink into the streaked mirror, she took a few moments to study her reflection. Hair looks passable, she thought, but her eyes…she saw more wrinkles around them than she remembered having. Susan wondered if she had bags under her eyes, or if what she was looking at was just a bad make-up job. What a mess. The only positive thought she had was that she liked her green eyes, and considered them her strongest feature.

"Jesus, I need a facelift, gotta cut out the cigarettes," she said in the beginnings of a whiskey-toned voice to the reflection. She laughed as she realized that she had been making the same vow for the last five years, just about every time she studied her face. There was hardly an inside place in the whole Twin Cities area where smokers could indulge any more. Smokers were frustrated, and everyone else loved it.

"The hell with it."

Fumbling for a cigarette, she ignored the indoor smoking ban and lit up a Marlboro in the restroom. At least there were no artificial preservatives. That was her constant rationalization. She took a few drags and dumped it into the toilet and flushed. As she entered her office, which was just a short distance down the hall, she found that Shirley, her secretary, had left a stack of pink phone memos on her desk. She pushed them to the side as she settled into her chair and watched the last streaks of light fade from the late February sky. She picked up a yellow photocopy of an abstract on colic from a veterinary journal. Ken Rollins would be able to help her decipher the medical jargon, but she wasn't sure she wanted to call him now. University vets weren't used to getting calls in the evening hours. They had students to handle that kind of thing. Yet, of all the vets at the University of Minnesota Veterinary School, Ken was the most accessible she knew.

There was a time when she would have been home now. Home with Randy. Gone with the rest of the government drones into the rush-hour traffic. That was before the horse murders started and the whole thing took hold of her and killed the best part of her life. Susan didn't like to lose, but this case had more holes than her kitchen colander right from the beginning. She had always relied on common sense to solve her cases. Criminals made mistakes. She just had to figure the angles, and that usually gave her a road map to their back door.

Hell, she wasn't even sure this Tremor thing fit the usual pattern, but the field office wanted her to lean heavily on the players. Everyone involved with the Florida horse mafia case from years ago was either dead, in jail, or quietly back on the horse scene. The American Horse Show Association had restricted their ability to show for fifteen years, but there were plenty of other ways to play the horse game. She even liked some of the people she had put in jail. She'd gotten to know their families, their kids. Maya, her niece, even rode with one of Buck Landers' nieces.

That was another sad case. Landers spent the better part of his son's show career in jail. He never got to see his kid ride in the Olympics. She was struck by how greed took him further away from his goal, rather than closer. The old man got involved in a mail fraud scheme trying to finance his kid's show career. And then, inevitably, got caught. His son was able to rise above the family shame and ride for his country, but it all seemed tarnished somehow. And it gave dressage a bad reputation.

Maya. That reminded her. Susan had promised she'd take her to a dressage clinic next week. She'd better call and arrange to pick her up after school. Still, she was nervous about Maya's involvement with the dressage world. Why couldn't she have been interested in barrel racing and riding at fairs and 4-H events? It gave Susan some comfort to know that just about everyone in the local horse business was aware that Maya was her niece. In fact, she made sure of it, figuring none of them would be stupid enough to mess with the girl. Sometimes a good offense was the best defense.

When her sister, Gwen, had gotten started in this whole horse business, she was so innocent. She had popped for big bucks to buy a horse for her only child, just to please her. Dressage seemed a perfect outlet for Maya's intelligence and physical restlessness. A seedy horse dealer in northern Minnesota saw them coming a mile away, and it proved to be an experience for them all. After years of investigating scams involving horses, Susan for the first time found herself personally involved in one. It was a tough lesson.

The dealer had taken Gwen for ten grand, promising that the horse was perfect for a ten-year-old. After the family learned a bit more about horses, it was evident that this one was much too large and spirited for a small child beginning in the business. But by then the little girl had fallen hopelessly in love with it. Gwen was faced with the choice of either inflicting emotional trauma by selling the horse, or risking serious bodily injury to Maya by allowing her to continue riding. Susan solved the family crisis by finding a small stable with a gentle trainer to work with the horse. Maya was riding a pony for the time being.

Susan's revenge on the dealer was well known locally. She tracked down both him and his contact in El Paso, who had run the horse from Canada with no papers, documentation, or Coggins tests. This got the dealer a small jail sentence for illegally hauling livestock. It also totally embarrassed the El Paso barn, which had several well-known horses on the show jumper circuit.

Susan had seriously plotted her revenge, and it was worth it. But maybe things had gone too far. Randy had thought so. He said she was getting hard. It hurt her to hear that from him. He never thought in terms of revenge. If he got mad, he seldom wanted to get even. And, not long after that, he was gone.

"Night, Susan." She was startled out of her preoccupation.

"Ho. You startled me. Night, Shirley. Are you the last to leave?"

"Yep. Just you and the security guards now."

"I really have quite the social life, don't I?" she laughed.

Shirley put on her long down coat, wrapped a scarf around her neck, pulled on a polar fleece hat, and hauled her all-purpose tote bag to her shoulder. "Looks like more snow."

"At this time of year it seems it will never end, huh?" And with that Susan picked up the phone and started returning her phone calls. Maybe she could catch a few people before they left.

She managed to contact some people and leave messages for others. She hit her e-mail, and cleaned that up. By then it was later than she thought. Her stomach growled and reminded her to look at her watch. One more trip to the bathroom, and then she too would close up shop for the day. She grabbed her cigarettes for another short one. Smoking on the street in the midst of howling winds and snow was tough. Better to grab a boost inside.

It was only after the bathroom door had swung closed that the figure in the navy coat reached around Susan's office door and killed the lights. With the help of a small flashlight, the figure quickly searched through the clutter on Susan's desk, slipping something into the front of the dark parka and stuffing a pink memo into a pocket. The rubber-soled boots were silent and swift. The figure saw the triangle of yellow color down the hall and knew it was a warning to leave. In an instant, there was no trace of the intruder's having been there, except for what was missing.

Susan was slightly annoyed to find the lights out in her office. She was sure she hadn't done that. Those cleaning folks and security guards were all so environmentally conscious—turning out the lights, saving energy. She fumbled a second, and felt some stirring of air. Now what? A window open? Nah. This was a new building. No windows opened anywhere. She wondered if she was just tired, and a bit jumpy from too much nicotine and caffeine, and not enough food. When she got to her desk she decided to give it all up for the night, go home, and use her last ounces of energy on the NordicTrack. If she felt really energetic, she'd heat a frozen dinner. Another exciting evening alone. What was left of it.

When she got off the skis, she felt the pleasant glow of sweat, and her mind was clearer. She toweled down, grabbed a bottle of La Croix water, and sat looking out the window at the glow of the city lights. She never tired of her view. Susan loved her high-rise apartment in the cradle of downtown Minneapolis. She felt connected while in the heart of "her environment," the working, playing, and sleeping place for a woman who loved to know and be known.

Randy had never felt comfortable here, and when he moved out, it gave her more sense of space—not worrying about him gave her the freedom to enjoy her place even more. She could run to work whenever she wanted, or she could grab a bite to eat whenever friends called or stopped by. She was a city girl in her heart and soul. She enjoyed going to the country as an outing, but she didn't feel as comfortable there as in the massive towers of cement, glass, and lights of downtown Minneapolis.

It had been a discomforting day. Seeing Carlos again, after all these months, had unnerved her and unleashed an undercurrent of sexuality she had not felt in a long time.

"I will not become involved with him," she heard herself say. "I will not allow it. I don't want to mess up a perfectly good relationship—a good business relationship. I won't." Somehow saying it out loud made all the difference, Susan thought. It became more like a vow that way. "Yeah, and you've given up smoking every day for five years, too." So much for vows.

And like it or not, she was involved with the horses. Her niece's troubles had put her on the local dressage map. It was a small biosphere. She'd have to dig in and adjust.

The phone rang. She decided whether she would let the machine pick it up, and on the third ring roused herself to answer it. "Hello?" All she could hear was breathing. "Hello?" More breathing. She was ready to hang up when the voice, muffled, low and slow said, "I have something for you. You'll want it."

"Excuse me?"

She heard the phone click. She quickly pushed caller ID. Up flashed "pay-phone" with a local area code and number. "Shit."

The adrenaline was pumping all over again. Her heart began to thump in her chest. The last time her ears buzzed like this, Maya was in trouble. "God, I hope nothing's wrong with her." She punched in Gwen's number. Five rings went by. Now her throat was dry. Six.

Someone picked up the phone and answered in a sleepy voice. "L'ho."

"Gwen?"

"Who the hell do you think would answer my phone at this hour of the night?"

"Are you all right?"

"Shit, yes. I was, until you called."

"Listen, don't get grumpy with me. I just had a scary phone call. Run and check and see if Maya is OK. I'll wait. Do it now."

It seemed forever before Gwen got back on the phone. "Yeah. She's fine. Sleeping like the old rock. What's up with you?"

"I just had this funny call. I got worried. Sorry. Listen. Do you use that security system in your house? I mean, turn it on every night, that sort of thing?"

"No. Then I would have to think. I am not worried someone is going to break in. I have nothing to steal. I'm not exactly the rich downtown lawyer, you know."

Sometimes Gwen's sarcasm peeved her. This was one time they didn't need to work on their sibling rivalry. She tried to ignore it. "Do me a favor. Arm it all the time, both when you're home and gone. Just for a while. I've got a bad gut feeling here."

"Now I know you're nuts. I've got a kid here. She runs in and out a thousand times a day. She's got friends. We've got the dog. Think again."

"Gwen, just do it. We'll talk later. I'm worried about someone breaking in." Susan implored. Her niece and sister were all she had left in the world for family, and it scared her to think of their getting hurt, or worse yet, her losing them.

"I'm in my warm bed, where, I might add, you should be. I've got nothing to lose here, Sis, like I said."

"Oh, yes you do."

"What's that?"

"Maya."

CHAPTER 8

▼

Carlos ran Britt's words around in his head as he waited for the engine to warm up. What she'd said was absolutely correct. And intuitive. "Even the unusual thing seems kind of normal…" What made her say that? Something about this case bothered him. It was too easy. The pieces fit together too neatly. Did she know something she wasn't telling him, or did she sense that it was too easy, too?

Something in his pocket prevented him from fastening his seatbelt. Tremor's nameplate. Too bad he'd forgotten to give it to Britt. Carlos smiled as he realized it gave him a good excuse to visit her again, and then he tried to banish the thought. He wasn't going to go there. Too complicated. Carlos wanted to keep his cases free of personal entanglements. He liked his life that way too, and it bothered him that he was seeing connections between himself and this girl that probably didn't exist. That he didn't want to exist.

He rubbed his hand over the brass nameplate, and then tried to put it into the glove box. A couple of maps fell to the floor before he realized that it was his .38 special Smith and Wesson that was taking up all of the space. It was a trite gun for an insurance investigator to have, but it would do the job if he ever needed it. So far he hadn't. He had forgotten it was in there. Actually, the gun was kind of his private joke. Thirty-eight specials were the staple of cheap detective novels. The gun always saved the hero's life, thereby giving an easy plot resolution. Real cases were much more complex and hard to unravel, especially the kinds of insurance investigations that required his expertise. Deadbeat workers' comp, arson, and fraudulent loss-of-property claims were real minor-league stuff. He found them boring.

That's what he liked about freelancing. He could pick and choose his cases. Right now, he wasn't sure he wanted to continue on this one. Maybe he should drop it. The cast of characters was way too familiar, and his gut told him that familiarity did, indeed, breed contempt. Yet he was the one who could advocate for Tremor. If he didn't, who would?

There were a lot of things about his job in general that bothered him. Carrying the gun was one of them. He preferred to think of himself as a man who could rely upon his intuition. His sixth sense had saved him before. The trick was to stay focused. The people involved in this case might cause him to lose that focus. He'd have to be mindful.

On the other hand, his investigative training in the military had taught him to rely upon the feel of things. For him, it worked well to sidestep active thought. It was the same connection he felt when he was riding well. He rehearsed the well-known phrases in his head: Let the horse carry you; don't carry the horse. Open and close the reins. Feel the tension, but stay connected. See and feel the whole picture.

On a whim, Carlos turned onto highway 55 instead of taking his planned route home. He drove past the rolling farmland west toward Buffalo and followed the County Road to Sally's barn. He knew what he needed to clear his head, and he was sure she wouldn't mind if he used the arena this late in the day.

Orion was stretching lazily across the eastern sky as he climbed out of the truck into the crisp night air. The lights were on in the indoor arena. He grabbed a duffel from behind the seat of the extenda-cab and made his way inside. He noticed there were two cars besides Sally's in the parking area, and then he checked himself. It was time to quit thinking like he was on the job.

He really liked this place. A small inheritance from Sally's father had paid for it, and Sally had done a good job building it. Rolling Acres consisted of a pre-fab metal building that housed the arena, a small lounge, and fifteen stalls. Nothing fancy, but the board was reasonable, the clientele friendly and middle-class. These were people who treated their horses as a hobby, not as an economic indicator. In addition, it was a place he felt was safe for him.

Settling briefly into the lounge area, he took a chance that no one would barge in and began to change quickly into his breeches and boots. He left the spurs in his gear bag. He always carried them because they once belonged to his father, but he figured he would never use them. Los Rios didn't need spurs when kindness would do.

"Hey, stranger!"

"Yo, Sally! Am I such a stranger?"

"Well, from the rear end, and only seeing your skivvies, I would say that was stranger than not," she laughed.

With a good humored out-breath, Carlos teased her back, "So did you get a good look at the Tasmanian Devil on the rear?"

"I could tease you about that, young man, but you are wearing boring black jockey briefs. Maybe I should get you a pair of funny shorts, to lighten you up, you know. I'd keep them here, so that your butt has more fun in the saddle."

Carlos loved teasing with Sally. For a woman in her fifties, she had so much life and vigor, and she always provided him with a few good laughs and a warm, open heart.

"I figured you wouldn't mind if I came to ride, and spend some time with my horse?" It was more of a polite question than a statement.

"You know, young man, you are welcome here if it's three in the morning, although I don't know if Los Rios would agree with me."

"How is he, my sweet woman?"

Sally almost blushed at the sentiment in his voice. God, she thought of Carlos as warmly as she did her own son. She would do anything to nurture him, and if that meant taking care of his horse, and letting him ride at all hours, she had no quarrel with that.

"Missing you. I love him up, but it's you that he looks for every day. You need to get here more often, you know."

"It looks like I will be around for a while. I'll do my best, Sally. Besides, I've been itching to do some work in the saddle again."

"Have you been riding lately?"

"You'll be pleased to note I just got back from a nice long trip to Patagonia."

Sally knew he spent all day astride a horse while there. "Good, your legs will be like trees instead of cooked leeks. Your equine buddy will appreciate that. Take what you need in time, dear boy. Enjoy."

"Thanks, Sally. You're the best."

With that, Carlos stuffed his gear in a corner, and went down the aisle to see his horse.

For a moment it looked like the stall was empty, causing Carlos's heart to race. The past crept into the present, blurring memory and time. His quickened pace prompted Los Rios to quickly raise his head from whatever had interested him on the stall floor and peer inquisitively through the bars of the upper door and snort. The sight of the familiar lopsided white blaze on the face of the big bay gelding made Carlos give a snort of his own as a sigh of relief flooded his lungs.

"Whoa, boy, don't do that to me!"

The horse pressed his nostrils toward the bars on the door, and man and animal completed a curious ritual. Carlos lowered his own face so that he was literally nose-to-nose with his horse. Man and beast began to breathe slowly and in harmony, as if they were taking in the essence of one another, breathing in and out for several minutes until their breath became as one. He had been told once that if he learned to breathe this way with a horse, the animal would never forget him. The horse would take his scent into memory forever. Carlos and Los Rios had grown accustomed to repeating the ritual as a kind of standard greeting. Each could assess the health and well being of the other in this way.

"Having fun without me, Rios? Sally's been taking good care of you, no?" It was times like this that his delicate lilting Spanish accent came out, a legacy from his mother. It added a touch of intimacy and softness to his communication and to him.

Carlos reached to unlatch the stall, but the gelding's big head pushed the sliding door to its full width before Carlos could grab the bridle that was hanging on the outside of the stall door.

"OK, boy, so you want to ride tonight? Let's see what you remember."

The arena was empty, and the halogen lights cast a bluish glow that seemed to intensify the whitewashed walls. Carlos swung easily into the saddle and placed the stirrups over the pommel, allowing Rios to feel the bit but walk unimpeded on a long, loose rein. Concentrating on the gait of his horse, Carlos closed his eyes and guided his mount in perfect diagonals across the arena, from K, to X, to M, switching directions on a perfectly straight line. He loved doing these specialized movements with Rios, and it seemed to intensify their attention.

"Hey, Sally, how long are you going to stand there? Your legs will get tired, yes?" The voice was still lilting and winning. He tucked his head under his arm to look at her.

"Don't think you are going to impress me with this riding with your eyes closed stuff!" Sally chided. "Rios told you I was here."

Carlos nodded, and with the slight duck of his chin coupled with almost imperceptible pressure from his legs and seat, he signaled the big gelding to begin to step in place. It was a stunning piaffe. Sally's eyes welled up at the sight of perfect harmony, and she quietly left the viewing area. She would talk with Carlos about his riding later. Better to let the boy have this time.

For Carlos there was no past, present or future. He was living and breathing totally in the moment, acutely aware of his surroundings, yet oblivious to them at the same time. The pulse of the blood flowing through the sinews and muscles of the big animal was in tune with the beating of his own heart. They were one. The past was vanquished.

CHAPTER 9

▼

It was well after midnight, and Susan was still rattled by the phone call and by that gut feeling that she was stepping on the wrong toes somewhere. Stepping on toes was a career hazard for a federal prosecutor. She'd thought she had gotten away from the interpersonal stuff when she asked for a transfer out of the civil law division of the U.S. Attorney's Office. She had been appointed to that office after a short postgraduate stint at a private law firm, where she specialized in civil fraud litigation. Idealistic and foolish, she really thought the federal appointment would give her a shot at changing at least a small portion of society for the better. Unfortunately, most of her time was spent on employment disputes, with the end result that she felt she had changed nothing, and only gotten more jaded. Actual accomplishments in civil fraud litigation seemed like small potatoes.

An appointment to the criminal law division opened up a whole new world, especially for a gal who knew her way around a database and computer networks. Someone had to be as smart as the crooks, and for a while they were more computer-literate than the prosecutors in her office were. Susan was renowned for her organizational abilities, and the databases she created were invaluable tools for the local office. The fact was that she really enjoyed investigating fraud of all kinds. Racketeering, mail and wire fraud, conspiracy, murder, arson, obstruction of justice—the whole gamut intrigued her. It was a game with real stakes. She used her research skills to outsmart the truly criminal, devious mind. These people were the lowest form of humanity in Susan's mind, and she fancied herself the one who held the sword of justice to eradicate the scum.

She hadn't counted on building a sub-specialty in horserelated insurance fraud. Her success with the Florida horse mafia case—was it really more than ten years ago?—had established her as the office expert on horse cases. And so a few years back, when a show-horse barn in St. Paul burned to the ground, the case naturally landed on her desk. The insurance company thought it looked especially suspicious, since the barn was so heavily insured and not one horse made it out alive. The 3:00 a.m. fire consumed the eight-thousandsquare-foot stable as well. Firefighters got there in nine minutes, but the facility had already been engulfed. Twenty-nine horses died, including two very valuable foals that had been recently weaned from their mothers. Besides the insurance on the barn, which totaled about $1.5 million, about half the animals had policies with various companies ranging from $10,000 to $50,000.

The largest mortality policy was with Lloyd's of London. Lloyd's hired Carlos to work with the local authorities on the investigation. There was obvious evidence of foul play, but the bigger question was, who had the most motivation to set the fire? Lloyd's had already paid out heavily in a similar case involving the Florida horse mafia. Carlos, the resident expert on the horse mafia, noted similarities to another mysterious barn fire, in California, where arson had killed an actress's collection of thoroughbreds. Susan had read the newspaper stories, with their horrible eyewitness accounts of the barn ablaze and terrified screaming horses throwing themselves at the stable doors.

Susan was quite sure that the files had ended up on her desk not only because of her previous success with horse crimes, but because of Carlos's determination to turn the thing into a federal case involving mail fraud and interstate flight. He had discovered that the same groom worked at both facilities. In addition, the groom had a minor conviction for fourth-degree sexual assault. Still, that didn't give her enough to order a grand jury investigation. Calling the jury was well within her discretion as a federal prosecutor, but Minnesota wasn't prone to using the grand jury system except in murder and certain political cases. She needed more to go on if she wanted to go that route.

So now, years later, the arson case remained unsettled—the first in what had become a long string of unsolved horse-death cases stacked up in her files. Even Ken Rollins at the University of Minnesota Vet School pathology lab was convinced he was seeing way too many mysterious horse deaths. She remembered his words, and his boyish, sincere face as he spoke about how frustrated he was. "My hands are tied. Geez, I wish someone could do something. You know, if the insurance companies would only press these issues a bit more aggressively…but the investigators don't seem to care."

All he was responsible for were the pathology reports, he told her. He wanted the insurance companies to worry more. The Agriculture Department, which worked closely with the vet school, agreed with Rollins but had nothing solid to go on either. And as much as Susan had tried to find a connection or pin something down based on their information, she always came up empty-handed.

All these recollections had jazzed her brain even more. Susan grabbed the remote and tried channel-surfing, hoping to distract her mind. A Columbo marathon caught her eye, but that only reminded her of work, and of Carlos. Carlos was quite Columbo-like in attitude, but certainly not in appearance. That was one of the reasons why Susan liked to work with him, never mind the other aspects of their relationship. And Carlos genuinely seemed to care about what happened to the horses. God knows, she thought she would never get him out of her office that first day he showed up on the arson case. Luckily, knowing Carlos had helped immensely later, when she was trying to straighten out the mess with Maya's horse.

Funny that the tables were turned. Now she was going to him again for help on a horse case.

Columbo said something about murders and car thefts being very hard to hide.

That got her attention. But why?

Columbo answered the question as it was forming in her mind. "You still have a body, and how do you hide the stolen car?"

She had case after case of horses that had mysteriously died, but no bodies. After necropsies required by insurance companies were completed, carcasses were sent to the rendering plants. Except, perhaps, for this time. Maybe, just maybe, they would be able to hang on to Tremor's carcass long enough to find out something. They were still finishing Tremor's necropsy at the U of M. There had been a backlog of cases due to a viral infestation at a swine processing plant up north in the Brainerd area. Tremor was still in a freezer, as far as she knew. Grabbing the phone, she dialed Carlos's number. God, he'll be mad at this hour. Somehow, she didn't care.

No answer.

Her laptop was still at the end of the bed. Susan logged onto the database labeled "Horse Deaths" and looked at her documents. There were at least nine cases dating back five years. Each involved horses dying for mysterious reasons. The ultimate cause was found to be colic.

She brought up Notepad and made a note on her computer: Ask Carlos about this. Things to check: Are expensive horses usually prone to this type of thing? Could it be something in their diets, or something else? She'd always had a nagging feeling about the amount of insurance payments in these cases. Were owners murdering horses for the insurance money? Why would they bother, when they could just sell the horse if they weren't happy with it? What's a $250,000 loss to a multi-millionaire, much less a small loss of a $10,000 horse?

These questions were driving her crazy, and keeping her up. No reason to stay up alone. She dialed Carlos again. This time she stayed on the line, letting it ring and ring. Funny that he had no answering machine. Maybe not so funny; perhaps a better word would be frustrating.

At last there was a fumble of the phone, a pickup, and then she could hear the receiver being put down again. There was a small snap in her ear. Damn! He was there. Why wouldn't he talk? She punched redial.

Finally, there were signs of life at the other end of the line.

"Whoever is there, call me in the morning. I'm sleeping. This is the answering service of Carlos Dega."

The phone was slammed down. Ah, at last he was awake enough to function. Susan dialed again. "If this is an emergency, dial 911," she heard, followed by another curt placement of receiver into base. Really, Susan thought, he is rude. She dialed again.

The second she heard the phone picked up again, she said, "Don't you dare hang up on me again, Carlos. This is Susan."

"What is so important that it can't wait? Our client is already dead."

"I've been thinking…"

"Just because you have a hyperactive mind in the middle of the night doesn't mean the rest of the world does, Ms. Prosecutor. Go wake up someone else. Call me at a decent hour."

"I've already called my sister, and she went to bed early, too."

"What do you call early, just for the record?"

"OK, OK. I get your point."

"Make it quick, Susan."

"I need you to go as soon as you can to the U lab in the morning. I have a real compulsion to hang onto this horse. We have to make sure that every test possible is made on this animal. I don't want another carcass sent to the rendering plant without a more thorough exam. Every exam done, in fact."

"You've got my attention. I'm up."

"Good."

"Susan, you've been through this before, dealing with the U lab. Do you know whose name is on the submission form? Who went in with Tremor and did all the paperwork with the pathology vet?"

"Yeah. I've got it here in the file somewhere. Frick, I can't find the paper file. I thought I had it. Let me call it up on my laptop. Here it is. Podsky brought Tremor in. He talked to Ken Rollins."

"So, are you saying that the only person who can receive information about the necropsy is Podsky?"

"That's a good question, Carlos. I don't have the submission form copy on my laptop. Sonofagun, where is that hardcopy file?" Carlos heard papers rattling and some mumbling in the background.

Carlos sighed. "When you find it, can you send me a copy?"

"You can find out faster yourself when you go to the U. So, will you get over there and talk to Ken? First thing in the morning?"

"Sure. I will go first thing, Susan. But you know the drill. Better get a subpoena ready for the info from the vet, or you and I will be in the dark for sure."

"Thanks, Carlos. And...sorry about the late call. What time is it, anyway?"

"I don't even want to know. Later...hasta mañana."

Susan heard the phone click. Mission accomplished, at least for the moment, although her mind still had the ceaseless questions.

What if it was murder? Even murder of a person would not be a federal offense, and therefore it would be out of her jurisdiction. The only reason the horse deaths showed up on her database was because of Carlos and his arson case. Horse killings would be an economic crime, and though they might be interesting to her, they would have no value...unless...Susan read through the field reports again. She had nine cases in her files, but there were references to similar killings throughout the Midwest and up and down the eastern seaboard.

Under "Other," she had logged a file about a valuable show horse that had been electrocuted at the Los Angeles equestrian facility. A short circuit had sent an electrical current into the horse's metal stall. The incident prompted safety investigations at the city-owned facility. The horse was insured for $300,000. Lloyd's of London took the hit on that one, too.

Lloyd's must put a lot of faith in Carlos, since he had been assigned to that case. If Carlos was good enough for Lloyd's, he was good enough for her. She didn't want to think of all the ways Carlos might be good for her. She wanted to sleep. She focused again on crooks and crime.

Swindling wasn't a federal offense, either, but...Susan closed the laptop and settled back into her pillows. Before she closed her eyes, she scribbled RICO on the notepad she kept next to the phone.

CHAPTER 10

▼

Unfortunately for Carlos, the routine part of his job was never mundane. It boiled down to this: He stalked death by picking apart the remnants of life. This was the part of the job he hated. The shadows of the soul were reduced to nothing more than tissue samples and vials of blood.

Knowledge was his weapon, his solace, and his curse. It could unlock peace of mind, or it could unleash a furious need for vengeance and hunger for retribution. He hoped this visit would put the whole matter to rest. Taking a deep breath to quiet his churning stomach, Carlos maneuvered his Dodge Ram past the hay truck that partially blocked the access to the University of Minnesota Veterinary Diagnostic Laboratory, tucked in a labyrinth of red brick buildings just off Gortner Avenue.

Pulling into the last visitor's parking spot on the far side of the hay wagon, he considered whether he should bother getting a parking permit, and decided against it. He knew from experience that the warning sign was more of a deterrent than anything else. Besides, the university police knew his truck. He hoped Ken Rollins would be in.

A fresh-faced student dressed in jeans and a sweatshirt was working in the intake conference room to his left as he approached the reception desk. Carlos made a mental note to ask Ken who did the intake work on Tremor. Sometimes it was initial impressions that counted most, and often those fine details never made it to the submission form.

"May I help you?" The pleasant-faced woman in her late forties was new to Carlos, and her greeting was as much a challenge as it was a friendly hello.

"Is Ken Rollins in?" He handed her his card. That action often served to validate his presence. "My name is Carlos Dega. I'm working on a case and would like very much to speak with Dr. Rollins if he is available."

Her face softened a bit, but not much, as she looked from his card to his face and back to the card again. It was only a business card, but she was treating it more like a photo ID. Carlos correctly assessed that she considered herself the guardian of the lobby, and he decided to respect her position, even though he knew he could take the stairway to the second floor and never be challenged by anyone. She seemed satisfied by this deference to her authority.

"Dr. Rollins is in the cafeteria. There is some kind of going-away party. I'll tell him you are here." She punched in an extension on the phone, never quite taking her eyes off him.

He was used to the stares. Minnesota was only recently being known for its Latin influences. He realized that he looked out of place. Good for her. Still looking at him, she moved her mouth closer to the receiver. "A tall man...I mean," she looked at the card again, "A Mr. Dega is here, Dr. Rollins...Oh...OK." She addressed Carlos again. "He said to come right on up. Do you know the way? Everyone's name is on their office doors."

"Yes. Thanks. I've been here before. I can find my way. No problem." When he smiled at her, it seemed as though a flashbulb had gone off in her face. She started to stand, and fell back in her chair. "Bye," she whispered as he turned and took the stairs in front of her two at a time. His smile seemed to affect women that way, no matter what their age.

He knew the way. Ken's office was halfway down the corridor, past one of the laboratories. The door was open, and Ken, who was on the phone, waved him in. Carlos settled into one of the chairs facing the cluttered desk. Looking up, he examined Ken's degrees, hanging on the wall behind the vet. His education was impressive. One framed certificate told all who could read the fine print that Dr. Rollins was a Ph.D. Another frame held the paper that proclaimed he was board-certified in veterinary pathology. As Carlos began to read the rest, Ken Rollins hung up the phone, jumped up, and pumped his hand over the paper heap that hid the desk.

"Carlos, it's a treat to see you again."

"You, too, Ken. You look busy. Is this a bad time to discuss a case?"

"No, not really. We had a party here, and so I had the bulk of the morning blocked off. It's a good time for me. I've had my coffee and donuts, so I should be able to think straight for at least an hour," he laughed.

For a man who dealt with blood, guts, and microscopic pathogens, Ken was amazingly jovial. Carlos had never seen him unhappy. He meant it when he said it really was a treat to see Ken. Carlos also deeply respected Ken as a professional. Ken knew his stuff, and had a great sense of caring for the animals, students, and clients he worked with. He wanted the right thing to happen. Carlos responded to "caring" and "right," maybe because those were motivators for him, too.

"Then I'll be sure to talk fast to catch you while your brain still is firing at top speed. Ken, tell me what you have on the Tremor case. First of all, do you still have him here at the lab?"

"Since we've worked before, you know the drill, Carlos. Are you on the submission form so we can talk freely about all the information? I'd love to hand the whole file over to you, if you want it." His voice was warm and deep. Carlos thought he should be singing bass in a choral group.

"Ken, I've been asked by Susan Lindstrom to look into this, as an independent consultant. I don't know what company carries the insurance, or who the primary vet is. That's why I'm talking to you—to get caught up to speed, and see what's happening. I just got in from a month's vacation in Patagonia. To say I have been out of touch would be an understatement."

The vet sighed. "So, we are talking off the record then? You don't get to go home with a file?"

"You and I know it is a matter of time only. I'll have a subpoena for the records as soon as Susan can pull it together."

"I want to help, and time is of the essence here, so let's talk. This case is weighing heavily on me. Tremor is a highprofile case. We don't get ones like this very often. It would be nice to pass it on, so to speak. Close the door behind you, will you please?"

Carlos reached with a long arm and slammed the door shut. "I'm listening. And, don't worry, I won't tell anyone we talked before we got the legalities out of the way."

"That's the thing I like about you, Carlos, you are discreet."

"I pride myself on it."

"Do you want to see the carcass first, and then we can discuss this?"

"You answered one of my nagging questions." He didn't say that Susan was the "nagging" part of the question. "I was hoping you still had the horse here."

"That's another thing I appreciate about you," Ken replied. "You have a natural curiosity and thoroughness. What I wouldn't give to have all investigators probe like you do. Do you know that most never—that's never-ever—come to the lab? In fact, most don't even call and ask questions over the phone. Insurance investigators for horses are a silent bunch."

"So I've been told. I don't know how they make judgments, myself, but I am a gut reactor, and being with the people and the animals is what makes it work for me."

"I had you close the door because this case stinks. I've gotten myself all nervous and suspicious. I don't know whom I can trust here. I put some students working on this, rather than the usual heads of the labs. I wanted some ignorance of past history, if you know what I mean."

"Sounds like a good idea to me, Ken. Clear thinking."

"It relieves me to hear you say that...I think."

"Are you concerned you have someone here in the lab who...what...will substitute information, or just be lax?"

"I don't even know what I am worried about. We've just had more horse deaths than we should, more insurance claims than seem normal. And there is no central body to gather information, no standard protocols for insurance forms, so who's to put this together?"

"I think Susan is starting to, Ken."

"You know I called her about this Tremor incident."

Carlos thought of Tremor's death as more than an "incident," but nodded, even though he was surprised. "It's good you did, Ken. You've got great instincts."

"Let's go see that horse." Ken pushed his donut-filled stomach away from the desk, and heaved himself up. "It doesn't look good, Carlos. I feel I should warn you."

"Yah. Thanks. This is never good. I hate this part."

Ken felt compelled to go on. "He was in a warm barn for a long night, and by the time the groom got the vet there, and the horse was brought in...it was a long time. We have some serious decomposition here, especially for winter."

"Who was the vet, anyway?"

"Local. The one Podsky uses for all his horses, when the owners don't care."

"What does that mean?"

"I don't have to tell you, Carlos, a vet is a very personal thing. But Podsky's choice here may have more to do with his desires than his client's. For him, I think this choice is a very personal thing. It's Lisa Anthony."

"Is she any good?"

"At what?"

Carlos groaned. "Oh, no. Not another maiden fallen at the feet of her 'protector'?"

"Something like that. Clouds the judgment, don't you think?"

"Mmmm. Better have a look-see, before those donuts wear off."

CHAPTER 11

▼

A radio was playing country music in the histopathology lab as Carlos and Ken made their way to the loading dock. The sign next to the stainless steel cooler door read, "Carcasses are incinerated or sent to the rendering plant immediately after necropsy is performed and are not available for pickup by the owner." Ken opened the latch and motioned Carlos inside.

"Go ahead, but let me warn you, it's pretty bad in there."

Carlos stepped across a large pool of Tremor's blood and viewed the carcass. It occurred to him that this thing was not Tremor; Tremor's essence was elsewhere. He decided to keep that thought to himself.

"Where's the head?"

"It was easier to do the brain tissue slides separately. We mounted the stained sections. They would have been ready for examination by our brain team twenty-four hours after being prepared by our computerized processor."

"Anything turn up?"

"So far, just routine…off the record, of course. There's something else I'd like your opinion on, though. Want to take a look?"

Carlos nodded an affirmative and averted his gaze from what was left of Tremor. This would be easier now that he had been able to dissociate the living, breathing Tremor from this shell lying on the cold concrete floor. He backed out of the cooler, careful not to track any blood onto the loading dock. As it turned out, that act of courtesy was unnecessary.

Ken unceremoniously grabbed a grappling hook and attached it to the anterior of the carcass, where the head used to be. A flick of a switch on the wall caused the body to be hoisted on a cable attached to an overhead track, which slowly transported its terrible cargo to the adjoining 3,400square-foot necropsy section. Blood and fluid left a road map on the floor. Tremor finally came to rest on a specially designed hydraulic table that was capable of handling his 1,600-pound weight.

Carlos told himself to take a deep breath. He definitely wanted to think with as much logic as he could muster. He'd been through this process hundreds of times, more than most pathologists had before obtaining their degrees. Thinking of the organ systems as a completed jigsaw puzzle, he knew, would help with the logic. See beyond the obvious, he told himself. Take the puzzle apart, and put it back together again. Notice the relationships among the organs. Are they the right color and shape and texture? He distracted himself by going through the standard necropsy checklist.

Tremor's carcass hung over the edges of the table, and this allowed for an excellent view of the abdominal and chest cavities.

"Tell me what you see, Carlos."

"Podsky said it was colic. Well, you and I both know that colic can mean anything from indigestion to a blockage. I've seen blockages, and I've seen twisted intestines, but I don't see that here. May I?"

Carlos pulled on a pair of latex gloves, and using a hemostat, expertly followed the previous incision of the pathologist. He retracted the rectal and peritoneal muscles, exposing the bowels underneath.

"I'm looking for red or black discoloration...I see a little green here in the colon. Whew...can't really tell what color it is...how long before you got him?"

"Longer than we would like. They had to cut a hole in the barn wall to get him out. It says on the submission form that Podsky had to get a front-end loader from a construction company putting in a housing development down the road. It was at least 60 degrees in the barn. Quite a bit of deterioration."

"So, what are you getting at?"

"Take a look at this."

Ken directed Carlos's attention to the abdominal cavity.

"You've got me here, Ken. I have no idea what you're seeing."

"Equine Anatomy 101, Carlos. See this area on the blood vessel...the cranial mesenteric artery. Could have been an aneurysm."

"I don't follow you."

"Look at these multiple areas of small perforations on the intestines...I know it's hard to see; so much of the intestine has rotted."

"Yeah, I'm with you...what's this tissue that's attached to the intestines?"

"Now, you've got the picture. That's the mesentery. It connects the blood vessels to the intestines. Block one of those vessels, and you kill the intestine…it's called an infarct."

"Kind of like a heart attack, only in the intestine."

Ken was animated now. He could sense that Carlos was thinking with him.

"Cut off the blood supply, and you can call it colic, but not the usual kind."

"You think that's all it was?" Carlos thought that maybe he was off the hook. He could just wrap this up and go home. There would be a big payoff, but that's what insurance was for. There was nothing the matter with that. Podsky had a way of being around when there was foul play, but he sure had nothing to gain from this one. He needed Tremor in the barn. Maybe this one wouldn't make Susan's files after all.

"Unless it was negligence."

Carlos looked up from the bloody cavern and gave Ken his undivided attention.

"How could an aneurysm be negligence?"

"Well, we usually see this kind of thing with strongyles. When the larva is ingested by a horse, it penetrates the wall of the cecum, right here at the beginning of the large intestine, and it develops and migrates to the arteries." Ken traced the path with his fingers over the horse's lower abdomen.

"Then what happens?"

"A couple of things can happen. You can get a ballooning of a blood vessel…that would be evidence of a larval infestation."

"Or?"

"Or, a clot can develop that blocks the blood flow and kills the intestine."

"Infarct."

"Right!"

"So, what's your theory? There is so much decomposition here; it's a wonder you folks got this far with this."

"I think these little perforations are indications of a larval infestation. I admit I wanted to believe there was foul play, but maybe I was too eager. It still bothers me, though. I can't understand how this amount of negligence could happen with such a valuable horse."

"Why is that?"

"Well, routine worming would have taken care of the problem…maybe these are old lesions. I can't be positive without more tests, but I can't really come up with any other cause of death."

"So, routine worming would prevent strongyles. If the horse wasn't wormed, there would be malpractice on the part of the attending vet, and there would be no insurance liability. Good try to get me off the hook, Ken, but a horse of Tremor's quality would certainly have had routine wormings. It's easy to check the records, though."

"I figured you'd say that, but I keep thinking about this one. There's got to be more, but if bacteriology, toxicology, and parasitology don't come up with anything, I'm gonna have to call it strongyles. Maybe he got a bad batch of wormer. I really don't see anything else, although I'd sure like to come up with something. All of his organ systems look so clean. This was a healthy animal."

"You save any blood?"

"Yeah, I labeled a couple of vials separately. Thought maybe there might be a reference sample on file somewhere. I want to check the samples for antibodies to strongyles."

"OK. Just don't use up all of the blood until I talk with Susan. See if you can keep a couple of extra samples. I'm not officially involved, yet. Any other tests you want to run?"

"We were able to get a fresh stool sample from the colon. I'd like to see if there are any ova present."

"A few more questions OK with you, Ken?"

"Shoot."

"Did the referring vet—Lisa Anthony, was it?—did she give you a detailed clinical history?"

"I'll have my student check. It's usually standard."

"We will have a subpoena. Make sure the report lists the body systems that require special attention…the ones you pointed out to me."

"Done."

"Has the insurance company contacted you yet?"

"Not yet."

"This case might get messy. Usually the insurance company will indicate if they want special testing. Are you saying the potential for litigation was not identified on the submission sheet?"

"I'm saying the insurer was not listed anywhere on the submission form. The attending vet signed for standard necropsy tests."

"Lisa Anthony?"

"You got it."

CHAPTER 12

▼

Getting up was bad. Madonna was singing "…you're frozen…" on WLIT.

"You got that right," Susan muttered as she slammed a hand down on the snooze button.

It seemed like seconds later when the commercial for Wells Fargo Bank finally convinced her there was no more hiding under the covers. Susan rolled over on her back, reached for the pack of Marlboros for a jump-start, and padded her way to the microwave in her small but efficient kitchen.

The hazelnut brew in the coffeemaker looked pretty thick, but she poured a cup anyway and set the microwave for two minutes. The murky liquid tasted worse than it looked, so she dumped what was left in the sink and opted for a quick shower instead. Not that she was on a time clock. As a special appointment, she was pretty much free to come and go in the office as she saw fit. However, Susan hated to miss anything, much less the good morning gossip at the secretarial workstation outside her office.

The sixth floor was the mother lode of interesting cases, as far as she was concerned. That's where the criminal cases were dissected, and no one knew more about what was really going on than the GS secretaries who did all of the word processing. The internal stairway leading to the civil division on the fifth floor was a reminder that she had moved up in her world in more ways than one. Not that she'd ever say that to anyone. Sometimes the civil cases would provide useful background for her investigations, so she wanted to keep a good rapport with her old colleagues.

It was a ten-minute drive from her apartment to the new Federal Courthouse. She still had time to run over to Third Street if she hurried. She could grab a cup of coffee and a bagel at Chessen's. The deli was the haunt of the locals in the building, and since she could see the place from her window, she knew she'd regret it if she settled for Shirley's coffee this morning.

As she pushed open the door to the deli, she saw two attorneys from the fifth floor and a retired federal judge who liked to hang around and visit with his old cronies. Otherwise the place was pretty quiet. Things would perk up at lunchtime if the fare at the courthouse cafe was as disagreeable as usual.

Mission accomplished and breakfast in hand, Susan walked around the building and entered through the atrium lobby. The three large potted plants next to the cafe looked pretty wilted. After signing in at security, she kicked her shoes off in the carpeted elevator just until the doors opened on the fifth floor. She hoped her card key reader was locked in her desk, because she couldn't find it at home this morning. Oh, well, this time she could act like an ordinary person and enter through the reception area.

Susan vaguely noticed that someone was at one of the public access terminals in the lobby of the reception area. The secretary nodded and buzzed her through the door to the right of the reception desk, while the Attorney General's eyes seemed to follow her from the wall as she passed in front of the many photos of "The General" that seemed to hang around every corner. One day she was going to count how many of those photos there actually were. Someone must have borrowed the picture of the president, because the Attorney General was all alone on the wall this morning. At least she admired her ultimate boss.

"Shirley, we have got to do something about getting rid of that tacky Tony Vinella print of Palace Avenue in Santa Fe," Susan whispered in her ear as she grabbed another stack of pink notes from the station. The phone calls could take all morning to return. It promised to be a long day.

Shirley rolled her eyes at Susan. "Stealing that picture could get you jail time," she informed Susan. Susan stuck her finger in her mouth and made a little gagging sound. Both of them laughed quiet little chuckles.

Unlocking the door to number 664, Susan was glad for the windows. Her hands were full enough with coffee, bagels and messages, and turning on the lights was too much. She pushed the door shut behind her, wriggled out of her shoes again, and kicked them in the corner under the drooping potted palm. Settling in her chair, she found a not-too-important file to use as a placemat for her breakfast. She didn't want to get rings on her nice desk. As she looked out her window and sipped, her eyes focused on the clock tower in front of her. The old Milwaukee Road railroad station once had been only two blocks away. The building was still there, of course, but it was no longer a train station. More's the pity. She was glad that urban renewal had saved the original structure. Maybe some day it would be restored to its glamorous beginnings and be used for trains once again. Susan thought about the snarl of traffic everywhere in the Cities and hoped commuter trains would come into fashion. The northeast view was pleasing to her, as the light came in all day, but did not produce a glare, especially when she worked late.

As she looked, around she was satisfied. Somehow, nondomestic as she was, she had put her own stamp on this little corner of her world. The stained-glass piece hanging at the top of her expanse of windows gave her joy, and the lights and colors reflected around her walls, washing them with rainbows. She had invited a decorator in, and the two of them had created a warm atmosphere that imbued trust, comfort, and security. At night, she would often work and phone at her large cherry-wood desk with only the green banker's lamp turned on. The surprise to all her coworkers was how neatly Susan kept her office. Her desktop was her only lapse, as that was stacked haphazardly with more than enough files for two attorneys. There were more files on the floor behind her chair. If she had her own private bathroom, that would have been stacked with files as well.

Susan called Gwen to apologize for the late-night alarm. Maya answered.

"Gwen and Maya's house. Whom may I say is calling?"

"Maya? Auntie Susan."

"Oh, yeah. Pretty cool message I learned. Whatcha think?"

"Great, honey. You are growing up. Is your mom around?"

"Yep…but asleep."

"Mmmm. I don't want to bother her again. I called her last night, and wanted to tell her I was sorry for waking her. Will you give her that message for me?"

"Sure, Auntie Susan. No problem. Anything else?"

"This isn't teasing you, honey. Don't talk to strangers. Don't go out without your mom for a few days. Stay close to grownups. Can you do that? There are some strange people around, and I don't want to worry about you. I mean, I want you safe."

"Weird. You know, sometimes you weird me out."

"Yeah. I know. Your mom tells me that too. Humor me, OK, honey?"

"Sure, Auntie Susan."

"Love you."

"Me too!"

Then she dug into the phone messages. She saw there was one from Ken Rollins and decided that was a good way to start. That case had kept her up half the night.

"Ken?"

"Your man just left, Susan."

"My man?"

"Your investigator. Sorry."

"What have you got going there, Ken?"

"He says you will have to get a subpoena to get the info from the submission form, and the test results."

"I take it no one who is really interested in this case is listed?"

"If you mean are you and Carlos on the form, then in a word, No."

"Can you talk to me yet, Ken?"

"Let's put it this way, talk to Carlos, get me that subpoena, and then we will meet for coffee someplace."

"Not you, too."

"What are you talking about?"

"Never mind."

"Ball's in your court, Susan. Then I'll call you when I get everything together here."

"Do you still have the horse?"

"Yes, and we will keep him for a while, but you will have to get on it in a hurry. We can't keep him too long. He's a big boy, and we have several cows coming in real soon."

"Thanks for calling me, Ken. Carlos must have been there early."

"He was. But that was good for me, too. Have you been up long?"

She knew that was a dig and chose to ignore it. "Bye, Ken. Thanks."

Shirley poked her head through the door. "There's an emergency phone call on line two. Better get it." The subpoena would have to wait, at least for this morning.

CHAPTER 13

▼

Podsky leered at Fiona Andersson's too-tight, full-seat Tempi breeches and what little they disguised as Fiona hauled herself into the three-thousand-dollar custom saddle that he had just sold her. Then he shuddered at his own reaction and thwacked his riding crop on the top of his boots as a kind of self-flagellation to hide his annoyance with himself. He would have to end things, but for now it was better to keep it on an even plane. Too much was happening too fast. He didn't need another scene like the one they'd had yesterday just before that insurance investigator showed up.

"Yah, dear, good, that looks good."

"I don't know, Sasha. Shouldn't I have more room between my seat and the cantle?"

"You look marvelous, my dear. Why not try a few leg yields and then trot a twenty-meter circle at C."

He was actually thinking she should lose a few pounds and give up her pathetic attempts at riding.

However, Fiona would never hear those words from his lips. As the wife of the sitting governor, she was too much of an asset to the barn and his reputation. He hadn't needed to get into bed with her. It was just too easy. A small flirtation had turned into a full-blown affair before he realized that the woman had fallen in love with him. He was used to wealthy, lonely women falling in love with him, but this situation had gotten too sticky. There had to be a way out, but too much was transpiring, and his usual charms and excuses were eluding him. He kept reminding himself to be careful. She was furious when she found him with Lisa.

Luckily for him it was the truth that Lisa was handling the insurance claim for Tremor. It gave him the excuse he needed to be spending a lot of time with her.

"I'm telling you, Sasha, it just doesn't feel right!"

"Yah, so, all right, then. Dismount and we'll see. You need to try to break in the leather, I know."

Podsky grabbed the reins as Fiona swung clumsily out of the saddle, losing her footing and falling against him. In spite of himself, he found the smell of her perfume tempting, and he did not back away as she continued to lean against him.

"Thank you, Sasha, dear. Whatever would I do without you? I'm so glad you are handling this whole mess with Tremor. It's so terrible, and with the Children's Benefit coming up and all...I just wouldn't be able to cope. Some insurance investigator named Carlos something-or-other called. What should I tell him?" Podsky hadn't counted on Carlos moving so quickly. He'd have to tell Lisa that Fiona would be giving a statement.

"You don't have to tell him anything, my dear. I'll handle it all. The barn was responsible for Tremor's care. That is my job. Don't you worry."

"Well, he was a big investment, and my partners could be important contributors to my husband's political career. I just hope everything goes smoothly. It's horrible what happened, but we could use the cash for the reelection campaign."

Not a tear was shed for the magnificent animal. Fiona was close to his heart, after all. He had discovered over the years that the true value of the horse lay in the prestige and money it would attract. This woman shared his vision, but she wasn't astute enough to realize her own greed. Tremor's death was a political inconvenience, nothing more. "I said, don't worry."

Fiona leaned closer again.

"Sasha, don't you think we could find another vet? I really don't like that Dr. Anthony. Are you sure she knows what she is doing?" Here it comes, Podsky thought. Be careful.

"This will be over before you know it, Fiona. Trust me. When things settle down, we'll take a trip to Puerto Rico and find you a new horse. I have a couple of leads already."

The thought of a Caribbean holiday alone with Podsky was enough to pacify Fiona for the moment at least. Maybe they could buy a much cheaper horse, have money for the campaign, and get away together again. She kissed his stubbly cheek and just about skipped away from him. Her obvious enthusiasm revolted him. He loosened the girth on the little mare.

"Fine, fine. Now don't worry. Why don't you stop by the spa and have a massage or a tan?"

Fiona was in a daze as she walked out to the BMW. It didn't even occur to her that she should have put the mare away herself. Puerto Rico and Podsky. It was so sweet of him to think of that. Did he think of their time together in the courtyard of that little hacienda in San Juan as much as she did? She could still recall the hours of flirtation and intimate revelations by the fountain. Maybe if they went back they could recapture the magic. Sasha looked tired. Maybe that was why he seemed so preoccupied lately. She was sorry they'd quarreled. Maybe Raja was getting to him. She knew things weren't going well between the two of them. Fiona figured she could nourish him in a way that Raja never could. This thought alone cemented her passion for him. Well, if this insurance matter got settled soon, they could be on their way to the Caribbean in a few weeks. Maybe sooner.

Fiona pulled down the lighted visor mirror and studied her pale face. The Minnesota winter had left her looking and feeling old. She grabbed the cell phone and punched in the number for the tanning salon. It was part of the spa Raja owned. It bothered her to go there, but it was the best health club in the area, and it helped her image to be seen there. The receptionist told Fiona she could have an appointment in two hours. Good. That gave her a bit of time to run some errands.

The girl at the front desk at the club looked like a poor imitation of a street-walker as she sat filing her nails and chewing gum. Her black leotard left nothing to the imagination. When she looked up and saw Fiona, she dropped the nail file.

"Mrs. Andersson. I'm so sorry. Let me get the bed ready for you." Fiona loved the reaction. It was fun to be recognized, and she truly enjoyed the pandering.

"That's all right, dear. You just go ahead." In a few minutes the girl was back.

"How long would you like to go today?"

"Well, it's been a while. Do you think I could last twenty minutes without turning pink?"

The girl studied Fiona's features.

"I think so. I'll put you in one of the cooler beds and keep it at nineteen minutes."

Fiona wondered if that one minute less would make any difference. The truth was that she was really uncomfortable in the tanning bed, but it was a necessary addition to her regular grooming routine, especially before a vacation in the sun. It was better to get that tan base and not have to worry about spending the day on the beach and burning. Even though her true hair color was more of a mousy brown, her skin was fair, and Fiona had found out the hard way that she could burn easily. She worried about frying in the tanning bed. It was quite the claustrophobic experience, like being pressed between the covers of a waffle iron. All that whirring and vibrating made her uneasy. What if something went wrong?

A poster of the girl in a bikini on some far-away tropical beach reminded her that all of the discomfort was worth it. She settled into the small room and took off all of her clothes except for her bra, to protect her nipples. She slipped out of the straps to avoid tan lines on the shoulders. An even tan would make her more seductive to Podsky, she thought. She fiddled with the tuner on the radio and tried the headset. By counting the number of songs played, she could guess how long she had been under the lamps and turn off the lights if she got too hot or uncomfortable or the timer was set improperly. She had heard of terrible burns sustained by customers of tanning salons who had fallen asleep under the lights after the attendant had forgotten to adjust the timer.

The governor's wife tucked a green towel under her ample rear and hit the start switch. She pushed the eye protectors deep into her eye sockets and adjusted the headphones on her ears. Taking a deep breath, she focused on the music, and that served to drown out the whirring and groaning of the motors on the bed as she pulled down the hood to within six inches of her face. It was hot, very hot, in just a few minutes.

The room fan wasn't working very well, and she reached outside of the bed to adjust the airflow on the small fan that was directed toward the opening in the bed. The breeze helped a bit, and Fiona settled into a reverie about Podsky. She could almost imagine that they were alone together on the beach again. The lights were awfully hot. She thought the girl had said this was a cool bed. The metal lid made her feel she was in a coffin. Maybe she was just thinking about it too much, or maybe it was her daydreams about Podsky, but she felt her sweat beginning to soak through the towel.

Turning her head, she glanced at the fan. It was still working. Only three songs had played and there were no commercials, so she couldn't have been in for very long. She leaned back and thought about Podsky again. The sweat was running into her eyes now. Maybe if she pushed the hood a few inches away from her face…the manicured hand reached around the edge of the metal cover for leverage, and what started as a soft tingling transformed into an electrical arc of 2500 degrees Celsius—a hot bed indeed. Fiona's last vision before she was overtaken by the flash was that of Podsky's face. Her sweaty body was a perfect conduit, carrying the surge through muscles, blood vessels, tendons, and fat.

CHAPTER 14

▼

Carlos was angry. It was a terrifying concept that the life of any creature could be snuffed out at the whim of a single human being. And if someone could summarily kill a beautiful sentient being like Tremor, the leap to killing a person couldn't be too far. He knew it wasn't healthy to carry around this baggage of anger as he drove—not healthy for him, and not for others. Road rage could be an easy response. He wanted to go to the stable to talk to Britt again, but maybe he might stop off at home for a nice long jog first.

Torn by anger, indecision, and the small little leap in his stomach at the thought of seeing Britt again, he drove on, not knowing what his primary interest really was. As he wended his way through the traffic snarls on Highway 94, he pushed the radio's preset button to MPR. Minnesota Public Radio always captured his emotions and imagination, and gave him mental space for mind wandering. It was a constant companion for him. Music opened a door for him to a world of order and beauty. Classical music was, for the most part, tremendously methodical, and its rhythm settled and organized his brain waves. Yes. He loved beauty and order. It was one of the many things he appreciated about dressage work.

Carlos found he had taken the exit for Highway 394. He was headed west. Already Mozart's Violin Concerto No. 3 in G was soothing his anger. He decided to press on to Podsky's stable to see Britt. He would run after that, taking all the time he wanted. He knew working out was his way of ordering his body along with his mind. More importantly, it discharged all his excess energy and anger.

Going out toward Chaska was a beautiful drive, and one Carlos didn't make often. He relished the transition from city to country. The undulating hills, with the snow covering broken corn stalks in fields put to bed for the winter, were like picture postcards from long ago. He felt he would be able to look over his shoulder and see a horse-drawn sleigh keeping pace with him on the track beside the road. Working farms were dotted between subdivisions of new housing. Animals grazed next to factories with smokestacks, their long hats of white steam dissipating into the leaden haze of winter sky.

The stable was nestled in a valley far enough out that it was still considered country. Urban sprawl was encroaching, but there was just the right amount of land to give the illusion of peacefulness and space. And illusion it was. Podsky's stable was no haven.

Several pieces of music later, Carlos was parking his car in the lot attached to the stables. He thought again how unusual it was to have a blacktop parking area for a local stable. Ordinarily people parked along the side of the road or on a gravel turnaround, anywhere they could find that was relatively close to the barn area. Land was valuable, roads expensive, and maintenance impossible, so barn owners generally left people to their own devices in finding a place for their vehicles.

There was no sun today, and the wind was tearing around the yard and paddock. It was bitter. February could be like that, brilliant one day, malignant the next. Wind chill combined with the dropping temperature could whiten flesh in less than a minute, unless it was covered well. The horses would be working inside today. Often they wouldn't work at all, if it got too cold. Something about the intense cold made the horses skittish, and they would act like naughty children.

Carlos strode through the barn door, expecting to be challenged as he was yesterday. It was eerily quiet. He could hear horses stomping in their stalls. He looked through the Plexiglas window. No one was active in the stable, no lessons being taught. He walked down the aisle. He wanted to avoid Tremor's box, but had to pass it to get to the area in back where he might find Britt. He kept poking his head into stalls, the tack room, and small aisles that housed difficult horses, or ones needing extra privacy. The sense of quiet was unusual. There wasn't even a radio playing.

At the door to the helper's lounge Carlos paused. "Britt?" No response.

"Britt? Anyone here?" He decided to sit for a minute, to see if anyone would show up. After about five minutes his waiting seemed silly. He then remembered she had living quarters above the barn. He found the stairs that wound up the outside of the building. Carlos dashed up the stairs, as they seemed to catch the full brunt of the wind. He pulled up the hood on his standard-issue Minnesota down parka, pounded on the dusty, brown door, and shouted. This weather was suboptimal for being outside for any length of time greater than two minutes. If she didn't answer on the next knock, he would call her from the car and leave a message on her machine. He banged his heavily gloved fist on the door again. With the wind beginning to howl, she might not hear him even if she was inside.

As he turned away, the door opened. Britt's startled face poked out around the edge of the door. "Oh. Carlos, is that you?"

Not waiting for an answer she opened the door wide, and pulled him inside. The wind whipped the door out of her hand, and banged it shut. A picture on the wall shook. She was pleased to see him. A huge grin was lighting up her face.

Smiling back, Carlos couldn't help but admire her wholesome good looks and the fresh-washed athleticism she exuded. There was some magnetism about her when her eyes opened fully, and she grinned with utter artlessness. There was no guile about this woman, and no artifice in her dress. She was wearing a heavy flannel shirt in bright red, over a thermal Henley white pullover. Her jeans were worn and comfortable, and did not hide the fuzzy bunny slippers she had pulled on over her thick red socks.

"Something smells good in here," Carlos directed his statement toward the kitchen.

"I've got some bean soup cooking on the stove. Very hearty. I've been up since it seems like forever and decided to get something going to sustain me. There's bread rising next to the pot, to keep it warm. I love the smell of yeasty things rising, don't you?"

"Hmmmm. Do I ever. That's why I hang out at bakeries whenever I get the chance. Fresh bread is my favorite kind of food. That and a really good cup of coffee."

Britt laughed. "From the look on your face, coffee must be a religious experience for you."

"Almost. But I prefer having coffee and then a separate religious experience. That way, I get both."

"Here we are still standing by the door. How ill-mannered of me. Do you, or, I mean, would you like to sit? Here, let me take your coat."

"I guess it's settled then; if you have my coat, I will be staying and sitting for a bit."

She gave him that open look, and twinkled like a little star. "Yes, in this weather you will be staying if I have your coat!"

She took his parka and ended up laying it on the floor by a vigorously growing spider plant. "It won't eat it while we're not looking, will it?" he asked. He wanted to see her twinkle again. She did.

"Just a sec. I want to put that bread in the oven, and then we can talk."

When Carlos was settled on a sofa covered with a handmade quilt, and Britt crossed her legs into a white wicker chair, he asked her the question that had been nagging at him. "What unusual things have you thought of, Britt, that might have a bearing on Tremor? No, wait; let me amend that statement. What things have you thought of at all over the last day?"

She sobered somewhat, but not entirely. "You want to know all my thoughts since I last saw you?"

It was Carlos's turn to tease, but he had lost what to say. He did, indeed, want to know what she was thinking, but didn't know how to say that. Instead, he just smiled. His teeth flashing in his angular face contrasted strikingly with his dark complexion. In the winter, most people in Minnesota had white, pasty skin. His was conveniently dark throughout all seasons. It often made him stand out. It was hard for some to picture that he was a local.

"Why don't you just talk to me about Tremor. Tell me how he thought, worked, what pleased him. What did you like about being with him?"

The tension that had been hidden in her shoulders released. She nodded, fixed her eyes on a spot on the white wall above Carlos's head and began to free-associate. As she talked, it became clearer to Carlos what the essence of Tremor was. He closed his eyes, and pictured along with her as she unburdened her heart and her love for the animal. She kept her monologue going for over twenty minutes. He found out how she came to be Tremor's groom, and all the little idiosyncrasies of the black. She was an excellent storyteller and kept him enthralled. Not once did she say "well."

A buzzer went off in the background, and he opened his eyes. Britt came out of her private space, her world of Tremor, and jumped up. "Ohmigosh. My bread is finished. Hold on there."

Carlos could see into the kitchen from his place on the sofa. The apartment was small, but it was homey, and it enveloped him with a sense of ease and comfort. It was hard to remember that just a short time ago he had been so very angry. It was also difficult for him to think this little oasis of domesticity was actually above Podsky's barn. Life was certainly filled with contrasts.

The bread smelled divine. His stomach growled. Britt must have heard it, as she looked up from stirring the soup and inquired, "Would you like to stay for lunch?"

"What a grand gesture. I surely wouldn't want to intrude, but it does smell marvelous. I didn't realize how hungry I was until just now."

"Perfect. This promises to be a good meal, and it seems a shame not to share it with someone who really appreciates it."

"Can I help?"

"Well…see the spider plant? If you would move it, we can eat on that table because it has leaves that unfold. Put the plant in the bedroom under the window there."

She truly was guileless. "Sure." As he went into the bedroom, he saw her double bed neatly made, and yet another handmade quilt put over it. There was a white iron headboard and footboard, with myriad pillows propped against the front end. It was neat as a pin. Carlos could resonate with that. It smelled of her freshness, and he was surprised that he felt so comfortable there, in her most private space. And he was torn. He wanted to remain objective with Britt. He didn't want his judgment on this case clouded with anyone or anything. And yet, he was unabashedly attracted to her. He couldn't remember how long it had been since he'd felt that way. It was pleasantly disturbing.

When he and Britt had finished the home-cooked meal—a rarity, it seemed to Carlos these days—they pushed back from the table and talked some more. Finally Britt stood up, and, with a start, looked at the clock. "Ohmigosh! Look how late it's gotten. I need to get down to the stable and get at a few things Podsky wanted me to do! I am sorry, Carlos, but I need to get to work."

"Me too. I'm afraid I forgot that I was here to ask you things; I got so carried away with the coziness of being here…being with you."

Britt smiled at him with those amazing eyes, leading him on while trying to whisk him out the door. They both reached over for his coat at the same time, bumped heads, and stumbled into each other, one acting as much like a gawky kid as the other. They laughed, Carlos with a deep hearty chortle, Britt with a giggle.

Carlos touched Britt's hair on the back of her head, then reached for her hand, which he missed because she put her face up expectantly for a kiss. Instead, he stroked her cheek with the back of his hand ever so gently, put on his coat in one swinging motion, and with a brief nod of the head said, "Thanks for lunch."

He swirled out the door and noticed the wind had died down to near normal levels. What time was it, anyway?

CHAPTER 15

▼

A small commotion in the hallway outside of her office distracted Susan from the call waiting on line two. A couple of paralegals and the youngest assistant D.A. were gathering around Shirley's desk watching her ten-inch Panasonic television, which served as a plant stand for a sickly fern that had been in the office at least as long as Shirley had. Technically, staff members weren't allowed to have televisions, but Shirley had been around for longer than the last three District Attorneys combined and often wrote her own rulebook. So much so, that she was able to sweet-talk maintenance into running an extra cable feed through the network conduit.

Ignoring the insistent blinking red light on the phone, Susan poked her head around the corner just in time to hear Channel Seven's lead anchor, Cindi Moreno, wrapping up a breaking story. Curious, Susan joined the growing huddle around Shirley's cubicle. Moreno was somewhat of a local celebrity, and easily recognized, not least because her face and that of co-anchor Frank Bartak loomed from a billboard over the I-94-694 interchange. Somehow the advertisement reminded Susan of Doctor Eckleburg's spectacles looming over George Wilson's garage in The Great Gatsby. Gatsby was the only novel she'd truly enjoyed in American Lit at Harvard. She saw the billboard as the modern equivalent of Doctor Eckleburg's moral stare over the roaring twenties. Channel Seven's news crew was the first to report on the failings and foibles of the Tom and Daisy Buchanans of the turn-of-the millennium Minnesota landscape. Now, Susan could see, Moreno was reporting from the county morgue at Hennepin General Hospital.

The content of Moreno's report jolted Susan's attention from the metaphor.

"Say, what?" Shirley shouted at the images streaming on the screen.

"It appears to have been an accident, Frank. Mrs. Andersson was visiting a tanning parlor and the bed apparently malfunctioned. The police say she died instantly of electrocution."

Even as she absorbed the strange news, Susan couldn't help wondering why Moreno wasn't more emotional. She had been friends with Fiona Andersson. Was it professional cool, or something else?

"Do we have any official word on how this happened?" asked co-anchor Bartak, from his perch in the newsroom.

"Nothing official yet, Frank. We do know from the local authorities that maintenance was done on the tanning bed yesterday morning. That may account for the bed being left in an unsafe condition."

"Do we know what exactly was wrong with it?" The camera pulled back for a wide shot just as some kid was waving a foam rubber finger with "number one" written on it behind Moreno's head. Moreno fumbled through her notepad for an instant before tossing her head in her trademark fashion and continuing. Maybe she was upset, Susan thought. God knows she herself had at times fought back tears in an effort to remain professional at all costs.

"Apparently the frame of the bed became energized when the power cord for the bed was inserted into a damaged wall outlet. The damage caused the ground prong of the plug to be inserted into one of the phase terminals. The metal casing on the tanning bed became energized when it was turned on."

"You mean the plug was twisted when it was inserted?"

"As I understand it, yes."

"Cindi, would it be accurate to call this a freak accident?"

"Actually, Frank, events like this are not uncommon, according to government reports on workplace accidents. In one case we found, a 24-year-old employee of a textile mill in North Carolina was electrocuted when he touched his loom frame. Same situation. The plug was turned the wrong way." Pretty impressive of Moreno to have that much background so fast, Susan thought. She made a mental note to try to hire away Moreno's staff researcher.

Shirley handed the phone to Susan without taking her eyes off the screen.

"You better take this call. The blinking's driving me crazy."

It was Pat North, one of the FBI agents involved in the ongoing horse killings investigation.

"You have a radio on?"

"Better. We have Shirley's TV."

"I can't believe it."

"What do you think, Pat? Foul play? Or could it have happened the way they say?"

"It can happen all right, but it usually happens in sleazy workplaces. Sweatshops and all. The governor's wife. Crap! Wonder if he'll still go for the re-election?"

"Probably. He might think he can count on the sympathy vote now."

"Can you believe that this is Cindi Moreno's story? Gonna make it harder for us to interview her on the racehorse case. Don't want to tip her off on any of the particulars of the Tremor investigation."

"What are you talking about, Pat?"

"Don't you ever read your faxes? Cindi Moreno's listed on the insurance payoff for both Tremor and that racehorse that was stolen from Canterbury Downs. Didn't she and the governor's wife ride together?"

"They were friendly on the celebrity circuit. Maybe more beyond that. Carlos told me that Moreno seldom showed up at the barn. At least that's all he's been told. He might want to check some more. I'll mention it to him."

"Something else that's pretty strange."

"Like what?"

"Guess who owned the tanning parlor?"

Susan was getting tired of playing twenty questions with Pat, and her irritation showed.

"I guess I don't really care, but if you think it's important..."

"Sit down for this one...Raja Podsky."

"You've got to be kidding."

"I'm not, I swear."

"How do you know all of this, Pat?"

"I'm pretty familiar with Podsky's file. Our Russian informant seems to have spread his business interests far and wide. Anyway, I'm more interested in Moreno's tie-in with the missing racehorse."

"You really think she's involved in a nefarious way?"

"Hard to say. Podsky fingered the groom that stole the horse, but he seems to have vanished off the face of the earth. The guy was a professional gambler as well as a race fixer, so we've been keeping an eye on the gambling halls and casinos, but no luck so far."

"Wait. You say the groom, or whoever he really was, was fixing races?"

"Yeah. They call it sponging. You insert sponges in the nostrils of a horse or two, the favorites, to adversely affect their performance. Takes somebody that knows the horse real well to get the job done. Thoroughbreds won't exactly stand still for that sort of thing."

"Podsky sure knows his way around the scumbags."

"Well, thanks to Podsky and you, Susan, we were able to get a warrant out for the groom on charges of wire fraud and interstate travel with intent to carry on unlawful activity. Thank God for RICO." Susan knew from first-hand experience that the federal anti-corruption law was a boon for agents like Pat. "I hear several animal rights organizations have put out a $50,000 reward for information on how to catch the groom in that case. Maybe something will come of it."

"Maybe. Right now, Pat, I want to get to Cindi Moreno."

"I read the first interview with her. Do you believe her story that she just likes to buy horses?"

"Could be, but she's had awfully bad luck with her last two purchases, wouldn't you say?"

"Maybe she is just hanging out with the wrong crowd. Could be innocent. A lot of people get taken in the horse business."

"Yeah, but she was smart enough to have insurance. Go ahead and interview her again, Pat, but keep me posted. I think I'm gonna lean on our friend Podsky a little harder."

"The news media might catch the tie-in with Tremor. That's the last thing we want right now. Too many particulars might spook the people responsible. His death was a big deal even to those outside of the horsy set. If I were you, I'd keep it strictly no comment on the details of the Tremor investigation for now."

"That will be easy. We don't have much to go on in the case yet. Anyway, Shirley will handle it. She's a master at stonewalling. And, Pat? Be careful not to spook Moreno, will you?"

"Who, me? We're FBI, remember? Talk later."

"Yeah, right." Susan hung up the phone and thought about Podsky. He was everywhere and nowhere at the same time. She had been ready to nail him on his involvement with unlawful transport of horses across international borders, based on the work she'd done on Maya's case, when he came up with the big break in the case of the missing racehorse. Tit for tat. Podsky had agreed to name names in return for immunity. Funny he left out the part about sponging. Well, what was she supposed to expect? Still, it pissed her off that Podsky was holding back on the race-fixing scheme. Was he protecting someone else? Or was it simply a matter of using information as currency? Don't spend it all in one place. Whatever it was, she was going to find out.

She thought about Carlos and realized that she was beginning to hate the rules of this game. Carlos had no idea that Podsky was her main informant. For that matter, Podsky had no clue that her office was behind the Tremor investigation. It was a dangerous game. Information brought protection and anonymity. She hoped the shield she had placed around Podsky wasn't misplaced…for Carlos's sake

CHAPTER 16

▼

The spurs on Podsky's boots snagged the chenille spread as he swung his bow-legged form across the bed he shared with Raja. He needed her now, but she was downtown dealing with the whole horrible mess at the salon. Fiona was gone. He felt nothing. How ironic that Raja was picking up the pieces. She was always the glue that held everything together, including his own pitiful life. He was feeling particularly sorry for himself.

Juggling Lisa, Fiona, and Raja was difficult but not impossible. In the end, it was always Raja he turned to. Never demanding of his time, she always opened her checkbook and her bed to him. God, he wished she were here. Things were totally out of control, and soon he knew the glare of the media spotlight would be on Grande Glade. The governor's wife was dead, and so was her horse. He knew he had to retreat to the shadows, but how?

He could turn to Kate, the daughter that was so unlike her mother, but would she have him? Beautiful Kate. Hers was the genius behind the arrangement that secured Tremor as the shining star of his barn. True, her flirtation with Fiona went a bit too far, but it did the trick. Fiona would have given Tremor to Kate had it not been for the little detail of the other members of the consortium. Actually, he never was certain whether it was he or Kate that Fiona really loved. When Kate left, it was his turn to receive the full force of Fiona's needs and affection.

At first, he didn't mind that. He too was seeking solace after Kate was gone. That was so like Kate to stir up feelings and then leave. And, oh God, he did have passionate feelings. It was infuriating and inciting at the same time. But that was Kate. He was aware that Fiona filled some of his needs, whenever he wanted her to. And she was greedy in her own way. He knew that. She wanted to be fawned over, and her husband was too preoccupied to do it—or to care.

Kate could never understand need—his, or anyone else's for that matter. Her body language begged to be needed. Arms around the neck, soft whispers in the ear. It wasn't his fault. He watched Kate with everyone. It was always the same. She begged for their love and encouraged all of them to need her. When they did, she left them. Left all of them with their needs—and love and hate.

He hadn't spoken to her in months. Raja said Kate knew about Tremor but was too busy with her tour to come home. Who was left for him? He had needs, too. After all, he was only human. Lisa. He could call Lisa. She would understand. She, alone, would comprehend the totality of what he was going through.

Everyone was so concerned about the unfortunate death of Tremor, including that insignificant insurance investigator, Dega. He pitied Dega. He could have been the world's top dressage rider, but he didn't have the balls to continue after that Julio fiasco. Too bad for him. Riders like Dega wasted his time with their quest for purity. What really mattered was the control. Podsky knew the key was to position himself so that everyone must come to him to satisfy their dreams, ambitions, and longings. Podsky congratulated himself on being so good at it.

Now they were coming to him for answers. Questions, questions, and more questions about the insurance policy. Next there would be more questions about Fiona. Didn't any of them know what it meant to lose a stallion of that quality? It meant everything to have him on the premises. Was it really so important to know the details of his death? Tremor was gone. Grande Glade would have to find a new niche. He'd manage. He always did. Podsky knew the needy would always seek him out because he alone could fill their longings. He had that power. And he loved it. He had taught his daughter how to manipulate in the same way, but it killed him a little bit emotionally every time she used that power on him. It was, he thought, his worst weakness.

Look what he did for Lisa. He made her. Now, it was up to her to handle the insurance investigation. He wanted no more part of it. That made up his mind. It was time for a vacation. Maybe Puerto Rico. He could stay at the hacienda he'd shared with Fiona. Let Raja and Lisa handle everything. Raja would be really angry if he didn't attend the funeral, but he knew she would let him get away with it in the end. It was time for a little vacation, but not before a quick goodbye with Lisa.

He toyed with the idea of changing clothes, but decided a shower at Lisa's would be more entertaining. The Jeep was gone. Raja must have it. The keys to her Cadillac Seville were on her nightstand. The damn car handled more like a boat, but it would have to do. As he looked out of the window to see if the Caddy was in the driveway, he noticed a Dodge Ram leaving the barn parking lot. Dega again. What was he doing here? The hell with it. He really didn't want to know anymore.

There was one more item that needed attention, though. The envelope was hidden in the back of his nightstand. Podsky tucked its contents into the vest pocket of his blazer. Then he made his way to the garage, set the house alarm, and climbed into Raja's car. Thinking about what he was about to do with Lisa made him smile as he turned the key.

CHAPTER 17

———————▼———————

Carlos knew he had stayed much longer than was necessary. By now the wind had died down considerably and the crisp winter air seemed to amplify every sound. His senses were already heightened. Emotion did that to him. Sometimes it felt like a small electric shock, but that passed in an instant. Carlos shrugged his shoulders to shake the sensation off and settled into the relative comfort of his truck.

His mind sorted methodically through the layers of emotion, like someone peeling the layers of an onion. Each thin veneer protected what was just below its surface, yet leading him to the heart of the matter. The fact was that Britt reminded him of Kate—Kate as she was when he first fell in love with her. They didn't look at all alike; they were more like day and night, flip sides of a very strange coin. The reminder was more on a gut level, a strange niggling feeling that Kate and Britt had some quality in common, and he pondered that.

Then, too, there was their age difference. She was probably close to ten years younger than Kate, which made her far too young for him to ever seriously consider as an emotional companion. Still, the connection was undeniably there. When he looked into her eyes there was a sense of the familiar. For a spiritual man, it made sense. For the practical man, a twenty-year age difference seemed insurmountable. Add that to the fact that he had relied upon his sense of spiritual connection with Kate before they imploded. That was before he realized how much she had been damaged. And it was far longer before he realized that kind of damage could not be fixed.

God, he hated Podsky for what he had done to his daughter. It came out in tiny bits and pieces. Conversations left unfinished. Revelations and half-truths that dropped from Kate's lips like bruised fruit falling to the ground. When Carlos asked the unthinkable question about her father, there was no denial. Instead she merely turned her head and blinked back the only tear he had ever seen her shed. It explained why Kate was so hard. So secretive and evasive. Is that what he was drawn to?

Why did he love such a damaged creature? Why did she reject him when she knew that he shared the family secret? Pedophiles were everywhere in the horse world. It was another one of the dirty little secrets, along with the cruelty and animal abuse. But even worse in his mind, her victimizer was her father. In anyone's language, that was incest. Why didn't she cling to Carlos for the love and support he offered as well as the opportunity for revenge? He remembered trying to convince her he could—would—be there for her, that they could beat this thing together. Kate had been his first experience with a soul so needy, so demanding care, and then rejecting love when it was offered in full measure.

Instead of her father, it was Carlos who became the victim of Kate's hate and revenge. By sharing her secret, he became another casualty of Podsky's reprehensible acts. By rejecting Carlos, Kate thought she could reject the truth of her father's abuse. By banishing Carlos, she banished the threat of exposure. Who would believe him? Indeed, who would believe her? And why, even as his head knew these things as facts, did his heart still feel like an oozing sore? He was frustrated and couldn't put it behind him. He had tried so hard, and she would not…or maybe could not…recognize his efforts. To be cruelly maligned when he had offered all of himself to her ignited his dramatic sense of injustice. Kate had been soft and gentle when they first began riding together. And then when he felt he could make things right for her, she left him, both physically and emotionally. The saddest thing to Carlos was watching Kate change from a lovely, caring person to a hardened, mean shrew, at least toward him.

Was history repeating itself in his attraction to Britt? She was like Kate, yet much more vulnerable. Kate always had that street-kid effect about her. Tough talk and bravado were her signature. It made sense why she was a runaway. Girls don't usually run away from home at the age of thirteen and live out of dumpsters with bottles of vodka hidden in their coat pockets. The eighteen-year old that told him the story seemed to treat it as an adventure rather than a tragedy. She was tough. She'd told him often, "Only the good die young."

Maybe he was just scared. Britt seemed so steady and responsible and, yes, vulnerable. He kept coming back to that descriptor. Maybe it was the vulnerability he was drawn to. Carlos the fixer. It was his acute weakness, and he knew it. There seemed to be more justice in the world when he personally saw that it was delivered. And his delivery system included exposing Podsky once and for all as an evil man hiding behind the aristocratic veneer of horses and money.

That's where Susan came in. She and Carlos were both intent on finding the source of wrongdoing, and they both loved to bring the perpetrators to justice. More than that, Susan was a mature woman who offered tantalizing thoughts to a man like Carlos. Yes indeed, Susan continually intrigued him, even when he didn't want her to.

The thoughts jumbled through his mind in what seemed like an instant as he headed down the long driveway, and he found he had already reached the main road. As he started to make the turn, some unseen force seemed to momentarily rock the cab of his truck, followed milliseconds later by an earsplitting concussion. A huge fireball caught his peripheral vision in the rear-view mirror. There was a second explosion, and the air inside of his truck cab got noticeably warmer as he spun the vehicle around in the direction of the sounds. It was at least a quarter of a mile back up the drive to the barn. He accelerated.

His first thought was of the propane tank that fed into Britt's apartment, but his trained eyes quickly determined that both the barn and the loft were intact. There seemed to be a vehicle fire close to the main house. As he got closer, he saw the hood of a Cadillac, its ornament still attached, resting up against the rooster weathervane on top of the barn. There was a huge conflagration in the driveway of Podsky's manor. The black smoke made it impossible to see, and the heat was so intense he couldn't get close enough to notice if anyone was in the car. The house alarm was sounding, probably set off by the force of the explosion. He grabbed his cell phone and notified the fire department, using the rural fire code number that was still visible on the post near the house.

Then the odor hit him. It was the surprisingly sweet smell of burning flesh. As the smoke cleared he could see the upper part of a human torso lying next to what was left of the car. Actually, it was more of a charred skeletal remain. He could discern a human skull, with the jaw permanently welded into a grotesquely silent scream. The lower half of a torso was absurdly wedged in one of the house windows, like a cat burglar in a B movie. Blood spattered the whitewashed wall of the barn, and there was other debris and flesh on the barn roof. Carlos checked quickly to make sure that there were no embers there as well.

The lower part of a leg was dangling from the plastic fencing. It was still clad in a riding boot, and the spur had caught niftily in the upper board, looking almost as if an invisible man were vaulting jauntily over the fence. It was the boot that caught his eye. It had a brown top like those usually worn by hunt seat riders. Only one person around here wore a boot like that. Podsky. Carlos's stomach churned with horror and emotion. The distance from the house to the barn was well over a thousand feet, and pieces of Podsky were scattered like roses in the snow.

There were sounds of sirens coming closer to Grande Glade. He turned to meet Britt as she ran toward him. He was grateful she was safe, and gathered her into his arms trying to shield her from the gore and horror.

CHAPTER 18

▼

The face on the Milwaukee Road clock tower read 6:12 as Susan took off her reading glasses and stretched back in the fabric-covered desk chair. She loved that chair. It seemed to cradle her as she worked hunched over in her characteristically myopic fashion. Podsky's thick file was spread across the desktop. Leaning forward again, she pushed the papers from side to side looking for the pack of Marlboros. Pat North's phone call had prompted her to attack the file again. She wasn't sure why, but something he said reminded her of Podsky's involvement in running horses across the border, and made her want to organize the whole thing into some kind of chronology that made sense.

Not that anything Podsky said or did made any sense. That was the main problem with him. He never seemed to have any driving ambition or motivation that would explain his shady comings and goings in the horse world. Money wasn't a logical reason. He had Raja's millions to fall back on.

She read the notes she had scribbled: Canadian Warmbloods. "Haul geldings with questionable breeding from the Canadian thoroughbred farms and pass them off as expensive German warmblood crosses to unsuspecting neophytes. When they ask for papers say that it's not really necessary to have papers for a gelding." Amazing how many people fall for that line. A classic con. Like selling steaks door to door. Convince people they are getting a deal and that you are doing them a favor, and it's incredible how fast they are willing to part with their cash. It was a real racket, tailormade for a con man like Podsky and his cronies in El Paso. Caught without a paper trail on the horses he was hauling across the border, it didn't take much at all to get him to rat on the gang that pilfered the racehorse in broad daylight right off the track.

Susan let out a low whistle. She pushed her glasses onto the bridge of her nose and started jotting more notes. She had been so anxious to nail the horse thieves that it never occurred to her at the time to question Podsky's knowledge or involvement. She mentally ticked off the various businesses Podsky was involved in—training, dressage, horse sales, managing Tremor's semen and that of one other stallion, but nothing having to do with racing. What would Podsky want with that racehorse? What was his interest? Every time Susan thought she had Podsky figured out, a new twist in his dealings showed up. Susan wondered if the dirty creep was up to another big double cross, but she just couldn't put her finger on it.

Then there was the race-fixing scheme. Why did he hold back on that one? Was he looking for additional leverage, or was he afraid? There was no such thing as an organized horse mafia…at least not since the demise of the Florida organization. Susan had extensive files on some of the players that were still operating small-time. She also noted all her computerized lists of bit players, grooms, trainers, and failed riders that stretched from the travelling circus to the stall muckers at the race tracks, but there was no overall organization or national loyalty that held them all together. At least, that anyone knew about.

For the most part, Eastern Europeans, who were happy to get a bed and a check at the end of the week, populated the travelling horse shows. They knew their way around the horse venues and were often available for a job that might yield a little extra cash. Many were in the States illegally with identities that changed from location to location. Susan wished she could get a better line on some of these shadowy figures. It would be such a huge break to have someone squeal on the larger fish in the pond, or finger someone who could be the means to enter into the inner ring of big operators—people with large cash payouts on their horse insurance policies.

Tremor's death was a part of the big picture. She knew it in her gut and yet still needed proof. But that was her job, now, wasn't it? No sense whining about it, she told herself. Maybe it was time to lean on Podsky a little harder, she thought again. Once she got the subpoena for Carlos, the two of them would have access to the intake reports on Tremor's necropsy. No problem. The judge was going to sign it today. Probably already had. She looked at the clock again. All the law clerks were gone by now for sure. It could wait until the morning. The truth could always wait. The expression of one of the old philosophers came to mind: "Truth, the daughter of Time." She was the one who had to learn patience.

That thought reminded her to pick up the phone and call Gwen. She hated to have her sister upset with her, or to worry. Susan's last phone call had been jarring to them both. Drumming her fingers on her desk, she hoped one of them would pick up the phone. No one seemed to be there. They were probably still at the stables for the evening riding lesson and workout. The answering machine clicked on.

"Hi. You've reached Gwen and Maya," a small voice said. "Leave a message."

Susan cleared her throat. "I'm sorry about waking you when I called so late before, Gwen. Everything seems to be fine here. I'm up to my eyebrows in work. I'll be in touch real soon again. Kisses to Maya. Be good, you two." She disconnected.

Susan found the cigarette pack and was ready to lean back and light up, but thought better of it. It would just take a minute to sneak into the john across the hall. There was no smoke alarm in there, and it sure beat hoofing it down to the pedestrian entrance of the building. She had to keep up the appearance of following the rules. After all, it was her job to prosecute those who didn't obey them. But, smoking! It was her continual rebellion against the State and its clean air legislation, the medical people, and the government. If one was a fighter, it didn't matter what the odds. The battle was what was important. At least that was the argument she always ran through her head. She hated to admit the bald truth. She was addicted.

Oh, hell, she thought. It doesn't matter. The building was deserted except for the cleaning crews in the law library. She was most always the last to leave. She was addicted not only to nicotine, but to work.

CHAPTER 19

▼

Charlie Branson twisted his five-foot, six-inch, 230-pound frame to get a better look at his watch. Damn. He was real proud of that Timex Indiglo. He could read the time in just about any situation, and he was in a real situation right now. "Looks like about six-fifteen," he whispered under his breath. He was getting damn tired of his tiny hiding place under the far back carrel in the eleventh floor Circuit Court Law Library. From the sound of things, the security guard had finished this hour's pass and he was finally alone.

Charlie wiggled out from under the desk. It didn't appear as if he had ever thought of dieting. He straightened his wrinkled polyester suit and tried to tuck his shirt in. It was too short, and pulled so tightly over his belly that hair stuck out through the gaps around his navel. He pulled a crumpled red tie out of his pocket and fastened it loosely while he waited patiently for the ticket to his elevator ride to the sixth floor. His annual clothes budget didn't allow for suits from Saks Fifth Avenue or Dayton's, but he wouldn't have to make much of an impression to get the job done. He was gently rubbing the smudges from his Timex watch face when the library door opened. A moon-faced kid was standing behind a government-issue gray trash barrel on wheels. Charlie grunted as he lumbered toward the perpetual adolescent. This was better than taking candy from a baby.

Fucking bleeding-heart liberals and their Americans With Disabilities Act. Blew a big fucking hole in the Federal Marshall's grand security system. Hiring folks with Down syndrome was a nice touch. Made his job easier. Made him think he was gonna be a bleeding voting liberal next election. Lots of advantages for a guy like him as well as the poor slobs with the disabilities.

"Hey, kid! Could you help me out? Must have fallen asleep in the books, and the elevators are locked down since it's after hours. I was working for Judge Lukes on a big case he's hearing tomorrow. Want to help?"

The kid looked nervous, but interested, at least in Charlie's estimation. He wanted to keep him going. This looked like it was gonna work.

"I don't know, mister. I'm supposed to stay on this floor until security comes back."

"That's OK. You're doing a great job. I'll be sure to tell the judge. Maybe he'll get you a raise. Like I said, this is a really big case and I have to get these notes here back to my office on the sixth floor."

Charlie waived a sheaf of papers in the kid's face. "I suppose it might be OK. Are you sure?"

"Yeah. I'll owe you one. Maybe I can fix it so you can watch a case in the big courtroom on the fifteenth floor."

That did it for the earnest helper. He'd graduated from cleaning the atrium lobby to the law library, but he'd never even been to the fifteenth floor. His friends would be impressed, and he'd be helping out this big-shot lawyer. Yeah, he'd do it. No harm done. Maybe he'd even get a letter from the judge. Sounded like the case was really important.

Charlie put a stubby arm around the young man's shoulder as he used his key card to open the elevator. Charlie slithered into the shadows in the back of the elevator before the kid could say goodbye. He punched the button for the twenty-second ride to the sixth floor. Chuckling on the way up, Charlie muttered to himself, "Candy."

In his job, his knack of being invisible, or at least not memorable, was an asset. The ride was cake. He peeked out into the hall. No one there. Just the night lights burning in the halls. He chuckled to himself. This whole, fucking you can't-break-this-security building was too easy, with a guy of his talents. There were a few offices with the lights still on, but that seemed to be from neglect, not intention. He went from shadow to dark space, and the adrenaline started to pump. He loved this part. Mr. Invisible Man. Yes, sir. Proud of his work, though, of course, he couldn't tell too many people about it.

He located the office he wanted. The light was on. Shit. Damn that Ms. Workaholic. Hadn't she given up and gone home yet? Maybe she forgot her light was on and left like the others. Otherwise it could mean another frigging forever wait like upstairs. Hours, even. He was getting tired of watching from the shadows. But he knew he'd better wait a few minutes to make sure Susan wasn't there. He had to be patient. There were still some things he wanted to look at, and Susan's office was a treasure trove of goodies for a man of his talent.

But he could hear a beer call him from the bar behind the Fed building, and Charlie had no more patience left. Best get on with this, he thought. He peeked around the corner, didn't see Susan, and decided he could quickly toss the place and be at the bar in five minutes.

Addiction or not, a smoke was definitely what she needed. Susan pushed the big chair away from the desk and padded barefoot across the hall to her sanctuary in the women's restroom. Someone had stacked some file boxes in the corner next to the mirror and she used one of them as a makeshift chair while she savored every minute of her illicit activity. The last drag started a minor coughing fit and quickly ended her brief reverie.

"Gotta quit," she promised herself for the umpteenth time as the butt sizzled to extinction in the bowl and the automatic flusher banished the evidence of her vice and her weakness to the bowels of the municipal sewer system. She wondered if the butt would make it to the Mississippi and chuckled at the thought of her office prosecuting environmental lawbreakers. Hell, the Bivalve Task Force was having more success stopping the invasion of exotic marine species than she was at making sense of what she was sure were horse murders. She couldn't even get organized enough to recycle aluminum cans at home.

Glancing in the mirror, Susan avoided studying her face and concentrated instead on her hair. She thought of it as her second-best feature, and for a moment she remembered the feel of Carlos's hand as he brushed the shock of hair from her forehead. Being involved with him, seeing him again, if only professionally, had stirred up a lot of memory and emotion that she wasn't really prepared to deal with at this time. Did she really need him on this case? He hadn't come up with much so far. But then again, that was his way. He worked from instinct. That much she knew. And his instincts were seldom wrong. He followed them like a wolf follows the scent of prey. Still, she had conflicting motives for calling him in on this case. She had to admit that it was exciting to see him again, if only for a crummy cup of coffee. He was being remote and enigmatic as usual, but then again there wasn't much they could focus on without the subpoena. What she had was another dead horse that might or might not make it into her files of "suspicious horse deaths."

Susan was having much more success prosecuting whitecollar crime. She and the D.A.'s office had received a lot of favorable press with her recent prosecution of a Ponzi scheme perpetrated by the CEO of a local investment firm. The guy bilked 185 investors of more than three million bucks by investing less than ten percent in commodity futures and then paying out the rest to other investors to give the appearance of profitability. Each investor received a monthly account statement that grossly overestimated profits and the value of each investor's portfolio. RICO made the case for her, and the guy pleaded guilty to four counts of mail fraud and one count of embezzlement. Pat North coordinated the FBI with the Commodity Futures Trading Commission. It was nice having all of the federal offices in one building, conveniently located across from City Hall. It seemed to have helped both communication and speed of networking.

"Stay focused," she told herself as she stashed the Bic in her pocket. The absence of the key card that she usually kept clipped to the pocket of her blazer reminded her that she had better find the thing before the Marshall's office got wise to the fact that hers was missing. They would have to re-key the whole system and issue new panic alarm codes if she couldn't produce hers when asked. Might as well spend a few minutes looking for the blasted thing before going home. At least she was the last one out tonight, so it was up to her to set the panic alarms and the motion detectors.

Getting to bed early was suddenly the best inspiration she had had in a very long day. Maybe her case was going nowhere, but she was going home for a deep protracted sleep. She heaved herself out of the small bathroom and thought about finding her shoes.

"Now where would that tag be," she wondered out loud. A long shaft of blanched color cast a triangular glow on the carpet outside her door. As she pushed the door fully open, the room suddenly went black, lit only by the subdued hallway lighting.

In a flash of an instant, someone was shoving a blunt object into her spine, and a fleshy hand was covering her mouth. She tasted blood as a stone on a ring cut her lip. She kicked backwards, aiming for the groin, with no effect. She was barefoot. The hand tightened over her mouth as she cursed herself for losing the proximity alarm that should have been attached to her jacket.

She jammed both elbows backward as hard as she could, gasping for breath as the hand dislodged from her mouth. Susan hated to do it, but she grabbed the banker's lamp from her desk and swung the brass base hard at the intruder's head. He let out a yelp. Susan was sorry to see her favorite lamp smashed. Now she was really angry.

"Hey hey hey...I give...I give...you don't have to hurt me for Crissakes...man that hurts...it really hurts!"

The voice sounded familiar and whiny. She thought about hitting the panic alarm on the wall before realizing that it wasn't turned on. What next? Run? She lunged for the wall switch, and as the room filled with light, she could see her attacker groveling on the floor. Charlie Branson lay in a sniveling heap, bleeding on her expensive carpet.

"Charlie, what in the hell do you think you're doing?" Susan wiped the blood from her chin in a feeble attempt to stop any further damage to the front of her suit.

"Hey, Susan, baby. I'm sorry. You startled me, that's all. No harm done. I'm outta here. Should I take the stairs or the elevator?" Susan, emboldened now, grabbed Charlie's shirt collar. She was about three inches shorter than him, but her anger seemed to make him shrink. "I should have thrown the book at you years ago and had your license pulled, but we had a deal, remember? So what made you think you could get away with breaking and entering a federal facility?"

"Hey, Susan. Breaking and entering is not my style. I prefer to think of it as creative reconnoitering. The only thing broken appears to be your lamp. Want me to buy you a new one? I know this guy..." Susan cut him off before he could finish by lifting her knee as if to give him a well-placed nudge.

"Assaulting a federal officer is just starters on the list of charges I could bring against you when the Federal Marshall's office gets their hands on you, Charlie."

"Well, maybe I got something you want."

Susan saw a floppy disk lying on the floor and picked it up. It was a backup copy of her horse files she'd made a few weeks ago. She hadn't even known it was missing; all the information was on her hard drive. "Can I add theft of federal property to your rap sheet?"

"I was trying to return it. I just borrowed it for a while."

"You mean this isn't the first time you've been in my office? Going through my files?"

So much for the Federal Marshall's security system, she thought. Maybe it was time to go over the surveillance tapes and see how many unannounced visits Branson had made.

Charlie made a feeble attempt to straighten his tie. "I'm a professional. I've been up here enough times to notice the flaws in the system, that's all."

"So, why are you stealing the information that you provided for me, Charlie? You've been one of my best sources on what's been going down at the racetrack. You've gotten more for me about horses than anyone. You're a great snitch, but now I find you're not trustworthy? And you'd accost me to boot?"

"We all gotta make a living, Susan. Sorry. I just knew you had the info really organized. Thought I'd save myself some time and borrow it back. Would have been no harm done if you hadn't surprised me. Hell, I thought you might be

Security or somethin'. A man's got to defend himself. Anyway, you're dangerous. Did you have to hurt me?" Charlie whined again as he rubbed the bruise that was starting to appear around the cut on his forehead.

So, what was she going to do? Charlie was pathetic, but a good, trustworthy source. OK, he used to be a trustworthy source. She hoped this was a small aberration. His boldness was stupid, but somehow predictable. She wasn't afraid of him, that's for sure. Should she turn him in or try to figure out what he was up to? And who would want her files on the horse business? And why? "Cut the crap, Charlie. You're gonna tell me exactly who you're working for and which side of the fence you're playing. If you don't, I will personally see to it that you are put away for a long, long time in the same facility that houses some of the very people you helped me convict. Now, wouldn't that be a pretty picture? Let's see, I might even notify them that you'd be coming."

Susan was bluffing, but she didn't think Branson knew it. Truth was, she was kind of fond of the perp.

"I'm working for the good guys, honest. You both want the same information, but they've got lots of money to throw around, Suz. I wanna get outta this line of work. If I pull this off it could mean early retirement." Susan glared at him. "Ya wanna pay me a little extra so's then I could afford to work only for you? Huh, Suz? Help a guy out here."

"Don't call me Suz or I'll have the Federal Marshall down here before you can take your next breath. And another thing," she narrowed her eyes and looked him up and down, "what you just said sounded an awful lot like blackmail. Are you thinking of blackmailing a federal officer doing her duty?"

He was so nervous he plunged on, totally ignoring what she had just said. "Tell you what, Suz, why don't we head on over to Lefty's Lounge and grab a beer? Let's talk things over civilized, you know." He was sweating like he was standing out in the sun in hundred-degree heat.

In a funny way, a night with Charlie and exotic dancers didn't seem like such a bad idea after the way things had been going. If she played things right, Charlie would spill his guts before the night was over. He was already strung out and on the edge of his nervous control. "OK, you're on, but you're also buying."

Susan put the disk in her pocket and set the panic alarm next to the stairway as she and Charlie made their way down to the pedestrian exit and out onto Third Street.

CHAPTER 20

▼

It was 3:00 a.m. as Susan pulled up to the frame house on Lyndale and disgorged Charlie into the gutter. The fibers in his cheap suit reflected the glow from the sodium vapor streetlight as he leaned against it and relieved himself before stumbling up the walkway to the three-flat that had seen happier and grander days. She watched as he fumbled with the keys and gave her a halfhearted wave as the foyer swallowed up his pudgy frame.

Susan remembered when this was a nice neighborhood. It used to be lined with American elms before Dutch Elm disease decimated the boulevards of the Cities. The workingclass tenancy died with the trees. Gangs provided death's refuge.

She remembered when she was nice, too. There was a time when it would never have occurred to her to spend most of the night at a strip joint with a washed-up private eye. In some ways she was closer to Charlie's world than to the safe ones of academia and law enforcement. She knew her targets and clients only too well. She was successful because she had learned to think and respond like the scum she was prosecuting. Where did that leave her? She was too much like Charlie. The thought scared her, especially with her soaring blood alcohol level.

Her hands shook as she removed the key from the ignition, realizing that she probably shouldn't drive. Getting Charlie to talk had required a lot of booze, and too much had found its way into her own system while she was trying to distract his attention from the girls. The city's decency laws had been violated before her eyes, but she wasn't on an undercover job, and frankly, she could have cared less about Lefty's Lounge's liquor license. Leave that to local enforcement.

She thought about parking her car right where it was and calling for a cab on the cellular, but in all honesty, she was afraid to leave her car in this neighborhood. In the morning it would have no tires or electronic equipment left. Shit. She got out of the car and managed to walk around it several times before the neighborhood, and the dark, drove her back behind the wheel. The cold air had jolted her enough to convince her it was probably OK to navigate the mile or two to her apartment. She started the car again, hoping the several Cokes she'd had along with the booze had helped dilute her blood level of alcohol. Traffic was just about nonexistent at this hour anyway.

Besides, the drive would give her the opportunity to digest what Charlie had told her. It made sense in some crazy way, and besides, he was too drunk to have made up such a complicated scenario. Even though Charlie was thoroughly unpredictable, Susan had learned from years of experience that his information was always accurate and that he prided himself on providing an honest answer if the questions were posed in an unambiguous manner. He would never lie to her, she thought, but she could never rule out deception by omission.

Leave it to Charlie to find a way to double his return on his time investment by working the same side of the fence twice. Susan wondered if the Channel Seven newshounds were aware of the fact that their journalistic standards were being severely compromised. Did it violate the rules of Journalism 101 to rely upon stolen surveillance to provide the backbone of what could be a Pulitzer-winning story regarding dirty dealings in the local horsy community?

Actually, Susan was certain the news organization had no idea that the information it was relying upon was stolen federal property. Charlie had his own reputation to protect. The whole approach by the Channel Seven producers was brilliant, actually. If her office had the money, she might have been tempted to stage something of the sort herself. Funny that Cindi Moreno, even with her faux ownership in Tremor, had been unable to unearth any more on Podsky than Susan's extensive investigations. Moreno most likely had never been on a horse other than the merry-go-round at Valley Fair Amusement Park. It was an undercover operation, after all, to create one big sting to penetrate Podsky's world.

Then there was the extra juicy angle that involved the late wife of the sitting governor. Actually, that was a bonus. Now Fiona was dead. That left the mysterious Randolph Decker as the last member of the consortium. Did Carlos have anything on him? And who was he really? Did he even exist?

So what drove Charlie to steal her files? Was it that he respected her organizational abilities and wanted to pass them off as his own in order to secure a permanent place on the payroll at Channel Seven? He knew what was in them, since he had been working with her on the racetrack fixes and the racehorse theft. The producers at Channel Seven must have thought it more than serendipitous that Fiona Andersson, Podsky, missing horses, and the death of the most famous piece of horseflesh in the Midwest were connected, if somewhat loosely. Had they figured out the angles? Were there any angles to figure out? Maybe it was just a case of lots of vile people being in the same place at the same time. Susan thought of L.A. like that. She'd wanted to move there until she realized that the bad people had gotten there first.

But it bothered her that Charlie had tried to blackmail her. She doubted he was as trustworthy as she had originally thought. And who was the heavy breather on the phone the other night?

Susan reckoned that if the biggest news organization in the upper Midwest was investigating the same people she and Carlos had zeroed in upon, there had to be something to it. But what, dammit? There was some thread that tied the whole thing together that was bigger than the obvious scam of horse killings and falsifying cause-of-death forms for insurance fraud purposes. Carlos was right about the horse business. Unless you could prove the bigger crime, the moral trespass was meaningless. A plan or conspiracy to commit an act of cruelty or abuse to a horse or any animal might not be illegal. It was immoral and unsporting, certainly. The American Horse Show Association was forever expelling members for foul and inexpiable conduct, but the ruling carried no legal weight outside of the organization.

It was up to her, Carlos, and Pat North to pin the crime on the perpetrators. It was time for a meeting, and the sooner the better. Maybe if they laid it all out on the table, they could at least get a racketeering angle put together. Up until now they were all working their individual territory. Carlos wouldn't like having to be a team player, but she would have to convince him otherwise. If they didn't get their acts together, Channel Seven was going to break something. The story would be explosive, and the fallout might unfortunately cover a lot of tracks.

Enough agonizing. What was done was done. She still had time to pull it together. Her resolve became all the more ferocious when she tuned the car radio to the half-hour local update and learned that time had run out for Podsky—and maybe her entire investigation.

She pulled over and did the only thing she could, but there was no answer on Carlos's phone. To hell with the indirect route. There was just enough alcohol left in her system to rationalize an early-morning visit to his house. She knew the way well. She needed to information, but more than that, she needed Carlos, even if he had never needed her.

"Damn it all to Hell, Carlos, open this door!" She was hitting it with all she had, but her mittened hands did not make much noise. The cold air was snapping her mind around, but the alcohol still had her inhibitions lowered. She pushed on the bell. Just when she thought she might have to give it up, the front door opened. Carlos stood there in his wrinkled Vikings shirt and bare legs. He ran his fingers through his richly black hair, yawned, and said, "Package delivery at this hour?"

"You drive me wild, Big Guy. Let me in."

"Just how do I drive you wild, Counselor?"

"Open the door, I'm freezing my ass off here."

"Do I need to remind you this isn't social hour? No. I sup pose not. From the looks of things you've already had that."

"Carlos…" She grabbed the storm door and pushed her way through like a quarterback stuck with the ball. What the heck. Make the play.

"Just for clarification, do you consider this still a decent hour to be up, or are we, in your estimation, approaching the middle of the night?"

"OK. For the record. This is the middle of the night."

"Good. I just thought I might be having a nightmare here and I wasn't really a sane rational person."

Susan sat down and put her head in her hands. "Oh Sweet Jesus. I feel a migraine coming on. I needed to talk to you, Carlos, because this case is going to make me crazy if I don't get some resolution, and get it fast."

"So, because you drank too much, and are having troubles with your work, you decided I could share in the fun?" When she looked up at him, and he saw how sick she was starting to become, he let up. "Are you going to puke? You look like a bucket would work for you."

"Yeah. That's a good idea. Do you have any peppermint tea? I know it's asking a lot, and deep in my heart I am sorry to wake you…again…but…" and then inexplicably she began to cry. Susan rarely cried, and surely never in front of anyone, much less Carlos. Her head now went between her legs and she started to sob.

Carlos went for the bucket and put the teakettle on. When he came back out to her she was curled up on the sofa. She was shaking even though her coat was still on. He pulled off her boots, put his arm around her, and stroked her hair. He didn't say a word. After some time she reached for the bucket and heaved her guts out. He took the bucket to empty it, then got the tea and came back to hold her again.

"I'm mortified. I really am."

"I know."

"Carlos, I've got to talk."

"I know." He was sitting close to her now, and they were both sipping tea.

"Do you have time to talk? I mean, do you mind, really mind if I talk?"

"I've got the rest of the evening, and, again, Counselor, you have my full attention in the middle of the night. This is becoming a right regular habit. One that I could like a lot more if it weren't the middle of the night."

She smiled weakly at him, a strong, determined woman who was just discovering that having someone to share things with was a pretty nice thing. She told him about almost getting knocked out in her office, the missing files, and her evening with Charlie. She felt the headache coming on more forcefully, but finished her thoughts, and her worries about the case. Somewhere in the telling she had put her head in Carlos's lap, and she felt him massage her neck and shoulders.

"That's my tale of woe tonight, Big Guy. I'd better go." But as soon as she sat up again, she reached for the bucket and used it. So much for the soothing effects of peppermint tea.

Carlos helped her lie down, cleaned up again, and got her a pillow and blanket. When he came back she was already asleep, and he tucked her into her makeshift bed like a small child.

She slept well, and late. When she awoke, Carlos was gone. By the front door was a note. The deep colors of the Oriental rug contrasted sharply with the square piece of thick white paper.

I called the office for you and told them you were sick and wouldn't be in today. Don't worry. I won't tell anyone about our one-night stand.—C.

CHAPTER 21

▼

As Carlos walked slowly up the steps of the Basilica of Saint Mary, he meticulously adjusted his topcoat over his olive green suit. In deference to the windy weather and cool morning air, he wore a wool muffler, which was an impeccable match to the overcoat. He covered his ears with his hands, as much to keep them warm as to drown out the sound of the massive bells. Even though they were housed over a hundred feet above the stair in the East tower, the sound was both melodious and deafening. He quickened his step.

He saw John and Iris waiting for him. They shared quick hugs, and John whisked them all inside. John gave his name to the usher at the door, who checked them off a security list. They were led past the old marble confessionals. He counted eight in all and wondered if people still used them, still confessed their sins. Had Fiona any sins to confess? The smell of flowers lay in the air, and that, mixed with the incense, almost made Carlos gag. Evidently the funeral of the governor's wife would be potent in many ways. He knew he was in for a long, very long, Catholic Mass.

Carlos was glad for the topcoat. The Basilica was always cold. He often came here for concerts, not Mass. He had not been an active practicing Catholic in many years, but the litanies and responses came without bidding. This was an impressive structure, and Carlos found his mind wandering to the architectural phenomena while waiting for the powerful and personal to the governor and his "dearly departed wife" to shuffle in, genuflect, and find their seats. He noticed those saying the rosary were mostly older women kneeling on sore and stiff knees. Others just sat. This was not a building that fostered friendship and conversation, but then, funerals did not promote idle chatter, in his opinion. John and Iris were equally silent. He was glad that he and John had been friends from childhood. With good friends like that, there was no need to talk.

The sanctuary area commanded his attention. It was unusual in that it was surrounded by marble pillars and a hand-forged wrought-iron grille, which depicted engraved scenes from the life of Mary after the crucifixion. On top of the pillars was a marble canopy that in its turn became the pedestal for the statues of the Apostles. The symbols of the Basilica were behind that, showing a pavilion of a half opened umbrella and a silver bell. Carlos watched as the governor, his daughter, and several men in dark suits filed in. There was an older couple, whom he assumed were Fiona's parents.

The priests followed them, and then, with a motion for them all to rise, the Bishop came in, resplendent in lush robes of purple and black. There seemed to be no end to the acolytes trailing behind, making the Bishop look like he had a restless tail. It occurred to Carlos that for all the hue and cry by Catholics about the simplicity of faith, the trappings belied the message. It became hushed in the Basilica, and the amassed choir began a slow, haunting Gregorian chant. The a cappella tune resounded within the acoustically perfect interior. The choir was excellent, not the usual church fare.

Wherever his eye turned, Mary was in evidence. He was struck whenever he came here how she pervaded each marble piece, every nook and cranny. On the top face of the canopy he could read, "Mater Divinae Gratiae." Was Fiona now thinking that Mary was the Mother of Divine Grace? Had she ever?

The service was far more pleasant than he anticipated. The choir members outdid themselves and reduced half the congregation to tears with each song they sang. After the Bishop gave the homily, which was too long and too preachy in Carlos's opinion, the choir began to sing "Agnus Dei" by Samuel Barber. He was able to meditate as he heard the tense melodic pull that was at the heart of this music. Again his mind went back to the old supplications as he registered the words. Lamb of God, who taketh away the sins of the world, have mercy on us. Grant us peace. There seemed to be many sins abounding. He cynically thought that either God wasn't hearing, or people weren't trying hard enough.

Carlos spent some of the moments looking around the sanctuary. He was most interested in the family of the deceased. No one cried, not even the young girl now missing a mother. She was the one who had been riding the little Arab when he went to interview Podsky. She looked detached from the event unfolding around her. He assumed that Raja and Sasha would have been here, if they hadn't been involved in their own funeral event. It was a wry and ironic thought. Raja loved this kind of pomp, and Sasha seemed to have had more than the passing relationship with Fiona. One didn't fight the way they had when he first came to interview Sasha if there were no passion somewhere in the relationship. But now that was for others to sort through. Passion died with them both. Odd they died almost at the same time. Very odd indeed.

As Carlos looked around the Basilica again, thinking of this coincidence, he thought he saw a small figure wearing a black Spanish lace mantilla leaning against a pillar off to the right side of the sanctuary, sheltered in a shadow. He instantly thought of Kate. But, if she were in town, she should be at her own father's funeral, not here. Although, on second thought, he wouldn't be surprised if she would pull a stunt like that—if in fact it was Kate. Maybe it was Kate that he saw at the airport, after all. He would never figure her mind out, or the passions and events that led her to become so twisted and bruised she could not heal into a compassionate human being. After the service he knew he would go to Grande Glade and "drop in" on Podsky's service. He would have to face Kate in person again, or face her forever in his dreams and subconscious. Now or later. Not one to wait, he decided it would be now. He would be in control of the timing, if nothing else.

The lines from the Rossini poem came to him, although the coffin was closed, and Carlos mused about the love, or love lost, between the governor and his camera-ready-smile wife. The horse barn kept Fiona busy, but who kept the governor busy in his personal hours? And, why not Fiona?

Carlos looked over at Iris, that gorgeous exotic woman who was married to his best friend. She caught him looking at her—she always did—and gave him the Mona Lisa smile. He wanted at that moment to ask her about love, and to know what she knew about deep caring and commitment. He thought she also might know about why the governor's family was not filled with an outward display of grief. Iris traveled in the same circles socially. He made a mental note to speak with her later.

When the choir began the Recessional, Carlos was startled to hear the opening strains to the "Song for Athene." Always with a judgment, he thought it pompous and presumptuous of the governor to choose the same song that was used for the "People's Princess," Diana, not too long ago. There seemed to be an overabundance of dying and burying these days. "Weeping at the grave creates the song: Alleluia," the choir sang. The juxtaposition was not lost on Carlos. He wondered if any others noticed.

The coffin was rolled out as the family walked beside it, touching it as the flower-laden box came down the aisle toward the main entrance, which was dwarfed by the magnificence of the stained-glass rose window of the Enthroned

Madonna and Child. The weakened morning winter sun backlit the window to create the perfect glow as the parishioners, no, the guests for the event, turned to see the last of Fiona Andersson. Carlos searched among the congregation for the small dark form near the pillar. Evidently, he had also seen the last of the figure in black lace, at least for now.

CHAPTER 22

▼

Driving to Grande Glade after the funeral afforded Carlos the opportunity to reflect again on women, and most particularly, Kate and Britt. Spending more than an hour in the Basilica, the Madonna's House, made him especially mindful of women. He did his best to be objective, and with a mental force of will, made a list in his head of the qualities he knew of each woman. It made sense to try to see what he was facing given the perimeters he knew he had. At the very least, he thought the exercise gave him structure and, through that, he might achieve a sense of control. Or the semblance of it.

Kate: Charming. Magnetic. Small in build. Attractive. Dark hair, dark complexion. Manipulative. Entirely untrustworthy. Slippery as a snake. Able to wind men around her little finger. Hated by other women, therefore, no women friends. Smart. Always into new activities. Athletic. Knows horses well, but not compassionate. Could be cruel to man, woman, and beast.

Britt: Guileless. Wholesome. Young. Naive. Freshly good looking. Tall. Blonde hair, light skin. Blue eyes that pierce like an ice crystal. Strong physically and emotionally. A loner. Finds refuge in animals and their care. Compassionate. Knows her own horses so well she can talk to them and get into their minds. Possible intuitive. Athletic.

With each woman there was an attraction. He had to admit that to himself. He knew what Kate could do to a man, how easy it was to get lost in her, and later be so hurt and confused it wasn't possible to dissect what had happened, or why. He had seen other men become obsessed with her, and like a person with a fly rod she snagged them lightly, hooked them good, and cut the line with the hook still in their mouth. In pain and swimming around, men would still come searching again for what had looked so good. He had been one of those men. Carlos rationalized it by saying to himself that he was only trying to help her. Yet he knew his Achilles heel was trying to "help." It had been his undoing before Kate, and he searched for the thought that would be the piece of flotsam to hang on to when faced with the whirlpool named Kate.

Britt. That would be the thought to hang onto. Comparing the two women had helped him see he liked the qualities Britt had. He could feel a gut connection there that could be good…not that he was truly looking for a commitment, or even a relationship, but he could hang onto those eyes, that nourishing self. He didn't need, didn't want, to be hauled into the maelstrom with Kate. He had learned that chaos did not breed more than momentary excitement and mental challenge. Its aftermath was akin to having a heart-lung transplant.

Carlos considered taking up prayer seriously. Soon. Like in the next five minutes. Maybe that would help him with the anticipation—dread—he felt about facing Kate, the enigma who was at the same time his love and his enemy. Former love. About to be former enemy, he hoped. He especially wanted to let go of the intensity of feeling for her. He wanted not to have emotional ties to her. He knew the bonds of fear and anger were stronger than anything in this world, and he wanted to let Kate go, for her sake and his.

The roads were no worse than usual for this time of year, and he made good time getting to Grande Glade. He could see the lights from the barn and house ablaze in the weak winter light. The familiar slate gray sky had ridges of pink and fuchsia that created a fan effect on the horizon. The color and softness in the surrounding starkness was a perfect backdrop to the wake.

There were cars parked everywhere. Some were very creatively stashed, because snowbanks, gates, and doorways made orderly parking impossible. Carlos was glad for his truck. He could leave it just about anywhere and still get out of the Minnesota muck or snow. In this weather a vehicle takes on high significance, he thought. Its reliability could mean the difference between living and dying. With all this death around him, he was glad to be among the living. He wanted to keep it that way.

Even in the cold, there were people on the porch to the house, holding drink glasses, chatting brightly and seeming to be quite happy. He smiled and took off his hat as he made his way through the people. He let himself in and looked around for Raja. She was buried deep in a circle of women who were dressed much as she was in amazingly colored caftans, beads, jangle bracelets, and hairdos that would make a wigmaker cry. Amidst all the flowing fabric, Raja was holding court.

"Oh my dear, that simply isn't so. No, no. Don't think a negative thought!"

The rapturous listener was nodding, making her head look like a fishing bobber in heavy seas. "I try so hard, Raja, I really do."

"There, there. Just keep at it. I must endeavor to do the same about my dearly departed Sasha. We are all in this world of tears to spread Light and Joy. Just remember that."

Carlos thought he might interrupt at that moment, when Raja looked up and he caught her eye. He motioned toward the kitchen, hoping it would be quieter there, and he could talk to her alone. One of Raja's admirers gave him a cold stare. He winked at the woman and smiled. She blushed and dropped her eyes.

The kitchen was filled with trays of food, and the caterer was busy trying to get the hot trays out of the oven and keep the table full. "Raja. I came to extend my condolences. You know I was here right after the explosion. I am sorry for your loss."

Raja looked at him with a completely blank stare. Carlos kept eye contact and waited. Sometimes it was his very best tool for getting information. Watch and wait. Hold the eyes. Be the last to blink. Raja at last batted her eyes at him. "Oh. I am rather speechless at the moment."

Carlos hadn't seen her speechless when he had first walked in the room. In fact, he rarely knew her to be speechless. Vacuous, yes, but not at a loss for words. "What are your plans now, Raja?"

"That will all be cosmically decided at the séance I will hold to try to get in touch with my sweet Sasha. We will ask him what to do, and get guidance from The Other Side." Quite ingenuously she asked Carlos, "Would you like to attend? It will be as soon as possible, while the spirits are still moving."

"I'm sure it will be fascinating, but I must respectfully decline the invitation."

Abruptly Raja changed the subject. "You know that Kate is in town, don't you?"

"In town? Or here?" He felt his breath go out long and slow. His subconscious was already programming him to slow down and be internally calm.

"Here. I think she is somewhere around." Raja waved her hand in her typical airy fashion, and indicated with a circular motion of her bejangled wrist. There were amethysts, sapphires, and tiger's eyes stuffed onto every pudgy finger. She actually seemed to glow. Carlos couldn't tell if that was from the heat of the kitchen or her New Age enthusiasms.

"I think I'll go look for her. In the house or the barn, what would be your best guess?"

Still with the ubiquitous wide-eyed stare she smiled softly and said, "Barn. Take care, she's upset. You know how that can be."

Indeed he did. He surely did know how that could be. Better to be psychologically armed, and therefore, forewarned. He'd take the help where he could get it, even if it was from Bernice.

Raja flowed past him, and smoothing her voluminous skirts beamed into the living room. Carlos was struck for the second time that day how the grieving survivor did not cry. Did not seem upset. Didn't even want to talk about the issue of being left, or sad, or a hundred other possible feelings. The day definitely had the atmosphere of being for the living. Who cared about the dead? Obviously, not those near and dear.

The wind had died down. Carlos unconsciously noted the weather. The cold had begun to deepen with the passing hours, and Carlos could hear the crunching of his feet on the snow- and ice-laden path. His breath made streams of white air in front of him. The barn was bright, but the party noises were behind him and faded into one muffled sound. The snow and cold could make noises sound like they had been packed up and put in a padded box.

He went to the truck and got his sorel boots. It wouldn't please him to ruin his good Italian leather dress shoes, and sorels would be much warmer for standing around in the barn. He tucked the finely textured wool of his pant legs into his boots, put his shoes under the front seat heater and hit the automatic door lock. On impulse, he reached back into the truck and felt in the glove compartment, to make sure his gun was still there.

Carlos found Kate standing in front of Tremor's stall. Her back was to him, and his rubber-clad sorels made no sound. She stood quietly, which seemed unusual to Carlos.

"Kate?"

Without turning she spat out the word, "YOU!"

Yep. In the flesh. Your mother said you were in a mood. Looks like she was right on."

Kate whirled on Carlos. Coming very close to his face she began what Carlos remembered as The Stare. He dished it back.

He tried to make conversation. "When did you get into town?"

"A while ago. It's hard to keep track of it all with so much going on."

"I am sorry for you and your mother that your father was killed. Please accept my condolences."

Kate started to soften around the eyes. For a moment he was standing in front of the woman he had known a long time ago. She leaned against a stall door, pursed her lips and said, "Isn't it the strangest thing…after all these years of my father living here safely, and now…in a flash…it's hard to understand that he's dead."

There was that wistful look on her face that he used to love.

"Is there something I can do?" Carlos was the ultimate helper, offering one more time.

Her dark eyes glinted malevolently. "God, I hate you. I still hate you after all this time." Her voice was low and cold. That was Kate, changing in an instant.

"I am to assume you aren't wasting any time or feelings on grieving for your father, then? And that would also be a rejection of the offer for help?"

"That's Carlos for you! Deflect from himself and change the subject. You ruined my life, I'll have you know. That's why I hate you."

Now he was totally baffled. He knew better than to get on the defensive and ask how he could have done that. He was the convenient target for her rage, and she let him have it full force. There was so much enmity he literally felt knocked back, and took several steps away from her. The maelstrom had started.

"What have you got to say for yourself? I demand an answer!"

"Kate, let's go into the lounge."

"No. We'll have it out right here and now."

"What's to have out? I wanted to help you, Lord Above knows I tried, and you seemed to ask for help. No. You begged me to help you a long time ago. But you have certain bizarre rules for those who are foolish enough to try to come to your assistance. I don't know your rules, and even if I could now learn them, I don't want to."

"See, that's just what I mean."

"I'm lost as usual with you, Kate."

"You only want to help me YOUR way, not my way. And besides, I wanted to be close to you, have you go with me all over the globe, be fun and fancy free. I wanted us to be the best horse riding and training team in the goddamn world. But, oh, no. You wouldn't do it my way. And my father. You could have helped me to deal with him."

"Kate. We've been through this before. I didn't want your dreams. I needed to have my own dreams. And, they were different. Because I rejected your dreams you feel like I rejected you. I would have helped you…" But he knew before he finished the sentence that he was starting into the same old cycle. Damn! Damn Kate! Damn himself that he kept getting sucked into it.

Kate started to kick the door to the stall. She beat on it with her fists. She swore. Carlos was reminded of the saying, "Hell hath no fury like a woman scorned." The horses were getting restless and began knocking against the walls of their boxes. The more Kate kicked, the more her kicks were echoed with the pawing of hooves.

"Kate. The horses are getting upset."

"I don't give a flying fuck."

And to Carlos that said it all. "So we leave it at this. At the same old war ground. Were you at Fiona's funeral this morning?"

"And if I was? What in the hell do you give a royal..." Carlos interrupted her. She had always had a swearing vocabulary that would have made R-rated movie directors proud. She could have taught them new words, in fact. "I saw you there. I just wondered why you chose Fiona's funeral over that of your father?"

"Why would I go to his funeral? He made my life miserable, treated me like property, and generally messed me up. I should celebrate his life? I'm glad he died. Do you think I really have even one tear to shed for that controlling bastard?" Defiantly, she added, "I thought I would see what the competition's funeral was like. Besides," and Carlos saw her face soften again, "Fiona stood up for me. She was good to me. We understood each other." Kate ended the sentence with a whisper.

"Then why did you come home?"

"I don't have to tell you a thing." Kate was belligerent again.

"Fine." He almost shouted the word. What a roller-coaster ride that woman was. Carlos exhaled slowly.

Just then a horse took a gigantic charge in his box and banged against a stall wall and whinnied. The door to the worker's lounge opened, and Britt came rushing in. "What's this? What's going on? Hush up, both of you!" She ran to comfort the most upset horse, and with soothing sounds reached for him in his stall. She grabbed some oats and gave him a handful.

Kate gave Britt a look that could kill. It was then that Carlos wondered whether Kate was involved in these deaths—out of spite for her father, or jealously of Britt? But, just how could she be involved? And how would Kate know Britt, at least enough to be jealous, or even care about her? He wondered how deep and how far her anger would carry her. It was a thought almost too sick to contemplate.

Britt turned to them both and with blazing eyes said, "Get out."

Kate spat at her. "Who do you fucking think you are to tell me what to do in my father's barn?"

"I am in charge of these horses until someone tells me otherwise. They are my responsibility. Obviously, you don't care what happens to them. Take your petty human problems someplace else. You're messing up the horses."

Kate pushed past Britt so hard she knocked her into the door of the stall. With a throaty voice full of menace, she whispered as she passed, "Enjoy your five minutes of being in charge. You'll be gone by morning." With that, Kate stalked out of the barn.

Carlos stood there helplessly. He watched Britt soothe the horses, and went to several himself to calm them. He came up to her at last and said, "I am so sorry. It's always out of control with Kate, no matter how hard I try."

Britt just nodded.

"Do you have a minute or two we could talk?"

It was then that she noted he was still dressed in his best clothes. She moved her eyes up and down from his shoes to his hat, and with a note of grudging approval in her voice told him, "Well, you look well behaved enough. Let's go up to my place. It could be my last night there, from the sound of things."

Carlos didn't know how to take that offer, but quietly followed her up the back stairs. Once inside, he removed his boots but sat on the sofa with his coat on. "I won't stay, Britt."

"I wanted to tell you I did remember something that might help you in your investigation of Tremor. I didn't want to take the chance that anyone might overhear us in the barn. I'm not sure if it has anything to do with anything, but it seems, all of a sudden, that no one is trustworthy and everything is suspicious."

"Do you feel that way about me?" Carlos asked.

"Oh, no! I didn't mean that. I was so taken aback by your altercation with Kate…well, I don't need to know about that…well…" and her voice petered out.

Carlos noted the "wells" had started again. She was rattled. "Tell me what you thought of. Don't worry about Kate. She never has been able to distinguish reality from what she makes up in her mind."

"I saw Podsky and Lisa Anthony with Tremor a few days before he died. They were in his stall and giving him an injection, it looked like. They finished up in a hurry when they saw me coming down the aisle, and when I asked why they hadn't called me to help with the horse, they just said it was a routine vaccination and they didn't need to bother me. Bother me? That's what a groom is for, don't you think? To help in times like that? I mean, I'm always there when they take the stallions I care for anyplace. What do you think it means, Carlos?"

"Was it recorded in his FEI passport?"

"That's the funny thing. After I saw them working with Tremor, I got worried that I had missed a vaccination date. It's my job to make sure these things are handled on time, and I thought the next one wasn't due for another month. I wanted to check the dates of Tremor's last shots—they would have been listed in his passport—but when I went to get it out of Podsky's desk, he was sitting right there. I asked him if I could see it, but he said he didn't have it. I was too embarrassed to tell him why I wanted it. This has never happened to me before. Missing an important date like that. I even went back and looked in Podsky's desk when he was out, but it wasn't there. I looked everywhere else I could think of and couldn't find it. That worries me, because I'm responsible for knowing where the horse's passport is, and I can't imagine how it could have gotten lost."

"It looks like the next order of business is to find that passport. Where should we look, Britt?"

"I'll ask Raja and get back to you. She won't think a thing of my asking, because it is customary for the groom to have it, or at least know where it is. She might not know where it is, but she would give me permission to search. Raja has so little idea of what goes on here in the stable."

Carlos stood. "Britt, you have a good sensible head on your shoulders. Thanks. You're a big help. If you need anything, or remember anything else, give me a call." He left her holding another one of his cards.

CHAPTER 23

Susan slid into the back booth at The Times, grateful for the dark paneling and subdued lighting. The bench was a horseshoe, and she positioned herself in the center, so she could see her colleagues as they arrived—assuming she could keep her head up and eyes open. The lunch crowd had gone back to work, so she had the place more or less to herself. She had purposely picked a spot as far away from the bar as possible. Even the smell of liquor was enough to reinforce her hangover and make her feel slightly nauseous. It would be tough to face Carlos so soon after last night, but having Pat North and Ken at the meeting would help her to refocus on the business at hand.

It was time to go over the case piece by piece. She had the subpoena for the necropsy report, and she'd told Ken to bring the medical files to the meeting. Carlos would have to work as part of the team now. It was time to remind him that he was working for her, whatever his private vendettas were. He was basically freelancing this case, and if he wanted to get paid, he'd have to be forthcoming.

Susan was horribly embarrassed about the previous evening, but she'd just have to get over it. She felt a slight bit of anger at Carlos because he was so cool, so in control. She, on the other hand, approached things with fire, and then regretted them later. Like driving when she shouldn't have last night. She was sure, positively sure, that she would never do that again. It was stupid. She knew it was her regret about her own behavior that fueled her anger with Carlos. But, she reminded herself, that was not productive. Being angry with Carlos hadn't changed his behavior before, and there were no signs that it would work now. Something was driving him, and it certainly wasn't a desire for a relationship with her.

"He's not worth it," Susan said out loud, drawing a puzzled stare from the waitress attending those in the adjoining booth.

Then the reality hit her again. Podsky was dead. It wouldn't be a federal case unless she declared him a deceased federal witness, but that might dry up the trail even more. Local law enforcement was handling the initial investigation. The case was all over the news. Car bombs weren't exactly a staple of southern Minnesota. Drive-by shootings usually dominated the ten o'clock news. But bombs! The media weren't going to let this dog die easily. Right now, she preferred that the federal horse angle not become news fodder.

Susan knew it would be only a matter of time before some enterprising reporter found out about the subpoena ordered by her office. All the public knew now was that the state had lost its most valuable equine star, the wife of the governor, and an illustrious horse trainer all within a few days of one another. If she couldn't tie the three deaths together in a meaningful way, she doubted that the local media would be able to either.

Her instincts told her that the whole mess could be a coincidence. She had seen crazier things happen. There were a lot of people who would have loved to see Podsky dead. As for Fiona, her demise read more like black humor in the article on the front page of the Star Tribune. The funeral must have been something else. The newspaper covered it in detail with great photos. Did she remember right? Did Carlos tell her he was going to the funeral? How did he get invited? And why would he bother?

Whatever her personal feelings about him, Susan needed Carlos on this case. He knew the ins and outs of the horse industry better than anyone else involved. He was a whole world apart from Charlie, and knew things from a first-hand perspective. Lloyd's of London had him on special retainer because of his insider knowledge. Why hadn't Lloyd's immediately put Carlos on this case? Was it because the claim hadn't been filed in a timely fashion? Did she just get to him first? Or was it something else? At any rate he wouldn't be working for Lloyd's now, since he had already agreed to work with her office. Which raised another question. Why would Carlos agree to work with her when he probably stood to gain more financially by working with the underwriter?

Yes, something was driving Carlos, and it certainly wasn't the money. That did not surprise her. She knew him well enough to know that he operated out of a private sense of justice. Horses were a very personal matter with Carlos. She wondered if he was holding something back. That thought bothered her. No matter what her feelings for Carlos, Susan wanted to close the book on Tremor and move on to something less complicated. She was starting to feel very tired and very old.

Susan pulled out her notepad and jotted a reminder to herself. There was something she'd read in Carlos's dossier. He was, after all, a federal source and required a background check. Sometimes she felt a tinge guilty, having so much access to very personal information about his past. There was a tie-in with Podsky or his daughter. Susan better refresh her memory later. Maybe that could explain why he was so intent on attending the funeral. Fiona was a major client of the barn and of Raja's New Age enterprises. But something else nagged at her memory. It would have to wait, since she felt Pat North slide into the booth beside her.

"Hey, Susan, you look like hell. Don't tell me you're losing sleep over Podsky. Hell of a way to go…you all right?" Pat motioned for the waitress to come over. They both ordered a Coke. Susan smiled weakly at Pat. She liked him. Solid family man. He had a wife, three kids, and a swimming pool in Shakopee. He was a brilliant investigator, but he liked to keep his involvement low-key for security reasons involving his family. He had nailed some pretty heavy underworld figures. He was largely responsible for the issuance of federal indictments against twenty-three people involved in the Florida horse mafia. After that success, he'd requested a transfer from the FBI office in the Northern District of Florida to the Minneapolis field office. Unfortunately for Pat, his expertise required that he pull together the indictment for the missing groom and race fixer that Podsky had fingered. He could be a big help, because he knew most of the scams. Besides, he was an expert on RICO laws, Susan's favorite catch-all for issuing indictments.

The Racketeer Influenced and Corrupt Organizations Act, or RICO as the lawyers called it, had been useful to Susan on many occasions. It was created expressly as a tool to stop organized crime. Since its inception in the seventies, it had been used with a much broader brush to include almost every area of business, law, and finance. That was helpful to someone like Susan who needed an edge for some of the smoky areas of crime—ones where it was hard to get convictions on the people involved.

"Did you hear how they cleaned it up?"

Susan rubbed her eyes, trying to shake off the headache she knew was coming again in full force. "What's that again, Pat?"

"Podsky. Did you hear how they cleaned it all up? Service Master. Can you believe it? His wife calls Service Master. I heard a rumor that part of him was stuck to the weathervane on top of the barn. One of the workers passed out. They called an ambulance when the guy fell off the roof and one of the paramedics was able to climb up there and retrieve it. Wanna know what part it was?"

Susan felt the room spin as the nausea hit her hard again.

She waved Pat off.

"Some other time, OK? I'm not feeling so good."

"Sorry, Susan." He looked sheepish. Susan also thought that he looked kind of cute in a little-boy way.

"I'm really sorry. I got carried away. Gotta go for the gallows humor in this job, you know?"

"Yeah, I know. It's just that I'm having a hard time holding it together today."

Just when Susan thought she might want to call off the meeting and go home, Carlos and Ken slid into the open ends of the booth. With somewhat of a flourish, Ken placed a four-inch-thick file in the middle of the table. It was the first time Susan had ever seen Carlos in a dress suit. She did a double take, even though it made her stomach lurch. He looked pretty good. Better than that, he looked terrific. He had loosened his tie slightly. Damn. Now she had to deal with stomach flutters along with the nausea.

"Your office served the subpoena last night. Not that I didn't want to share it with you anyway. I hope you know that." Ken looked stern.

Susan reached for the file. "Yeah, Ken. I know. First thing I want to get clear is who ordered the necropsy? An extensive one is pretty expensive, right?"

Susan was looking at Carlos out of the corner of her eye, but he seemed to be evading her glance. Never mind, she thought. She could count on him to be discreet about their late-night encounter.

Ken continued, "About four to five hundred dollars. Not a whole lot for the wealthy set, but nothing to sniff at either. To answer your other question, Lisa Anthony ordered the necropsy."

"Is she the vet for Podsky's barn?"

"His and a lot of the other breeding facilities in the area. Seems she has just about the best reproductive kitchen facility in the Midwest."

Susan's curiosity was definitely piqued about Dr. Lisa Anthony.

"Anything else I should know about her?"

"Just rumor," Ken said.

"What kind of rumor?"

"Well, like maybe she and Podsky had something going."

"That wouldn't surprise anyone. Podsky was in everyone's bed, including his daughter's from what I have on file."

Susan felt Carlos shift uncomfortably next to her. Now what's THAT about, she wondered.

She looked at Ken.

"So, Dr. Anthony orders the necropsy. Pro forma right?"

"Yeah, the insurer would require it. Lloyd's of London doesn't like to pay if it doesn't have to, right, Carlos?"

Carlos still looked pretty uncomfortable. He evaded Susan's stare, and nodded at Ken. "I'm not working for them now, but, yes. Have you heard from their underwriter, yet?"

"Just a phone call requesting the necropsy report. You're the first to see it."

"How much was the policy?" Susan wanted to know.

"Two mil."

Susan was considering motive. "OK. So they have a two-million-dollar policy on a horse with stud fees of $100,000 a session. So would you agree that it wouldn't make any sense to kill him for the money? He was worth more to the consortium alive than dead."

Pat was on track with Susan. "Podsky was certainly capable of killing the horse or having someone else do it, but he had no financial incentive, unless someone paid him off to do it. But why?"

Susan thought it was a good time to spill Charlie's surprise.

"Get this, boys. One of my best sources tells me that Cindi Moreno's interest in the consortium was backed by her news organization. They were putting together some kind of investigative piece on fraud in the horse industry and used her to buy into Podsky's operation."

Pat groaned. "If they go with any kind of story we might as well say bye-bye to any future indictments. Tracks are going to be covered faster than you can say Tremor's Dead."

Susan went on.

"Let's look at the other two. Fiona Andersson is conveniently deceased, but it looks like an accident. The only lead we have on Randolph Decker is an unoccupied houseboat in Miami Beach. Same neighborhood where they found Andrew Cunanan, I believe. It's a very nice, large houseboat. It's owned by a corporation, and now we're working on tracking down the principals of the corporation. Hopefully, we'll find out soon. Could be a dead end, but you never know."

Pat let out a low whistle.

"You know, if you tried to put all of this into a book, no one would believe it. Most of my cases are like that. Maybe I should quit and become a writer. Be a safer occupation."

"Motive and opportunity."

The group looked up in unison as Carlos spoke. Susan took the lead.

"What are you getting at, Carlos? I think we are all familiar with the basics of a criminal investigation."

"Sorry, it's just that it doesn't matter what the news organizations are doing or what story they come up with. We should focus on what we know and go deeper. For instance, was there life insurance on Fiona? As they say, follow the money."

Susan had to agree that he had a point. She also was relieved to hear him use the first-person "we" when describing his involvement in the investigation. Maybe he would be a team player after all.

"OK, Carlos. So what did you and Ken come up with at the necropsy?"

It was a logical place to start. Carlos nodded and deferred to Ken.

"It was a very thorough necropsy. My best guess is that it was a strongyles infection."

Susan was incredulous. "You're telling us that one of the most valued horses of all time died of worms? How could that happen?"

"How did he get worms, or how did they kill him?"

"Both, I guess. Just don't tell me that we have been spending tons of the tax-payers' dollars on the case of a horse that died of worms! Anyone have an Excedrin?"

Pat set a bottle of Extra-Strength on the table, and Susan hungrily swallowed two, then another one for good measure.

Ken continued, "It's all in the report. This kind of worm can cause a blockage in the arteries leading to the intestines. All I can tell you is that the marks were there, although pathology couldn't come up with any signs of active infection. It could have been the results of an old infection. Anyway, a blockage would have stopped the blood flow to the intestines, and that's what probably led Podsky to believe it was a bad case of colic. Horses die of colic all of the time."

Susan looked at Carlos. "You think that's all there is to it?"

"It's possible, but things are not always what they seem," mused Carlos. He was staring off into the distance, and Susan didn't know if he was focused on the issues at hand or his mind was someplace else entirely.

"Hey, come back and join the living, Carlos…you're gonna have to be a little more specific."

"I was just thinking of a case that has been causing some controversy on the West Coast recently. A very expensive show jumper stallion…the flagship of a breeding operation…died of a rare parasite. Necropsy showed there was no natural port of entry. The owner has posted a big reward for solid information leading to proof of foul play."

"Motive?" Susan challenged Carlos with his own method. Now he was proving his value to this investigation. She felt her choice was vindicated.

"The owner feels it was a reaction to her environmental crusades in Southern California. If her breeding operation were to be destroyed, maybe she would be forced to put up or shut up."

"What does the science say? And why didn't you mention this case to me during our review of the necropsy?" Ken was obviously annoyed.

Carlos was unmoved. "I wanted to go back and review my files before I added another question to the mix. The veterinarians are taking a conservative approach. They feel the parasite could occur naturally in the environment. Although the chances of natural infection are slim, they are still higher than someone injecting it on purpose."

Susan wondered who came up with those odds. "So, let's not reinvent the wheel, guys. What was the approach on the necropsy on that California case?"

Carlos flinched at having to go over the gruesome details. "A urine test finally revealed the presence of halicephalobus deletix just days before the stallion's death. At that point he had lost eighty-five percent of both kidneys, much of his brain, and his vision was totally destroyed. Further tests on frozen semen showed contamination by the parasite."

Susan pushed the files back across the table in Ken's direction. "OK. Start running some tests on Tremor's blood and semen. I assume you have some samples on file."

"Blood, yes. Semen, no. But it's not that easy, Susan."

Susan was holding her head in her hands. All this talk about bodily fluids was getting her queasy, and the Excedrin was getting her buzzed. "Would someone please explain why?"

Carlos pushed a glass of water toward her and waved the waitress away as she approached with a stack of menus. Pat and Ken looked at each other, as though they sensed a bond between Carlos and Susan that went beyond the professional.

Carlos pretended not to notice the reaction of the other two men. Men seemed to have a primal, almost paranormal sense of the chemistry between one of their own and a woman, he thought. "We have to know what we are looking for. When you run a tissue or blood test it has to be for something specific. There are hundreds of things we could be looking for."

Susan groaned. They all turned and looked at her.

"Or nothing." Carlos continued. "Maybe this case is just one big fat nothing...or we could be looking for a needle in a haystack...pardon the pun."

Ken was frustrated, too. Trying to get some forward motion going, he offered, "My best differential diagnosis is colic due to a strongyles infection. A semen sample would be helpful at this point. I could run some random tests for other pathogens."

Susan suddenly sprang to life. The caffeine in the Excedrin combined with the Coke was working its magic. "I think we need to go back and use what we have to fill in the blanks. Here's what I want you to do."

Susan was beginning to sound like a drill sergeant. "Carlos, I want you to visit this Dr. Anthony veterinarian. See if you can get some semen samples for Ken. She ran the breeding operation, so that should be no problem. If she was banging Podsky, it would be interesting to know if she is distressed by his sudden demise."

She looked at Carlos for some sign of agreement with her plan.

Seeing nothing but his professional blank stare, she continued, "Ken. Great job on the necropsy. We've gotta find something for you to look for, but in the meantime, would you mind doing some research on colic for me? Anything you can come up with that might disguise itself as colic. Put some of your University researchers on my payroll if you have to. I need something solid to go on."

"You won't have to pay us, Susan. A lot of the docs have been suspicious about these insurance cases for a long time. An awful lot of horses seem to have been dying of colic. They will be happy to know that someone is finally taking their concerns seriously. You won't have any trouble gathering research, believe me."

"Thanks, Ken. Just don't let them get too carried away with other cases that bother them. Keep them focused on what happened to Tremor. Make copies of the report if necessary...I don't need a lot of wild theories...I want answers."

"Saving the best for last, Susan?" Pat North raised his eyebrows and put his chin in his hands. He got a small laugh from Susan.

Then Pat's voice grew serious. He knew what his assignment would be, and he also knew he wasn't going to like it. There seemed to be no escape from this horse business. "Maybe I should put in for a transfer to narcotics? Right now even that rat-hole assignment seems to hold more cheer than the pathos of the horse world."

Susan and Carlos looked at him with questions in their eyes. Susan queried, "Are you serious?"

"Maybe, maybe not. What have you got for me?" Pat responded.

Susan wasn't about to give up on Podsky's connections to the horse underworld. "Pull out all the stops on the missing race fixer, Pat. Podsky knew more than he was telling us. I'd also like you to lean on that guy in El Paso who was running the horses across the border. If we can prove conspiracy, we can open a RICO investigation and maybe flush some more of the vermin out of the woodwork. It would, at the very least, give us more authority to look into Podsky's affairs."

Her own choice of words made Susan feel sick again. Her distress did not go unnoticed by Carlos. He deftly took charge. "Pat, Ken…you two go ahead and order. I think our fearless leader here needs a little fresh air."

With that simple statement, Carlos gently put an arm around Susan's shoulder. She looked up at him gratefully. He guided her out of his end of the booth, into her coat, and propelled her through the door to take in the crisp afternoon air.

Pat and Ken were left with each other and an obviously frustrated waitress.

CHAPTER 24

▼

Carlos spotted the antique shop on the north side of 55 that signaled the left turn onto County 14 and his entry into the horse farms near Buffalo. Dr. Lisa Anthony's operation wouldn't be hard to find. Falling Oak Farms had seen its ups and downs but was still regarded as the ultimate breeding kitchen in the upper Midwest. Fact, fiction, lore, and just plain rumor swirled around its history as one of the area's most valuable pieces of real estate. An eccentric millionaire had pumped over a million dollars into Falling Oak's construction in the late sixties. Since then, the bedroom communities north of the Twin Cities had begun to fill in the agricultural real estate that once surrounded the enterprise.

Carlos himself remembered mucking stalls there when he was nine or ten years old and trying to earn the money to buy his first pony. His father was barn manager at Falling Oak then. That was just before his father went to work for John's father. He smiled fondly at the memory of how he had then become such fast friends with John that people used to refer to them as "the twins." Falling Oak was the jumping-off point for both his father and himself.

Carlos shook off the thought, not wanting to revisit that particular memory. It would cloud his vision, and he needed clarity, not nostalgia.

Falling Oak was now in the hands of Lisa Anthony because the millionaire tired of overseeing the finances of an operation that was doing little more than breaking even. Like many with too much money and time, he found that the myopic dream of running a horse operation lost its allure once it was realized. And the dream was realized beyond all reasonable expectation. In its heyday, Falling Oak boasted five miles of white board fencing, three fifteen-stall barns, an indoor arena, a complete veterinary hospital with radiology and laboratory, and a caretaker's house. A three-story log home was magnificently reflected in the ten-acre pond at the bottom of the knoll that overlooked the barns.

When the millionaire tired of his project and fled to Arizona to golf away his middle years, a fish farming operation was able to secure the property for less than half of its original cost. It was a write-off for the millionaire and a debacle for the fish farm. The operators realized too late that restrictive environmental zoning laws and local opposition tied to fears of groundwater pollution would result in mitigation costs that would effectively shut down the operation before the first fish could spawn.

The fish tanks were removed from the barns in time for a deal to be struck with a manufacturing firm that dealt in electronics. That deal fell through at the last minute when the fish farmer held out for too much money and the manufacturer found cheaper acreage two miles closer to I-94.

Just when the fish farmer was sweating his creditors, Dr. Lisa Anthony stepped up to the plate and offered slightly less than he paid for the property. In addition to taking a loss, he had to finish restoring the barns, repaint the white board fencing, and hang the old Falling Oak Farms sign back in its original place along the roadside. He was glad to do it to get out from under his mountain of debt. That was less than two years ago, and the operation had already re-established its former success and notoriety among the racing crowd at Canterbury Downs as well as the general horsy set in the surrounding hills.

Susan's extensive research and his own memory gave Carlos at least a sketch of the history. He would fill in the brush strokes as he conducted his visit with Lisa Anthony. She was expecting him. He thought it was surprising that he was able to contact her with one phone call, without an answering service or recording intervening. That was unusual for a busy veterinarian who also ran a breeding kitchen, he thought. It could be his good fortune, but it seemed out of place; it spoiled the symmetry of Falling Oak Farms. He would remember. Carlos liked to assemble the complete picture in his mind. He was not fond of looking at the shadows, but it was all part of the job, and if he wasn't too emotionally involved, it was easier to do.

Susan was his opposite. She would not rest until she had found the truth. Like a photographer who overexposes a shot to shed light on the texture and detail in the shadows of a photograph, she would examine the nuances of every case until the image of truth materialized. To Carlos, that seemed like forcing the issue. He preferred the patient approach, but he had to admit that when they combined forces the investigation became relatively seamless. Somehow, in spite of all of their obvious differences, they were able to pull together.

"Like a matched team of horses," he said out loud. Their personalities and styles were different, yes, but when they focused their energies in the same direction, the load was noticeably lighter.

The oversized tires on the Dodge Ram skidded on the blacktop as Carlos just about missed the driveway entrance to Falling Oak. This was not the time to be thinking about a woman, he reminded himself. He was amazed at how much he found himself thinking of her. She'd pounced into his life again, and it was having an effect on him. He had been having a fine time being a loner, or at least that's what he had been telling himself. With an effort, he brushed thoughts of Susan aside and headed down the driveway.

No horses were visible in any of the ample pastures that lined either side of the driveway. This was not uncommon for a breeding operation. The contract stallions would be inside waiting their turn to service the mares, while the "teaser stallions" did most of the work. Dr. Lisa Anthony's job as veterinarian was to make certain that the proper amount of sperm was ejaculated into each mare.

In addition, she would oversee the "kitchen" that would cool semen for transport. Mare owners who elected to use transported semen for artificial insemination incurred much less expense and, theoretically, much less risk to their mare. They did not have to transport their mare or worry that she would not stand for the stallion. It was a good option for the semen producer, and Lisa Anthony was one of the first reproductive veterinarians to successfully merge both processes. Falling Oak Farms certainly had the space.

Carlos found the whole process distasteful for humane reasons; it was too much of an assembly-line approach, all in the name of efficiency. It wasn't an unusual setup; it just didn't meet his approval.

He felt the same way about the contract farms for the production of mares' urine. It sickened him to think of row upon row of pregnant mares constrained so their urine could be easily collected. The poor horses were not allowed outside and stood for months with catheters inserted into them so that no urine would be wasted. The more "humane" facilities used catch cups, but it was still slave labor as far as Carlos was concerned. The pharmaceutical companies paid dearly for the substance, which they then used to produce estrogen supplements for women. The foals were then killed, auctioned, or rendered so that the mares could be immediately bred back to a state of pregnancy. And many were bred from kitchens like the one Dr. Anthony ran at Falling Oak Farms. It was part of Carlos's job to visit these enterprises from time to time, but he didn't like it. That was certain.

He parked his Ram in one of the spots labeled "Visitor" and adjusted his sunglasses as a lone horse caught his eye in the pasture to the left. He walked up to the fence, a natural response on his part. Horses seemed to call him, and there was seldom a time that he would pass up the chance to commune with one or at least give it an affectionate pat on the neck. He would much rather be visiting with a horse than humans.

Carlos noticed that she was a very attractive mare and most likely highly bred in the German tradition. She was probably a Westphalian or Dutch Warmblood. He wasn't sure since she was blanketed, but she was a big and beautiful bay with two hind white socks and a small snip on her nose. Friendly, too. She nickered softly at Carlos and walked slowly toward the gate, leaving the ample pile of alfalfa in the hayrack.

The mare was clearly a pet, and Carlos wondered why she was alone in the paddock. Perhaps she belonged to the doctor. It would be highly unusual to have a client's mare outside in this weather.

"Do you like her?"

Carlos feigned surprise at the question, acting as if he hadn't noticed the woman's approach. He had actually been aware for several minutes that someone was watching his interaction with the mare. He didn't bother to turn around.

"She's beautiful. Well put together. Dutch Warmblood?"

"Very good. Not many people would pick up on that. Most people think she's Westphalian. You certainly have an eye for breeding. Have we met?"

Carlos turned toward the woman's voice and noticed right away that she was attractive, late twenties to early thirties. Her long blond hair had been pulled back into a tight bun at the base of her head. She was slim yet muscular. The blue lab coat highlighted her violet eyes and also told him her name. He shifted to face her and extended his hand. She looked him directly in the eyes.

"Carlos, Carlos Dega. You must be Dr. Anthony? Dr. Lisa Anthony?" He feigned a submissive stance. It might draw her out and disarm her, but probably not. His instincts told him otherwise. There was a certain toughness to her classic beauty.

"Mr. Dega. I've been expecting you."

Lisa Anthony extended a well-manicured hand and Carlos took it, assessing what he could about the character of the woman through the simple overture. Unfortunately, there was nothing in her touch that provided the opening he was looking for. On a hunch, he tightened his grasp for a millisecond. Nothing. She withdrew her hand and he realized that she had won the initial encounter. That usually didn't happen, and he was caught slightly off guard. She would be difficult, he calculated, but the nature of his job often made initial encounters adversarial.

Interviews with the veterinarians seldom had this component. Their job was to submit the detailed clinical history along with the request for necropsy in insurance cases. On occasion, owners preferred to retain the animal's carcass, and the necropsy could be performed by the referring veterinarian. He would start there. It would give him a conversational opening.

"Thank you for seeing me on such short notice. I've always loved this place. Does it still have the diagnostic lab?"

Dr. Anthony turned away from the paddock and her body language was enough to indicate that she wanted Carlos to follow. She was slightly suggestive in her walk, and several times she coyly looked over her shoulder as she led Carlos toward the lab.

"Well, yes and no. The equipment is still there, but I'm afraid that our breeding operation has been monopolizing all of my time. I really didn't expect it to take off the way it did. Between managing the on-site breeding and shipping the frozen semen, I'm afraid I don't have much time for a clinical practice...other than follow-up ultrasounds. You've been here before, then?" With one hand Carlos removed his sunglasses and held the door as they entered the office area. Typical vet's office. Organized clutter, and stacks of journals piled in the corner.

"Not officially. I groomed horses here as a kid." No harm in letting out that bit of information, he thought.

"I imagine things have changed quite a bit since you were here last. Feel free to look around. When I got your call I was a bit confused. Are you working for the underwriter on the Tremor case?"

Interesting that she would call it a "case."

"Not this time. The District Attorney's office asked me to follow up on the necropsy. With everything that's happened in the last few days, I'm sure you can understand why."

"Actually it's very frightening. I was Tremor's vet, after all. I've already looked into extra security. Do you have much experience with this sort of thing—car bombs and all? Who ever would expect such a thing here of all places? Poor Mr. Podsky. His family must be devastated."

Mr. Podsky. Nice touch. Was she really scared? Hell, he was.

"I know this must be overwhelming, but I have just a few questions that I'd like to clear up. Is there a reason why you feel you need extra security? Something Podsky may have said about Tremor?"

"Well, with one of Tremor's owners being electrocuted and his stable manager murdered, the reason for my concern should be obvious. And, no, I don't have any other information about Tremor other than the fact that he was a great horse. Probably the best of our lifetime."

"But you were his personal vet. You did sign the necropsy submission forms. Why didn't you do the necropsy yourself?"

"I'm really not set up for it. Besides, I just felt the university lab could do a more thorough job. I also don't have a cooler big enough to hold a carcass long enough to keep the tissue samples viable."

Again he said, "But you were his vet. Did you handle routine exams and vaccinations, that sort of thing? I thought you said you were too busy for a routine clinical practice?" Carlos pressed her.

"I did. But what vet would turn down a request to oversee the medical care of the most famous horse of our generation? I'll be honest with you, Mr. Dega. It's still a man's world in my profession. My inheritance bought this place, but to keep it going I have to do a lot of PR. Tremor was good for advertising and good for the business."

"Then you might be able to help out with the necropsy after all."

She motioned for Carlos to take the chair to the left of her desk. He moved the stack of journals to the floor and sat down.

"In what way?"

"Well, for one thing, the carcass was left for too long in the warm barn and the lab was unable to get a viable semen sample for testing. Would you happen to have any on file?"

She laughed.

"Absolutely not. Tremor's semen was as valuable as the gold in Fort Knox. No one kept any samples as far as I know."

Unlikely, but not impossible, Carlos thought.

"What about recent blood samples?" Playing a hunch, Carlos fished a little. He couldn't be sure just what Britt had witnessed, but neither, he figured, could Lisa. "I interviewed the groom, and she recalled that you took some samples a week or two ago. An uncompromised sample would be helpful as a comparison."

"She must have been mistaken, Mr. Dega. I stopped by to give a booster vaccination. No blood was drawn. Sorry I can't help you. What does the necropsy indicate? I haven't heard the results."

Now that was interesting. Was the woman that busy? No time to follow up on her most famous patient?

"Intestinal infarct due to strongyles."

"What?"

"Strongyles. I know that could be embarrassing to you, but don't worry. It looks like it was the result of an old infection. How long were you caring for Tremor, anyway?"

Lisa Anthony was agitated now and didn't seem to hear the question. "Is that information confidential? Strongyles! If that becomes known I'll be the laughing-stock of the Midwest Veterinary Association. This can't be. There must be another reason!"

"I'm afraid that's what the report has been able to come up with so far. There are a score of blood tests that could be run to look for something else, but we don't know where to start. Besides, the intestinal infarct was unmistakable. That's why a baseline blood sample would be very helpful."

"Believe me, I wish I had one. How long ago do they think the horse was infected with strongyles? I've only been working with him since he's been at Grande Glade. About a year, I think. I'll have to check my records." Carlos had just what he needed. There was no reason to prolong the interview. He rose to leave and handed her his card.

"If you can think of anything, please call. I'm sorry you don't have a copy of the necropsy. I'll make sure Ken faxes you one ASAP." Carlos noticed that she was hardly listening.

"Yes, certainly, right away. Strongyles! Are you sure? This can't get out!"

"There is no reason for it to. The insurance underwriter and the D.A.'s office have the only copies outside of the two of us. The university lab has the complete file, of course. I'm sorry you didn't know." Lisa Anthony looked truly stunned, pale and suddenly dwarfed by her surroundings. It was as if the news of the necropsy results were more devastating than the other events surrounding the case. Carlos was certain she was surprised and very worried about her reputation at this point. He was also convinced that she would go to any length to protect it.

CHAPTER 25

▼

It was almost happy hour before Susan felt like she could really focus on the Tremor files. Shirley had fortified her with cup after cup of her strong brew, and that, along with several gulps of Mylanta, saw her through the hours after the meeting at The Times. The investigation was floundering. She knew it and didn't like it.

Pat North was complaining loudly about wasting taxpayer dollars on the search for the missing groom. She had to admit that it was one of hundreds of seemingly loose ends that were ever-present in the horse industry. Sometimes it would pan out, like it did in the Florida horse mafia case, but more often one blind alley led to another one, each populated by shadowy figures that seemed to vanish into the ether.

Pat was frustrated, sure, but her instincts told her he was scared. Maybe he wouldn't want to dig deep enough, and that would cost the investigation. It might be time to think about assigning someone else to his portion of the case, but that would lose valuable time. He knew more than anyone where the maze led, and it would take a new investigator months to assimilate what Pat knew, if it could be done at all. She would have to find a way to motivate him. The gambling groom was key if only because of his ties to Podsky.

She lit a Marlboro and didn't bother to retreat to the restroom. Everyone was gone, and the defiant act of taking an illicit drag somehow made her feel a little better. Her private line rang.

Quickly exhaling she picked up the receiver.

"Susan? It's Gwen."

"Yeah. Hi. You just caught me smoking at my desk."

"Something's not quite right here."

Susan's stomach lurched again. "What? What's wrong?"

"Listen. Maya's not home yet from her riding carpool. You know, I trade with a few other moms so we aren't driving all the time. I know I laughed at you the other night, but now I'm a bit concerned."

"Does this happen very often? I mean, does she ever get home late?"

"Sometimes, but this mom is usually so reliable. The weather could be a bit iffy here, but, maybe not. I just didn't know what to do. Are you still worried about something happening to Maya? Any crazies you're dealing with still out there?"

Susan sighed and took another drag on her cigarette. Her hands were shaking. "Yeah. That particular crazy is still out there. I don't like this."

Gwen was uncharacteristically warm. "I really appreciate your caring so much about us, Susan. I feel so alone at times like this. I don't know what I would do if anything happened to Maya."

"Let's be rational for another half an hour, OK? Then I'll call you back. If Maya isn't home by then, we'll both panic. Call in the troops. Whatever it takes. Whaddaya think?"

"OK. Yeah. OK. Gosh, I hate this part about being a parent...and maybe I hate having a crime-busting high-profile sister just a little bit, too. Why couldn't you have gone into business?"

Susan snorted, snuffed out her Marlboro on the bottom of her shoe, and said, "Take it easy, Sis. It will be fine. I'll call you in a bit."

She thought about her niece, and all of the heartbreak that the dealer in El Paso had cost her and probably hundreds of other children and amateur riders. The guy ran several other neat little scams. Another one was running jumpers from Canada that had sustained soft-tissue injuries that were all but undetectable except by the most sophisticated ultrasound methods. Ken had helped enormously on that one, when he realized that otherwise sound horses had injuries that would lag behind any radiographic evidence. A lot of buyers would ignore a bad front flexion exam if the horse were otherwise sound. Impossible to prove, but at least Susan was able to get the guy for hauling horses across the border through International Falls without proper papers.

Crooks always slipped up somewhere. She never met one who was a Rhodes Scholar. Her thoughts were wandering. Smoking did that to her. So did nervousness about Maya. An index card with her all but illegible scrawl caught her eye.

It was the Columbo quote. Well, not exactly. Susan had written, "Horse murders are hard to hide because you have a body"...or in this case Tremor's body.

That was the linchpin. She and everyone else on the team were being distracted by the maze. Everyone with the exception of Carlos. It had annoyed her that he was so dogged about Podsky. Maybe it was some old vendetta. Something about Podsky's daughter. But he was right. It was, after all, one particular horse murder that they were investigating. It WAS murder.

She was sure of it. There was no other way to explain Podsky's sudden demise. What did Podsky know? Who was threatened enough by what he knew to resort to killing him? There was no such thing as coincidence, that she knew. They were fortunate. Tremor's body was still in the freezer at the U. There was no hiding WHAT had happened to Tremor. The questions were who and why…and how Podsky figured into the whole mess. Maybe it was time to take a lesson from the news team that set Cindi Moreno up as a front. A little investigative reporting was in order. Charlie wasn't really interested in her extensive files on the horse industry. It was the information on Tremor that he was after. That meant the news team didn't have enough to break a new angle on the story any more than she had enough to indict for insurance fraud. Ken's necropsy report wasn't among the stolen files. There was absolutely no reason for her to be playing defense on this one.

She had the power to subpoena all of Moreno's notes if she wanted, but that might shut down their investigation. Better to let them continue. Right now they had nothing, but they might turn up something interesting that she could use later. If they threatened to blow the case, she could probably get the judge to issue a gag order. Let Channel Seven do all the reporting it wanted to on fraud in the horse industry. It was time for her to follow Carlos's lead and focus on the specifics. She had gotten carried away with the big picture. And she suddenly realized that she was beginning to get carried away with Carlos, at least in her mind.

Seeing him again last night stirred up the old feelings on her part, but she wasn't so sure about him. He was tender, that was for certain, but there was a distance in his touch. Susan also thought that he was spending more time than was absolutely necessary with the young girl who was Tremor's groom. That information probably accounted for her middle-of-the-night intoxicated visit. God, she hated to admit that to herself.

And Susan wasn't going to set herself up for competition with some other woman—girl, almost. Especially not now, when she and Carlos were in the middle of an important investigation. Work always seemed to draw them together. The intensity of their focus on the mystery inevitably spilled over from their professional relationship until their personal chemistry ignited. Last time it was with less-than-good results, Susan reminded herself. Yet, she wanted their relationship to be held together with something more than just the baling twine of work. Susan thought she might have been too hard last time she and Carlos worked together. Randy had started calling her SuperBitch. Maybe this time she would be able to look beyond work to the personal. Maybe…

Thinking of the personal, she dialed Gwen's number. It rang three, four, five times. Susan bit her cuticle. "Come on, come on, answer…"

"Gwen and Maya's place. Whom may I say is calling?" Susan shuddered with relief. "Baby?"

"Hi, Auntie Susan!"

"We were worried."

"Yeah. So Mom said. Just some bad traffic, and one of the girls had a longer cool-down with her horse, stuff like that. No big deal. Want to talk to Mom?"

"No. Tell her I called. Watch out for strangers. You know the drill…"

"Gotta run for supper. I'm starved!" And with that the phone clicked in Susan's ear. This personal stuff was emotionally draining. Work was much easier.

CHAPTER 26

▼

The room was darkened to the point of blackness. Around the huge oak-clawed dining room table was a circle of people, holding hands and wearing crystals. Somewhere in the distance could be heard the sound of Tibetan singing bowls. The people began to hum in tune to the tone of the vibrating bowls. Even though it was a cold February evening, the room was hot. Heavy wool sweaters, knobby textured pants, and knee-high socks kept everyone even warmer.

Raja's voice could be heard in a rattling whisper. "Sasha. Come to us. Speak through any of us. Give us a message from your new level of consciousness. Tell us the wonders of your life, of what awaits us when we make our transition to the other side! We quietly await you…"

After a period of thirteen minutes, Raja spoke again. "Speak through any of us, Sasha. Or send us a sign. We have your riding crop here on the table. Move it so the tail points north, just like the north star. Tell us you live!"

Someone cleared her throat. Otherwise, there was no movement at all. The proverbial pin could have been heard hitting the floor, had it decided to drop at that moment.

More time passed. Nothing. Raja tried again. "My husband. We release you to the world beyond. We are not trying to hold you here to earth. We see your spirit spiral heavenward. Go in peace, even though your earthly ending was so violent."

Hands began to get clammy. The throat cleared again. Faintly at first, another voice began to speak. It was halting to begin with, but the feminine voice had a definite masculine quality and tone. One of Raja's oldest students began to sit up more in her chair. "You all must know there is more to life than what you think you know now. Remember to think upon each other, and the departed soul of

Sasha with understanding and compassion. You will soon find out things you did not think were possible. We on the other side of the veil beg you to reserve judgment. Things are not as they seem. There are those among you who would want you to believe one thing, and lead you away from the larger truth. Do not be fooled! Look to Sasha's first loves for answers."

The voice coughed. There was a moan. All the participants were riveted to their chairs.

"We would like to speak more, but we cannot at this time. Sasha is still in a state of deep rest after his explosive ending. This was a very traumatic thing to happen to his soul, and he is being nourished here. Contact us again in a fortnight. We will have more news for you then...Good night." A huge sigh escaped the medium's lips, and her head fell forward and banged on the table.

The lights gradually were raised, showing Raja visibly shaken. Her flesh was a light pea-green color and had a waxy sheen. She seemed unable to focus her eyes, and her hands nervously pulled at her scarf. Someone leaned over the poor passed-out medium and shouted, "Get her some water. Somebody—open the window! It's too hot in here."

It was then that Britt quietly let herself into the room. She had never seen a séance, and had been listening with fascination in the hallway, leaning against the doorjamb, cocking her ear to catch the breathy voice of the woman speaking in low moaning tones. She knew she should have waited until things got back more to "normal," but her fascination had propelled her forward to see what was happening. Filling the doorway, she stared at the passed-out woman with her forehead still plastered onto the oak table. Others stood around the table, fanning, gasping, and looking a bit wild-eyed. From dead calm to frantic bustle. The contrast was amazing to Britt.

Raja looked up in time to see Britt's quizzical expression. She rose from her chair so swiftly that her chair piled over backwards and hit the floor with the thud that only solid oak furniture can make. She pointed at Britt and said loudly and deliberately, "She's the one!"

"Excuse me?" Britt said.

"You, you...wolf in sheep's clothing! You are the one the spirits are talking about!"

Britt was stunned to the point of stammering. "I...I...I don't know what you are saying. Or...or...why."

"We'll have none of you at Grande Glade! We've been warned. It would be foolish of us to keep you here another minute! Leave!" She waved a jeweled hand,

and there was a movement of air around the room, as though someone had opened a door. Only no one had moved, not one inch.

Britt still didn't grasp what she was being told. "Of course, I will leave all of you alone. I apologize for interrupting. When can I talk to you? There are some things about the horses, especially Tremor, that I need to ask you. I was wondering where his FEI passport is."

"FEI passport?"

"Yes. You know, the document with his medical record?"

Raja went into a swoon. She sank into her chair, passed her hand over her eyes, and croaked, "Water. Water please. I feel faint." Now the group had two woozy ladies and one confused groom to deal with. Things were falling apart fast.

One of the other ladies—a sweet one whose name Britt thought might be Marilyn—came up to her and whispered in her ear, "She was awfully shocked about the reading tonight, and of course, the loss of her love Sasha...maybe you should come back later, dear."

Raja looked up, and said, "It is all too much for me to see you, Britt. You must pack up and go. The vibes are bad for me to see you. It reminds me of all that has been taken from me. Be gone by tomorrow morning."

Britt stared. "Tomorrow morning? Surely you're joking?"

Marilyn quickly assessed the situation. "I'm afraid she's right, dear. I think it best if you go. It's best for all of us." With that she deftly wheeled Britt around by the elbow, and gave her a little shove toward the door.

"But...but...I have things I need to do. Things that have to be discussed."

Sweetly, but very firmly, Marilyn said, "Not now, dear. Not now, or ever, dear. Raja has spoken, and we can't upset her any more. You can see that, can't you? Now, you go, and say your little horse good-byes."

All Britt could respond with was, "Yes, ma'am." She looked back into the room she had always considered, until this moment, warm and friendly. Her last mental snapshot was of shocked, pale faces, all around the table, and two women stirring and looking rather dazed. Britt thought she must look the same way. She certainly felt it.

She stumbled out into the cold night, and instinctively looked up to the stars for guidance, to give her some sense of normalcy. Something had to stay the same, since all her internal senses were reeling. Maybe she could find security in the rightness of the black sky with its twinkling lights of hope and constancy.

Just as her world stopped spinning, and her breath came more evenly, Britt heard the sound behind her of crunching snow. She half turned, expecting a verbal barrage from one of the séance members. It was Kate.

"You got what you deserve, you bitch," she told Britt ever so quietly.

"What is it with you, Kate? You are home such a short time, you don't know the first thing about me, and already you hate me. I have never done a thing to you."

"Ah, as Marilyn would say, my dear, you have done far too much. Don't try to fool me, as you have the others. We're on to you."

To Britt, the last hour was fast becoming a strange alternate universe. All she could think of was the horses left in her care, and the one who had been in her care but was now dead. "What of the horses here, then. Will you take care of them?"

"We took good care of Tremor, didn't we?"

The malice in Kate's voice made Britt weak in the knees. All of a sudden, she felt very vulnerable, even though she was much taller and outweighed Kate by a good 50 pounds. Britt was looking into the face of evil.

Now she couldn't wait to leave. It took all of her training to remain rational. She tried to think of herself riding a bucking, thrashing horse, keeping herself calm in order to subdue the animal. Kate was like a wild animal. Britt knew she must not let Kate smell fear or she would attack—maybe even physically.

"Well, then. Well, good. I guess I can leave with a clear conscience. I'll go then."

Kate smirked. It was clear that she was pleased that this little untidy business with Britt would soon be over. As she watched Britt walk over the snow-covered path, she shouted one last warning. "Don't show your face here again. Ever. I hope we are very clear!"

Britt turned, looked her over for at least thirty seconds, and said, "Oh, Kate. You are very clear. I would not miss your intentions."

Then, when she looked up again into the star-studded night, there was order in her private universe, at least for that moment. It didn't matter that Kate had threatened her again. Raja had just lost her husband, and was upset. It wouldn't hurt to try to apologize later. Maybe Raja would understand and not fire her.

CHAPTER 27

▼

In the far recesses of his mind, Carlos knew it was so deep into the night that no one on earth could be alive, much less awake. It was the phone ringing again that forced him into a semblance of consciousness. His first thought was of Susan. He wasn't sure if that was because he was dreaming of her, or that she was the only person he knew who would call him at that hour.

He struggled to find the receiver, feeling drugged. It had been a few days since he had slept well, and it was difficult for him to come up to talking level.

"Susan, stop calling me like this. I'm dead."

He wasn't sure why he kept the receiver up to his ear; maybe he was too tired to put it down. Perhaps it was the tremulous tone of voice that truly got his attention.

"Hello??? Carlos???"

"Yessss…" A long drawn-out sigh followed the tenuous statement. "I hate to bother you at this time of night, but…" and then the crying started.

"Who is this?"

"Well, it's Britt."

Carlos was sitting up now. "What on earth??"

"Well, you had said that I could call you at anytime, and I just didn't know where to turn, and well, I thought I could handle it myself, and then I found out I couldn't and so, well…"

"Britt. It's OK. Settle down. Yes. It's just fine that you called me. Don't worry about that. What has upset you so? What's happening?"

"Well, I talked to Raja and I don't know what happened, but she kicked me out. I thought it would come, but not now. She doesn't have anyone to look after the horses except a few of the transient hands, and I thought she needed me to figure out about Tremor, but she doesn't care about that, and told me to have my gear moved out by morning. I've been up half the night trying to pack, and I don't know what I'll do, or where I'll go." She started crying again.

Carlos never knew what was the manly thing to do when a woman started to cry. So he sat on the phone and waited until Britt could talk again. Eventually she sniffed into his ear, "I hate to ask, but could you come and pick me up?"

Without thought he said, "Of course. I'll be there about seven a.m. Will that be OK for you?"

"Oh, Carlos that would be wonderful! Thanks. I don't have much, and I think you and I can put everything in the pickup. Now I have a better idea what will happen." And with that she hung up.

Carlos was glad she had a better idea of what was going on, but he surely didn't. He looked at his watch. Now he knew why he always slept with it on. Five o'clock. He struggled out of bed, found his jogging clothes on the floor, and pulled them on. He would have to remember to wash them soon. He didn't care. One more jog, one more sweat.

It was dark and slippery. He didn't think about the cold. With his vision sharp, he tucked a small flashlight in his pocket, just for good luck, and pulled on all the warmth he could find as he made his way to the front door. As he silently opened and closed his front door, so as not to awaken his neighbors, he felt his breath catch in his throat. Damn. It was cold and hard to breathe. He pulled his turtleneck up over his mouth, and got swallowed by the cold and the steely darkness.

When Carlos pulled up at the back of the stable at the bottom of the stairs to Britt's flat, he saw that the porch light was on. He took the stairs two at a time, even though the ice was still treacherous on them. The door opened before he could ring the bell, and the red-eyed Britt again pulled him inside.

She flung herself onto his chest, and he reflexively put his arms around her. She sobbed, "I have been trying to think what I did wrong, what I said to deserve this, and I just haven't found a clue. I feel so…so…cheated. It isn't fair. I don't want to leave the stable this way. I did a good job, and I am being thrown out like a thief in the night. It really is too much. What is going on here, Carlos?"

"We're both clueless here, Britt. I'm as surprised as you are!"

She had started crying less loudly. "Thanks."

"No. I mean that. There is something going on here that isn't right, and you just got caught in the crossfire. I can honestly tell you that you have done all that would be possible for the horses and your employers. This isn't about you, Britt."

"Do you mean it?"

"I couldn't be more serious. Now, let's get some action going here, and get you started on a new direction."

"What is your thought?"

Carlos laughed in spite of the gravity of Britt's situation. "I was hoping you would tell me."

"Well, that's why I called you. I have no idea. I mean, well, I didn't plan to have to leave my place at the crack of dawn with no references, and a dead horse in my past. That Raja! I asked her for a letter of recommendation, and she wouldn't give it to me!"

By this time Britt was sitting on one of her packed boxes, looking for a tissue. Again, Carlos cursed himself for not having a clean handkerchief in his pocket. It seemed like he needed one almost daily for some upset female. In the end she got some toilet paper and loudly blew.

"Here's the hasty plan, then. We'll pack up our trucks, and go down the road to a fine diner I know. It's an old-fashioned farm place, and we'll stoke up with the idle farmers and talk more. How does that sound?"

At the loud growl of Britt's stomach they both laughed. "I guess that's the best strategy for me," she said.

As the dawn gave way to morning, and the warm rays of the sun mingled with the crisp air, the two-truck caravan left the gates of Grande Glade. As Carlos turned to look up at the big house, he saw a curtain move in the living room, and he wondered who would be looking at them so early in the day. He had his suspicions, but then, he was suspicious by nature. In his rear-view mirror he watched the light go on in the kitchen of Raja's house.

Over steaming cups of watery coffee, Carlos and Britt eyed each other. Carlos thought she was sizing him up, but didn't say anything. She had entrusted herself to him, and she needed time to adjust to the situation, and what he had just suggested. She sighed. "This coffee must be an offense to you."

"In this setting there is something fine about it, don't you think?"

She was nonplussed at his attitude about the brew, when she knew it was important to him, but then she was learning a little of his chameleon nature and his ability to enjoy things when they were in sync with their surroundings. Britt smiled.

She had a beatific smile, he noted. He was reminded of an innocent angel-child. It brought out the protective feelings he had toward all things pure and guileless, and he felt the urge to keep her safe, so she would not be sullied and become bitter like Kate.

"So, Carlos, tell me more about this Sally. She must be good-tempered, since she didn't seem to mind you calling her so early. But are you sure she's really willing to take in a stranger? With no references?"

"More than willing. When I asked her, she was delighted at the thought. She says she'll put you up in her guest room until you can find a place of your own. She has just gotten several new horses and is feeling a bit stretched. At her age, she could use an extra gentle hand, and there is no need for a letter of recommendation with her."

"It sounds settled, then. And the sun isn't entirely at its full strength. What an amazement to me you are, Carlos. I'm a bit overwhelmed, along with being overjoyed. This is better than I hoped for."

"There is only one payment I extract for this, Britt. And, I am dead serious about it."

"What's that?"

"You are to tell no one that I keep my horse there."

"Why ever not?"

Carlos's chin grew firm, and his eyes took on a strange glint. "Because I told you not to. There is no discussion on this point."

Britt was obviously confused, but kept her grateful silence. She knew that this was territory she would not be able to enter unless Carlos let her. And he was certainly not inclined to now. She let it be. They ate their eggs in silence.

When Carlos had gotten the check, Britt began to get up to go. As she reached for her truck keys, Carlos put his hand over hers. "I didn't mean to sound so harsh." His eyes held hers for a moment, and again he felt very protective of her. For a moment he thought he might know what emotions fathers have for their daughters.

"No. I know. I didn't mean to pry. It's OK. Really."

As he moved his hand to put on his hat, he asked, "Did you get Tremor's passport?"

"No. That's the continuing peculiar thing about this. Every place I looked for it, I couldn't find it. It wasn't where it should be. It just wouldn't have gotten misplaced like it appears it is. I am very careful about these things."

"Did you get a chance to ask Raja about it?"

"Yes, but that was when I interrupted her séance by mistake. And that's when she got mad and told me to pack my things and get out. Her friends practically pushed me out of the door. When I went back later to apologize, things only got worse."

"Can you remember what she said?"

"I hardly had a chance to explain myself. I told her that you needed the passport for the insurance investigation. Then she screamed that you must have 'put me up to it,' and told me to get out."

"Thanks, Britt. I'll take you out to Sally's, and then I have some calls to make. Will you be all right?"

"Sure. Really, Carlos. Don't worry about me any more. Let's go."

Sally greeted Carlos with her usual warmth, and Britt was openly impressed with her set-up. Carlos handed Britt over to Sally's capable hands and quietly went down the aisle to his sweet horse love. Forehead to forehead they communed. They breathed into each other, and Rios nuzzled Carlos. He crooned to the horse in Spanish while running his hands over his neck and body. Carlos loved Rios' scent and let the horse lean into him and rub himself on Carlos. It wasn't possible to tell whether horse or man was getting or giving more nurturing.

After doing the morning's grooming chores, he whispered in his horse's ear and left as he had come…with hushed tones and quiet footsteps.

He looked for the women, and seeing no one, got into his truck and drove off. Some people needed to be spoken to, and sooner was much more to his liking than later.

CHAPTER 28

▼

Carlos was used to being lonesome. In his estimation it wasn't really a negative condition. But as hard as he tried, he realized that he had never gotten Kate out of his system. He didn't love her, he knew, but his sense of defeat, or perhaps his failure to get through to her and bring about changes, still nagged at him. He wanted to make it right with her somehow, and yet he continued to miss the mark. He could not get over the profound sense of sadness and frustration this brought him. Deep down he knew that was the main reason he didn't want to take this case to begin with, but when Susan had handed him the pictures of Tremor, fate had collided with his attempts to evade it. It was time to face the truth and maybe come to terms with what was left of his feelings for Kate. His protectiveness for Britt brought out the realization that he still felt the need to reach Kate somehow, even though he suspected it would be a losing battle.

His confrontation with Kate at Raja's gathering had unnerved him and left him off balance. It stunned him to realize just how guilty he felt about leaving Kate all those years ago. Their problems were as much his doing as hers. He could take responsibility for his part in the relationship. What Kate did not comprehend was that he had shared her dreams. It was Podsky's methods of realizing those dreams that revolted him. As much as Carlos had loved Kate, he wasn't willing to finance their equestrian careers on bogus insurance claims or underhanded methods of horse care and training.

He had looked the other way emotionally regarding Kate for too long. He knew she continued to do what she had suggested to him those long years ago. In a way, his current job was a kind of repentance. He would work to stop people who thought they could profit off the backs of innocent animals because they couldn't speak and didn't have a human to do it for them. It was a way for Carlos to balance the ledger: Kate doing immoral deeds, and him correcting ones like it.

Did Kate actually expect that he could continue to pretend that he'd never met her or her father? Time hadn't given him someone else to love. He thought that time had bought his escape from the truth, but who would have envisioned Podsky being arrogant enough to open his old bag of tricks? The question was why. He'd had more than enough money from Bernice's Polish inheritance.

Like the undead of Carlos' Latin heritage, evil had become presentable in the form of the polished Podsky. Susan was right when she suspected that Podsky had ties to the Florida horse mafia. Would they want him murdered? Did Podsky know something that would draw attention to their whole messy operation again? A car bomb sends an unmistakable message that you are pissing off the big boys. Maybe Susan was getting close to something really big. Her investigation had certainly turned up the heat on the insurance fraud angle.

It had been almost five years since horses had mysteriously begun going down on the circuit. Rios was almost one of them. If anyone even suspected that Rios was still alive…Carlos stopped himself. Time to focus. His secret was safe. Carlos knew there was talk behind his back about his "troubles." He never let on he knew of the whisperings. He would have been far more troubled if Rios had died, but the horse was his, and safe. Let tongues wag. He wasn't going to correct the equine grapevine.

Carlos thought about his mental appointment with Lisa Anthony as he parked his truck at Falling Oak Farms. He felt that this whole bizarre puzzle had begun here. Hopefully it would soon end. He adjusted his sunglasses, and for a moment the place looked like it had ten years ago. Maybe it was the sweet smell of the earth under the melting snow. The sensation took him completely off guard. He tried his best to shake the feeling, but it left him unsteady. Time to get on with it. He reached back into the truck and grabbed the Tremor files before heading for the office. The door was unlocked.

"Excuse me?"

Lisa Anthony was clearly annoyed with the intrusion as she stood up from her desk. Her violet eyes darkened. She drew her mouth into a fine line and clenched her jaw.

Carlos threw the file on the mahogany desk and exposed the pictures of Tremor.

"What's this all about, Mr. Dega?"

"Let's go over the Tremor death again."

"You are interrupting me, and interrogating me in my own office? You have a real attitude problem. You aren't the police."

"This horse was the star in your crown. I would think you would, as a matter of course, want to give him a little time in death since you were his caretaker in life."

"Mr. Dega. We've been over this ground."

"What is your problem, Dr. Anthony? Are you so unconcerned? Last time I was here you asked about the cause of Tremor's death. What if I told you we've gone over this case again, and come up with a new diagnosis?"

"Now, why would you do that, Mr. Dega?"

Carlos sat on the edge of her desk and looked piercingly into Lisa's eyes. "What I have been wondering is how a fine horse could go down so suddenly." Carlos looked around at Lisa's facility. "And I have been wondering why you have not been more actively involved in trying to find the cause of death. It would seem it would be in your best interests to get to the end of this case as soon as possible. Yet you are, shall I say, coldhearted about it all? The only thing you seemed to be concerned about so far is your reputation. That is minor compared to a great stallion like Tremor."

"What has that got to do with your visit? Surely you have other things to worry about besides my attitude."

"There were no markings on Tremor. Not one. He was not rushed to the Vet School after he…" Carlos paused for effect. "Podsky did the paperwork, not you. It was as if you already knew what you needed to know about Tremor."

"And your point is…?" Lisa was forming a bead of sweat on her upper lip.

"He was electrocuted, wasn't he?" Carlos leaped up and shouted. The cords in his neck stood out, and each muscle group could be seen.

Lisa Anthony may have been surprised at the outburst, but she wasn't about to give up any ground. "I have absolutely no idea what you are talking about, Mr. Dega."

Carlos waved one of the eight-by-ten glossies in her face. "Look at him. Not a mark on him. What can do that? He was your patient. Do you really think he died of worms?"

"Honestly, I…"

Carlos cut her off. "I've seen this before. But I didn't want to remember. It's Podsky's signature. Isn't it? No trace. Very clever. Electrocution is impossible to prove and makes for an easy insurance claim. The question is why, Dr. Anthony. There was nothing wrong with Tremor, nothing that would kill him, that is."

"Mr. Dega, I'm asking you nicely to leave. You are upset, and at the moment, uninvited here. If you refuse to leave, it will be very easy for me to call 911 and resolve this matter."

"Go ahead, Doctor…if that is what you are? Did you help Podsky? Maybe you knew how to perfect the technique? On second thought, Podsky didn't need your help. His techniques were renowned. Weren't they? It's so simple. You asked him how he did it, and then probably used the wires and clips for a little sexual game after your nasty little job on Tremor."

Carlos knew he was on dangerous ground here. He was losing his focus, but the rage was unleashed and he didn't even want to contain it now. He shouldn't play this card. He was guessing about their sexual relationship, but he didn't want her to know that. "So, where are you hiding Tremor's passport?"

That got her attention. "I have absolutely no idea what you are getting at…coming in here like this and making all kinds of wild accusations about electrocutions and lost passports. I would imagine that Tremor's groom is in charge of his passport."

"She says that it disappeared. I wanted to look at it to see if he really needed the vaccination you said you gave him, and if you bothered to record it at all. Isn't it true that a horse of his caliber that travels internationally must have all of his vaccinations in a passport? An FEI requirement, I believe."

"We certainly kept his vaccinations up to date, if that is what you are getting at. But we had no plans to have him travel. We could run the syndication between Falling Oak Farms and Grande Glade."

"I'm more concerned about what might NOT be in the record. The groom thinks she saw you drawing blood, not giving a vaccination. Now, why would you do a blood draw on Tremor?" He was bluffing, but he wanted to force something out of this poor excuse of a veterinarian.

With anger getting the better of him, Carlos had failed to notice Lisa Anthony's manicured hand had reached quietly into the desk until he saw the polished silver barrel of the designer revolver that was pointed at him. Lisa waved the revolver at Carlos, and he took the hint and sat down on the desk corner again.

"So you did find something on the blood draw." It was a shot in the dark, but he had nothing to lose at this point. "What if I told you the lab at the U of M is doing some blood work of its own?"

If Carlos thought Lisa was going to cave in under his accusations, he was dead wrong. She handed him a roll of duct tape. "Just shut up and get on the floor.

Tape your ankles together. Do it tightly, please. Now, lie down on your stomach, hands behind your back."

Carlos thought about trying to overpower her, but the look of the gun barrel pointed at his gut made him think better of the idea. This woman was resourceful. She taped his hands together tightly with the duct tape, and double checked his ankles.

"Now roll over and sit up...over there against the door."

With a struggle, Carlos complied. He pressed for more. "Who wanted Podsky dead? And why don't they want you dead if you know what he knew about Tremor?"

Lisa said, "It won't matter to you in a few hours, Mr. Dega. Too bad to have to mess up a handsome man like you. I bet you look just great astride a horse, or..." She let the innuendo dangle.

Carlos couldn't let it go, even in his compromised position. "Maybe it was you all along."

Lisa blanched.

"You killed Podsky."

She laughed a hoarse, brittle laugh. "Honestly, Mr. Dega. Your imagination is finally getting the better of you. And I really don't have the time to deal with you right now. Nice try about the university. The problem is that I have an appointment with Dr. Rollins this afternoon to go over the lab results. I don't think anything unusual has been discovered in Tremor's blood work."

She rested a jodhpur-clad boot on his shoulder, momentarily chucking him under the chin with the toe of the boot. "Now, you wouldn't want to make me late for my appointment with Ken, would you?"

Carlos jerked his head away from the gesture. "Was it worth killing Podsky?" The door to the lab swung open.

"There were a lot of people who wanted to see my father dead, Carlos, but Dr. Anthony wasn't one of them."

"Kate."

She walked up to Carlos and stood over him, as if she were admiring some species of insect. "I like this posture on you, Carlos."

"What are you doing here?" This was making no sense to him.

"Lisa and I had a few things to discuss. You are a bonus surprise."

"Why are you so positive Lisa wouldn't want your father dead?"

"Let's say there is some evidence that points to the contrary." Kate glared over at Lisa, and Carlos was pleased to see they didn't seem particularly friendly.

Lisa handed Kate the gun and put on her sorels and down parka. She jangled her car keys and said, "You two can continue your reunion at a later time. At least until I figure out what I am going to do with you, Carlos. Kate, would you hold the door while I get our guest settled into his new accommodations?" Lisa motioned Carlos to his feet. She took the gun from Kate and waved it.

"Now, do you think you can hop this way to the car? Kate, would you open the trunk?"

Kate hesitated. "Maybe we are going a bit too far with this."

"My dear, it has already gone too far. Mr. Dega…the trunk please." She put the gun in front of his face with the barrel pointed directly between his eyes. The tone of voice he heard coming from Lisa certainly did not match the look on her face.

Carlos had no choice but to comply. He hopped to Lisa's car, conveniently parked near the door. He rolled over the bumper and into the trunk. He heard Kate say again, "Lisa, I think you are going a bit far with this bluff."

"Oh, it's no bluff. We need to get rid of this pesky investigator."

"Well, I don't think this is the thing…"

The lid closed and the darkness at last gave him the moments to search for his locus, the center of his calm, once again. He hoped that there were no exhaust leaks as he heard both women get into the car. The engine purred smoothly as the car leaped forward. Carlos heard the radio go on, so their conversation was lost to him.

Damn!

Damn! Double Damn!

After all the meditating he had done to work on his temper, he knew he had lost ground with himself. Much as he had tried, when it came to animals and helpless humans, Carlos couldn't avoid trying to rescue them, even when they were dead. And now he couldn't even rescue himself from his own stupidity! It galled him. He was more upset with himself than he wanted to be, and tried to shake off the self-recriminations and home in on his present situation—which, he had to admit, wasn't good.

Trying to listen to the music to keep track of the time, Carlos let his mind move to problem solving. It wasn't the easiest task. He had no gloves on, and his hands were feeling like ice cubes tied behind him. He felt he was losing sensation in his left leg because he was lying on it in an awkward way and wasn't able to move it. He was too tall for the space. Stretching out or rolling over wasn't a possibility. His large quadriceps muscles were threatening to go into cramps and spasms.

First, he realized, it was time to quickly adjust his perceptions of Kate and Lisa. It was not his usual thinking to believe that women could be so brutal and cold-blooded.

Next, he had to admit to himself that at times like these, being a loner was a distinct disadvantage. If he had a partner, he would be missed. Someone would be waiting for him. Cold as he was becoming, he started to sweat, thinking about his lack of support. Maybe the time was coming to change the loner stuff. He hoped he'd have the chance. When he got out of this—if he did—he vowed to build more relationships. Positive ones. Right now, he had to deal with two negative relationships. Fine state of affairs, Mr. Dega, for being such a smart-ass.

He figured eight songs had been played. At three minutes a song…no wonder he was getting more stiff and cold by the minute. Soon, he would stop worrying, and just want to sleep. That would be his worst enemy now, wanting to give up and sleep. Cold could make a person lose enthusiasm. Hypothermia was sneaky that way.

The radio went off, and he was startled back to attention. He felt the adrenaline surge again. Maybe he could throw them off guard when they opened the trunk, and kick the gun out of Lisa's hands.

As the trunk lid came up, Carlos realized his hope was futile. He could hardly move. And Lisa, with the gun, was standing quite far away. It was Kate he was looking at. He looked her in the eye, and piercingly said, "You were right. This has gone far enough. You don't need to do what Lisa tells you. You're a woman who thinks for herself."

Lisa simply said, "Get out."

Carlos tried again. "Kate, this can all be worked out. There's nothing that has been said and done that calls for this action."

Lisa was getting impatient. "Kate. Get him moving. Don't just stand there and stare at him."

Carlos tried a new approach. "You have sunk to a new low, Kate."

"Shut up. I don't want to get smooth-talked by you anymore."

"This is common sense, not smooth talk, Kate. Don't do it. You'll be forever tied to Lisa, and the freedom you want will never be yours, unless, of course, you want to kill her, too."

"Shut UP! SHUT UP!" Kate screamed. "Get out!"

He forced a smile and tried for charm. "My dear, I would love to accommodate you, but I am so stiff, I can't move without help." That was no lie.

Lisa said in a menacing tone, "Watch him, Kate. It's a trap."

His head lifted up, and Carlos said, "You'll both have to shoot me in the trunk, then, and that could be very messy. Whose car is this? You'll have blood, traces of me all over in here. Either way, you will both have to lift me out."

Kate came closer. Carlos couldn't help himself. He winked at her. She drew her right arm back so fast he hardly saw it coming, and it connected squarely with his jaw. His head fell back onto the carpet of the trunk. He didn't feel the cold anymore.

CHAPTER 29

▼

Carlos knew he was shivering. It was that awareness that provoked him to slowly open his eyes. He saw white. His face was numb, and his head was twisted around his shoulder in a crooked V shape. It seemed he was face down in a freezer. Yet when he cautiously moved his head, he could see that the white was indeed real. He was face down in the snow. He was lying next to a tree and was surrounded by deep woods. He was able to pull his neck straight, bring his knees up to his chest, and flop over onto his back. That effort alone caused him to pant. The blow to his face had made him woozy. Carlos decided to wait until his stomach settled down and his ears stopped ringing. He knew that if he moved too quickly he'd pass out again.

There were chickadees flitting from one low-hanging aspen branch to another. A loud camprobber was scolding a squirrel. The oak leaves forming a canopy above him were a deep copper. They faintly swayed in the breeze, creating a rustling effect, as though some beautiful lady had just swept by in a billowing taffeta ball gown. Carlos was reminded of the qualities of the oak—that of strength and endurance. He would try to capture those qualities for himself. Now he would need both.

It was a normal day in the woods for the animals and birds. For him, it was distinctly not normal. Nothing about his situation or the way he felt was normal. He lay there for a few more moments and then came out of his reverie with a start. He had no idea how long he had been there. Carlos looked around for the sun and discovered he could see nothing of the sky. The woods were too deep, and the branches above him too thick.

He rolled onto his knees and promptly fell over again. This was going to be a first-class case of misery. With effort, he rolled again to his side, pulled his knees up to his chest, turned his face toward the snow, and braced his forehead against the ground. Then he put his knees against his chest, tucked his toes under him, and pushed up. He swayed to a crouching position, and from there, squatting flatfooted on the ground, he pushed up to stand. Warily, he sighted his eyes toward a tree and stood and focused on it for several minutes. The nausea lessened slightly.

He looked around and saw a stump from a tree that had collapsed in a recent windstorm. Rolling over to the stump, painfully, and deliberately, he slowly worked his way into a sitting position and pushed his hands against the jagged points of wood. He slid the duct tape over one of the shards, and frantically began moving his hands up and down behind him. It was harder to do than he thought it should be, and he hurt like hell, but the more he got his body moving and the heat rising, the better he felt. Action. That was his forte!

He strained against the wood and pulled forward with all his strength. Whoever invented duct tape did too good a job of it. It wouldn't give way. He started the sawing motion again, and meanwhile listened for sounds, hoping to hear something that might offer him help. If he could find the road, he might hail a car. He leaned forward another time, to put more pressure on the tape, and found himself with a face full of snow again. But, blessed relief, his hands were free.

He unwound the tape from his ankles. He rolled it up again, carefully as he could with his awkward iced hands, in case he might need it for something. He pushed himself up against the tree stump, tried to get his legs underneath him, and heaved himself up to a standing position. He ached, and his limbs seemed to be asleep, but he flapped his hands to his sides, and up in the air, jumping and stamping his feet. A million little needles seemed to prick at his extremities, but, as far as Carlos was concerned, that was a good sign. A very good sign. Even the pain of circulation returning was positive. He was thirsty and thought of water. He grabbed a handful of snow and took a mouthful.

It was then that he became aware of his bladder being full. With his smile askew, he remembered what Ben Franklin—or was it Mark Twain?—had said: "Never pass up a chance to relieve yourself." So he did, right there by the helpful tree remains.

He reached into his pockets for hat and gloves, and was glad for the automatic Minnesota preparedness. Every coat he owned had gloves and a hat in the pockets. Then he began to move from the shadow of the larger trees, crouching and moving as if he were tracking an animal. The activity helped. He could breathe again, feel again, DO something. Doing was important. Doing was life itself.

He saw the cut through the trees and surmised that was the road. His suspicions were confirmed. The two women didn't want to take time to drag him too deeply into the woods. He hoped he was too much effort, too. It gave him some small satisfaction to think he inconvenienced them, even if slightly.

Looking behind him, and then forward, he tried to decide which way was the Way Out. In this cold and all the snow, it was easy to get turned around, and any disorientation could cost him his life. If he felt like sleeping, he would be a goner. The adrenaline began to pump, and he stood in the road and tried to figure which direction would be best. There was one set of tire tracks, in and out, but which way was which?

Carlos started to jog and checked the slant of the weak sun trying to glimmer through the trees. If he didn't know where he was going, at least he wanted to know where he had been. He continued to follow the tire tracks until he came to a small bend in the road. The tracks stopped. The snow was messed, and he could see where he had been unceremoniously dragged. It was hard on his pride to look at the spot. Well at least he knew this was the wrong direction to get to the main road, wherever that might be. Turning and checking the slant of the sun again, he began jogging down the road. He tried to keep the jog light, not too fast, not too pressured. He didn't want to end up sweating, wasting his energy and then getting cold. He knew he could keep this pace up easily for ten or twelve miles, as he did that on a regular basis, but after that it could get dicey. He breathed. He watched the birds. He jogged.

After several miles he heard a sound. Carlos thought about yelling, but didn't. He'd wait and see who and what was making the noise. He needed to be cautious right now. He headed off into the woods and slipped through the trees. He tried to keep up a light jog, but the snow was too deep once he got off the road.

He circled around the sound and came upon a stuck car. He ducked behind a large oak trunk and watched. He worked on breathing through his nose so as not to draw attention, although the noise from the car would have covered his sounds.

Lisa's car was deep in the snow, its front end angled into a pothole. Lisa was trying to rock the car, and Kate was digging around the front left tire. There was ice behind the other three tires that made it impossible for them to move the vehicle. The more they had kept the car running, the more the exhaust had formed ice under the car. Carlos noticed for the first time that the sleek little car was an Audi sport model.

He moved through the trees again, sneaking up on the car's right side, since both women were intent on the left front. He knew they needed someone to push them, or they needed to build a ramp out of the ditch for the front tire. He hoped they wouldn't think of the solution for at least a few more minutes. Lisa got out of the Audi to look again at the mess they were in. Kate's fiery temper was causing her to lash out at Lisa, and the two of them were both dangerously close to slugging it out with each other. They were yelling and gesturing and blaming each other. Perfect.

Carlos sneaked from tree to tree until he was even with the back of Lisa's car. He watched the women. They were still absorbed with the problem in the front of the car. He decided he would have to take a terrible risk. Carlos crouched down on his now near-normal-feeling hands and knees and ran to the back of the sport coupe, quickly sliding down behind it. He waited and hoped they wouldn't walk to the back of the car. He had to have good timing to pull off his own rescue. This particular model of Audi had a small design flaw or two, and Carlos used one of them to his advantage. Once the car was unlocked, all he had to do to gain entrance to the trunk was to push the button by the back handle. He peeked under the car and saw the two women still screaming at each other. Carlos gently pushed the trunk button. He lifted the lid as minimally as he could, and rolled back inside. He hated to do this, but it sure beat being lost in the woods in the deep of winter. Quickly he pulled the lid down, and held it closed by holding the built-in handle. He slowly released his breath.

Soon he heard both front doors close. Carlos pulled the trunk lid closed tightly. He didn't want to give himself away by having Lisa see on the control panel that the trunk lid was open. Suddenly he was thrown violently forward as she gunned the car ahead. His extra weight in the rear end and the wood pieces they had stuffed into the hole did the trick, and they were out. Both women shouted, "Yessssss!" at the same time, and Carlos shocked himself by making the sign of the cross on his chest.

This time he could move, albeit gingerly, and he discovered the jog had helped him get the kinks out. He wasn't cold now. If the ride wasn't too long, he'd still be mobile when the car stopped. He was waiting for his moment, and he had no doubt now that it would come. After another half an hour, the car stopped. He heard Kate say, "Lisa. Don't call my house. I don't want to upset my mother or have her suspect anything. She really is fragile and couldn't take anything else. I'll call you."

"Since when have you been so concerned with your mother, Kate?" Lisa said acidly.

"Listen, bitch. We're in this together."

"So, what has that to do with dear Raja?" Sarcasm dripped from Lisa's voice.

"OK. I don't want anyone, not even Raja, to know you and I were ever together. If you call, she could get suspicious."

"Raja couldn't find her way out of a paper bag."

"Leave her out of this, Lisa. I don't trust you, and you don't trust me. I think what we did to Carlos was uncalled for. I've got to get this behind me as soon as I can. It's entirely conceivable that when they find Carlos's body, it will be murder one for both of us."

"They'll never suspect us, and it will be months before anyone comes across his remains in the woods. Besides, after the animals get through with him…all I can say is identifying the body won't be easy, if possible at all."

"Give me a few days to finish things with Raja," said Kate. "Then I'll be out of the country again, and we won't have to worry about watching each other's backs, or mouths."

"Sure, Kate. Give yourself a break here. We did the only thing we could."

"Three days, Lisa. I'm telling you. I'll be gone in three days. Don't call, don't come around, don't mess with anything at our stables. Understand?"

"Got it." And with that the car door slammed, and the car roared away. Carlos, surprised again, was thrown back onto the wheel cover. He bit his lip to keep from yelling out. His kidney got nipped. He was beginning to feel like a frigging ping pong ball.

It was another thirty to forty minutes before the car stopped again. This time Carlos was more than grateful for the cessation of movement. He was cold, tired, sore, hungry, and mean—and, on top of it all, carsick. If he got his hands on Lisa now, he wasn't sure he would be able to keep from strangling her. He heard her footsteps recede in the distance. Patience. He needed to count to one hundred. Wait. Don't blow it now. It took all his nerve to wait. He was hoping she was keeping that appointment with Ken Rollins.

The Audi had a split seat system and he pushed on the back seat with his hands. It wouldn't budge. There must be an inside mechanism to make the seat move. He knew it should. Now he was frustrated and more anxious. Wouldn't that just take the cake, to get this far to safety and be stuck in this trunk? He rotated onto his back, and bunched his powerful legs up toward his chest. He heard voices outside and froze in mid-motion. He inhaled to the count of three, and exhaled to the count of four. The voices faded. It sounded as if their owners were walking away.

He gathered his strength. He hoped he had guessed right that the seat that was movable was on the passenger side. He pumped his legs together and kicked with all his strength. The top of the seat moved, and smoothly enough to make a German engineer smile, the seat folded down next to the rear of the front seat. He crawled through the opening and over to the other seat, and unlocked the door. He looked behind him and returned the folded seat to its original position. He'd broken the latch, but he wedged it back where it should be. He let himself out of the car and smiled with satisfaction. He was standing in the visitors' parking lot of the University of Minnesota's Veterinary School.

CHAPTER 30

▼

Carlos was feeling particularly smug about his escape, but he had no time to emotionally luxuriate, as fate in the form of a particularly overzealous University security officer cut short his self-congratulatory celebration.

"Hands in the air, lean against the car and spread 'em!" Carlos had had enough for one day. "What's the problem?"

"I said, turn around and spread 'em!"

Having the second gun in as many hours pointed in his general direction was enough to convince Carlos to submit. He turned around and leaned against the passenger door. Pudgy fingers poked and prodded during the shakedown.

Finding nothing, the guard relaxed his tone of voice, but not his demeanor. "Turn around and face me, but keep your hands where I can see 'em. Can you produce your license and registration for this vehicle?" Carlos slumped against the Audi. Based upon his disheveled physical condition, he had a good guess what was coming next, but he tried to explain anyway.

"Actually, this isn't my car."

The guard was feeling pretty feisty about now. He pressed his cheek to the microphone clipped to his left lapel. "I have a probable car theft attempt at the vet hospital parking ramp. Request city police backup."

The dispatcher's voice came through the static well enough that Carlos correctly guessed that a city squad was on the way. Blood from Kate's blow was still fresh in the corner of his mouth, his clothes were torn, filthy, and wet, and to make matters worse, he had forgotten to zip his fly after he relieved himself in the woods. No wonder this guy had made him for a car thief, pervert or worse.

"I don't suppose you'd believe that I am the victim of a kidnapping, would you?"

The pudgy guard was having too much fun now. "Yeah, and my grandma is the Queen of England. You got any ID?"

The guard kept his beady eyes on Carlos's hands as he searched his jeans pockets for his wallet. Carlos figured it would be too much to ask to find it, and he was right. It could be anywhere, but it wasn't on his person. He tried pleading again, but not before he zipped his fly.

"I know this is hard to believe, but I was kidnapped in the trunk of this car…well, not exactly, I kind of hitched a ride because I was left bound and gagged in the woods…"

Carlos stopped himself before his captor interrupted because he suddenly realized how ridiculous it all sounded. He felt tired. Very tired and very defeated.

"All I know, buddy, is what I seen. You crawling back-asswards out of that pretty lady's car. Looks like you got it all dirty inside, too. Nice leather seats. A shame. A real shame. You got a name? What are you, Mexican, or something?"

The overt racism didn't phase Carlos at this point. The existentialist moment was almost too much, and he found himself starting to giggle. "My name is Carlos. Carlos Dega. You won't believe it, but I'm an insurance investigator working with the U.S. Attorney's office on a possible insurance fraud case."

The guard let out a low whistle. "Suz! You the guy been working with Suz on that Tremor case? Yeah, sure. Carlos, she said. That you?"

Carlos was stunned beyond belief. He played the linguistic game just for the absurdity of it all.

"Yeah, that me."

"Well. If it isn't Suz's Carlos. If that don't put the nail on the cake I don't know what does. I'm Charlie Branson. Suz ever tell you about me? Ho ho ho, wait'll Suz hears about this. This'll even the score for sure." Mixed metaphors aside, Carlos certainly did recall Susan's story about the private eye that was stalking her for information on the case. He didn't remember the guy's name though.

"Well. How do I know for sure that you are Charlie Branson or whoever you say you are? Susan said you were a private eye, working for the local TV station if I remember. If so, what are you doing here?"

"Oh, I'm him all right. So, Suz talked about me, huh? Think I've got a chance with her? I always knew we had a kind of chemistry going, you know?"

Carlos could smell the testosterone, and he could also hear a siren about three blocks away.

"So, you gonna have me arrested, Mr. Branson?"

"Hell, no. Suz will be really happy if I save your ass. No problem. I'll just call in a false alarm." Charlie leaned into the microphone again and had the dispatcher call off the squad.

"Isn't your boss going to be ticked off that you called in a false alarm to the city? You're calling it off just like that, no explanation?"

Flush with possibility, Charlie was walking frantically in circles, changing direction every second pass or so. "Piss on this job. I took it just to be closer to the vet lab. I'm getting paid good money to try and figure this one out. That lady really did kidnap you then? I seen her here before. Dr. Lisa Anthony. Those tall, thin women always give me the goose bumps, know what I mean? Those legs go all the way up to there, don't they?" Carlos was feeling queasy and his head was spinning, but Charlie's observation about her being here had him wondering.

"You've seen that woman here before?"

"Yeah, two or three times in the last week or so. Always this time of day. That's why I took this shift today. Been trying to shadow her. Figure what's up. Then you come crawling out of her car and I figure you're either trying to steal the car or you're after her. Either way I figured I had to put you on ice for awhile. The competition in my business is pretty tight. You coulda been another shadow. Who could know?"

Carlos put his fingers to his lips and motioned to Charlie to follow him and step around the corner. From the anonymity of the late-afternoon shadow, the two men watched as Lisa Anthony bolted from the glass doors of the veterinary building. She threw a small plastic bag into the front seat and raced the Audi down the street.

"Well, don't that beat all, eh, pardner?" Charlie emphasized the word "pardner."

Beat up and tired as he was, Carlos turned very slowly to Branson. Keeping himself in tight control, he looked him straight in the eye, and said haltingly, "When did we become partners?"

Something about the way he said it made Charlie shift his porky weight uncomfortably. "You know, we're both on the same case, I helped you out here, buddy. I coulda had your ass in a sling. But, me, you, and Suz, we're in this together, wouldn't ya say? I mean, isn't it worth somethin' to ya to have me working with you?"

"Are you trying to shake me down, Charlie? You've been tough on Susan, and now...spell it out for me, what are you saying?"

"Hey. A guy's gotta make a buck; you know what I mean? Just wondering if I couldn't be some help, that's all. I've got stuff to offer you, and maybe you'd want to help me out in return, that's all."

"Let's get this clear, Charlie. IF, and that's a big IF, we work together on this case, then we all share information. Like nice guys. No one pays a partner to be nice, to do what's right. Is this something you can understand, Charlie?"

Charlie was nodding so hard Carlos was afraid his head might roll off his neck. "Sure. That's what I meant, too."

It seemed like a long way home, and Carlos was losing momentum. He had another errand to run, and thought he better get on it. "OK, Charlie. Here's the drill. If we work together on this case, you take your calls from Susan and me. Before you drop your info at the TV station, give us a chance to put our heads together, and really bust these slimeballs. Someone is doing crappy things, and it isn't just to horses anymore. How 'bout it?"

"Yeah. That's more like it. A team." Charlie grinned. Carlos winced.

"So, Charlie, I'm going to run in and see what Lisa took and threw in her car. Call the police again, and see if they can pull her over for some other violation and get what is in the car. It's got to be pivotal to this whole case. I'll call Susan. I've got to run upstairs and talk to the vet."

"Yep. Sure, pard."

Carlos jogged up the stairs to Ken's office. He wasn't there. Carlos searched all the small interview offices and checked the staff break room. No Ken. He stopped a tech as she came by in the hall. She stood and stared and then started to back away slightly. He grabbed her by the arm and blurted out, "Where's Ken?" He sounded more frantic than he wanted to. It scared her. She backed away a few steps more.

The tech managed to point downstairs toward the necropsy lab. Carlos patted her shoulder as he sprinted by her. "Thanks. Sorry to startle you." This day was definitely out of control. What the hell.

Taking the stairs two at a time, Carlos hit the huge open lab at a dead run. Startled students looked up at the wild man entering the room. "Where's Ken?"

A young woman looked up from a cadaver and said, "What's going on here? Do you have security clearance?" She stripped off a latex glove, and went to the phone on the wall to call security. He leaped over to her and said as quietly as he could manage, "I think he is in danger, or in trouble, and we all need to help him. I just came in from outside talking to a security guard, and he's working on this too. I know I look a sight, but I have just come in out of the frigid woods…"

She dropped her arm, and one of the other students offered, "I think I last saw him going to the cold locker. I just happened to look up, and saw him go in there."

"Oh, shit! That's it!" Carlos raced to the cooler around the corner and called as he went, "One of you please help me with this door. It looks as if it has been wedged shut!"

Several students came running, and they worked on getting it open. Carlos shouted into the other room, "Maybe you had better call security after all." The door yielded to their efforts in a few frantic minutes, and they swung the door open. There was Ken, lying face down on the cooler floor. There was blood all around him, and an open wound on the back of his skull.

Carlos bent down and felt for a pulse on his neck. Faint and slow, but nonetheless there, was a small pressure under his fingers. "Let's get him out of here, and someplace warm," he said to the students. They carefully rolled Ken over, and they lifted him up and carried him to a clean necropsy table. Someone found a shock blanket and put it over him.

"I called 911," he heard someone say.

"Ken, Ken, buddy...hang in there." Carlos looked fleetingly over Ken's body for the source of all the blood. It couldn't have come from the head wound. There were no rips in his clothes, no place from where blood seemed to be pouring. He covered Ken again, and held his hand. He thought he was going to cry, but found instead that he was starting to sway and to see small white dots in front of his eyes. He sucked in some air and bent over to stick his head between his knees.

After the paramedics had taken Ken to the hospital, Carlos slowly walked back to the cooler. He went in again and looked around. Most of the pooled blood seemed to come from a new animal that had been hung on one of the huge grappling hooks. It was hanging right above the spot where Ken had been lying. Carlos felt himself let his breath out in measured doses. He looked over at Tremor's remains and wished he knew what was in the bag that Lisa had thrown into her car.

He leaned over the drain and threw up until he had dry heaves.

CHAPTER 31

▼

Carlos told the cab driver to wait while he went into his house to get cash. He hoped he would find some in the jar on his dresser. He looked for his hidden key under the drainpipe, and couldn't find it. He fumbled in the wet rotting peonies, and, lacking any better thought, tried the front door. It was unlocked. He looked at the driver, put his hand up and went inside, wondering if there was someone there who shouldn't be.

He quietly slipped off his shoes, and slid around the living corner to the bedroom. No one there. Maybe he just forgot to lock the door in all his distraction this morning. After he paid the driver, who had thoughtfully walked up the steps and was waiting at the front door, Carlos went to the bathroom and started the tub. Carlos was going to have a nice long soak. A really long soak. One that might last until tomorrow.

He dumped his wet clothes on the floor, and gratefully stepped into his long-awaited respite to thaw his bones and ease his sore muscles. He let his head sink under the water and slowly bobbed up and down. He added more hot water until even his dark Hispanic skin was pink. He scrubbed with a loofa, feeling as if he wanted to peel off the layers of depravity he had been exposed to by those two desperate women.

He started to perk up in mood and began singing a lullaby his mother had sung to him in Spanish. He was alive, Ken was alive, and he would make sure that Lisa would pay. It was then that he smelled the odor of frying onions. It startled him. He grabbed a towel from the rack above his head, and dripping, wrapped it around himself. He tiptoed out to the kitchen and stared in amazement. He heard a hearty laugh, looked down at himself, and started to laugh too.

"Well, Big Guy. I had heard through the grapevine you weren't looking too well, but I can see with my own eyes that you look just fine. Very fine, in fact."

Still laughing, Carlos searched Susan's eyes. Then he pointedly looked her up and down and said, "I didn't know you could look so good in a barbecue apron. Do you cook often?"

"Why don't you slip into something less comfortable, and we'll talk about all my skills?"

"Is it soup?"

"Yep. I heard that you'd had a bad day. Weren't feeling well. Your new partner thought you looked pretty bad, too. I thought a little tender care and homemade soup—with this good bread I picked up at Great Harvest—would put you in shape to finish this case."

"Are you the key thief?"

"Will I get time if I tell you, officer?"

"What kind of time would you like?" Carlos's eyes twinkled, and bunched around the corners of his dark lashes. He looked at Susan and thought she was more attractive than usual, standing there in her stocking feet and no spiked heels. It made him notice how small she was, especially next to him as he towered over her from the doorway.

"Now, there's work time, and private time. Which would you like to discuss?"

"We've got lots of talking to do, it would seem," Carlos said.

"Get your clothes on, Carlos. I never thought I'd hear myself telling you that!"

Not in any hurry to get dressed and hit the cold streets again, Carlos grabbed a robe from behind the bathroom door and sat down at the cherry table that served as both kitchen and dining room table. Pulling out a matching wood chair, he never took his eyes off Susan. He was enjoying having her in his home, with him. He remembered his promise to himself in the trunk of the car about trying to build relationships and not be such a loner. It seemed, at least for the moment, that Susan was dropping her tough façade. She was warm and social.

"Carlos?"

"Hummmm?"

"You're staring at me."

"Oh. I was thinking. Did it bother you?"

"You just have this way with the very direct gaze. It can be disconcerting sometimes. Did I do something that got you staring?"

"Besides being you? Yes."

Susan let out a small sigh. Carlos watched her lovely chest rise, and then fall with her deep breath. "Oh, geez. OK. What?" She saw where his eyes landed and blushed.

"You look lovely. Soft and feminine. Not the usual tough ADA-Ms.-Kick-Ass demeanor. You looked approachable. And I've had a very wicked day and realize I need a friend or two that I haven't had before."

"Geez, Carlos. You bring this up now?"

"You asked. I thought you wanted to know."

"Let's finish this case, and see where we are then, OK?"

"Sure." Carlos looked bewildered.

"I do want to be your friend. And…I like it when you stare at me like that. I want to talk about this more, Carlos, I truly do. Let's just get to safer ground for now."

Bringing the conversation to business was like trying to turn the Queen Mary around in a bathtub, but Carlos struggled with it and said, "You told me that you had heard about me through the grapevine. I suppose that by 'the grapevine' you mean our 'colleague,' Branson. How did you know where to find me?"

"You left quite an impression at the University. Charlie flashed my pager, but by the time I got there I guess you had already flagged a cab. Hope you left it in better condition than the sidewalk. Are you ready to eat?"

"Not really. How 'bout sharing a St. Pauli Girl with me?"

Carlos looked so forlorn that Susan turned the heat off under the soup and sat with him at the table, each with a cold bottle of beer in hand.

"What about Ken?" Carlos asked.

"Don't worry. I already spoke to the hospital. Ken's just fine, but he's going to have a headache for at least a week."

"You seem to know an awful lot that I don't." Carlos was feeling upset now. He wasn't quite sure why. This whole thing with Susan had given him an emotional sideswipe. "What's this business with you and Branson?"

"I told you before, he's been working a different angle on the case. I thought all this shadowing of Lisa Anthony would go nowhere. With Charlie, it was almost a case of legal stalking, and I thought it would keep him out of your hair while you were working the horsy set. Luckily for all of us you both flushed her out of the woodwork at the same time."

"I'm sure she's the one who killed Tremor, and she did it by electrocution. I've got a long story to tell you about what a bitch she is. Not only does she kill animals, she's working on eliminating people, too."

"What Charlie mentioned to me didn't include that."

"Susan, did Charlie try to blackmail you?" Carlos was still looking at her with liquid eyes.

"How did you know?"

"He tried to do the same thing with me. Of course, it was under the guise of just needing a few extra bucks to do a nice job for us."

"He's a bigger creep than I thought. I knew he was shady, but I thought he might have some loyalty to us, you know, work with the white hats." Susan was biting her lip and had begun to wring her hands.

"Did Charlie say anything to you about a package or bag that Lisa took from the lab? He was going to try and get a handle on what that was...she clearly took something. If my suspicions are right, it would reveal her motive for killing Tremor. I know the how. I just need to find out the why."

Susan shot straight up from her chair and ripped off her apron in one movement.

"Oh shit! That little weasel. He's not going to tell us anything, is he?"

Now Carlos was on the move too, pulling on a pair of jeans that were draped over the back of the couch. A gray hooded sweatshirt went on next and he was pulling on his sorels before Susan could recover.

"If Charlie took any evidence from the car, you can bet your ass he isn't going to give it to us. We've got to find him before he goes to his employers in the media. What a twotimer!"

Susan was fumbling for her car keys when her cell phone rang.

"Lindstrom here. Great. Thank you, Shirley!" She turned to Carlos. "Let's move. Charlie is at the hospital. I had a guard posted there since Ken may be a witness. If Charlie did find something, he doesn't know what it is, since the guard caught him dressed as an orderly trying to pump poor Ken for more information. We'd better hurry. They can only detain him for so long unless I have him arrested, and I really don't want to do that."

Susan's '89 Audi was parked illegally a half-block from the house. It wasn't half the car that Lisa Anthony owned, but Carlos was grateful to be sitting upright instead of crammed in the trunk. Before he could sit down, Susan took an empty Coke cup and an indeterminate Wendy's wrapper and tossed them unceremoniously into the back seat. Carlos peered over the headrest and noticed at least a month's worth of similar debris scattered in the back seat.

"Geez, Susan. Haven't you ever heard of recycling?"

Susan looked at him as if she didn't comprehend what he was saying. Then she got it.

"Oh, yeah. Guess I should have this thing detailed."

Carlos fastened his seatbelt while Susan shot him a side long glance that was part flirting, part ribbing. Her spikeheeled foot jammed the accelerator to the floor as she bullied her way through the late-afternoon traffic.

It took less than fifteen minutes to reach Hennepin General. By the time they found their way to Ken's floor, they could hear Charlie halfway down the hallway, cursing and chattering in an increasingly high-pitched voice. When he saw Susan, he bolted in her direction, taking the security guard totally by surprise.

Susan motioned to the guard and mouthed the words, "Lay off."

"Suz, you gotta call this guy off. I know my rights. You gonna arrest me or what? I though we was helping each other. You know?" Susan grabbed him by the collar and hauled him to a chair in an adjoining waiting room.

"Hand it over, Charlie."

"Whaddya mean?"

"You know what I mean, you little weasel. Hand it over or I'm going to add assaulting a federal officer and illegal entry to federal property to the other long list of charges I'm sure I can drum up. Give! Now!"

"OK, OK. But I'm gonna lose a lot of time and money on this one. How about we go fifty-fifty?"

Susan stomped a spiked heel within millimeters of Charlie's sneaker-clad big toe. Charlie blinked and reached into the front pocket of his borrowed scrub suit and produced a vial of what looked like blood.

"Mind if I take a look at that?" Carlos was interested in the tube.

Susan handed the vial to Carlos. He looked it over carefully before gripping it tightly in his fist.

"This makes me wonder about what Britt said." Susan was the one getting annoyed now.

"Will someone please fill me in? I'm getting awfully tired of this case and especially you." She shot Charlie a meaningful glance, but Carlos seemed to think the admonition was meant for him. He looked hurt.

"Not you, Big Guy. Sorry. Just tell me why this tube is so important."

"It was something the groom said about thinking that she saw Dr. Anthony give Tremor a vaccination shortly before he died. A horse that travels internationally needs a passport, just like we do. All vaccinations are required to be entered into the passport. So that record can tell you when a horse is due for a shot, and also when he actually gets one. Funny thing is, Tremor's passport is missing. I don't think Dr. Anthony was giving an immunization that day. I think she was more interested in taking Tremor's blood."

Susan released her death grip on Charlie's arm, removed her heel from the vicinity of his shoe, and gave him a pat on his balding head. He rubbed the spot and remained totally tuned into what Carlos was suggesting.

"Why? Was he diseased or something? I thought the tests came up negative for everything but colic. What's going on, Carlos?" Charlie whined.

"Susan, I want you to give me three hours, and then I want you to join me at Grande Glade. There's something else I have to check out. Be discreet, and don't make a big show of anything. Got it? Three hours exactly."

"I don't know. I don't like the idea of you playing cowboy."

"Look, you asked me to help on this, and I need to put the final pieces in place. I'm the only one who can do it, and I need your trust. And," he looked meaningfully into her eyes, "you are the only one I can trust. So, are you with the program?"

"Anything that will wrap up this case once and for all," she said melting to his persuasion. She wanted to put business before pleasure, but it was getting harder to do that by the minute. Before Susan could finish the sentence, Carlos was on the elevator. For the second time since she started on this case she felt real fear. The first time it was for her niece, Maya. This time it was for Carlos.

Leaving Charlie with the guard, Susan entered Ken's room. If he couldn't tell her what she needed to know, her fears would turn to reality. Of this she was certain.

CHAPTER 32

▼

There was a feeling of vacuum in Ken's hospital room. The curtain was drawn against the dwindling winter light, and Susan thought Ken's skin looked especially dark against the crisp white sheets. The bandage around his head suggested the beginnings of a mummy. She pulled up a straight-backed chair and, before sitting next to him, stared into his face looking for some sign that his great intelligence was still intact.

She felt a stirring behind her and thought that a nurse was coming in to check on him. As she moved to make space for the caretaker, she felt a large, warm hand on her shoulder. It was Carlos again. As she turned toward him, startled, she tripped over the chair and fell into him. He caught her around the waist, and she looked up at him and smiled. Neither of them wanted to speak and wake Ken. Carlos steadied her for what seemed like a short time, when he heard Ken's deep voice rumble, "Are you here to see me, or each other?"

With that, Carlos dropped his hands, and faced his accuser, "Ken, buddy. You had me going there. I have to admit you really had me scared. But, now that you seem to be back in the land of the thinking, we need to get your input, and I hate to do it this second, but we are under a bit of a time crunch. Can you help us out?"

"I thought you were on your way out?" Susan queried.

The rich voice from the bed said, "Was my being knocked out that serious, that you had my funeral all planned?"

"Of course not, Ken. I just said goodbye to Carlos in the hall. He's the one I thought was on the way out. I'm as surprised to see him back as I am to see you awake."

In spite of the day from Hell, Carlos laughed for the second time in an hour. "I ran out to the parking lot and realized I don't have my truck. It's still out at Lisa Anthony's. I came with you in the candidate vehicle holding the most recyclable material in the Twin Cities area. I need to borrow your car."

"While you're here, stay a moment. I was going to ask Ken what Lisa stole from him, and why."

Ken moaned. "Shit. She stole something?"

"You mean, you don't know anything?"

"The last thing I remember was Lisa asking me to show her Tremor's carcass one more time. I tried to convince her that was no longer our focus. It was the blood work that we were looking at, and some tissue samples. She got agitated, and I thought she looked kinda strange."

"What do you mean, strange?" Susan asked.

"Lisa has always been the cool and collected one with me, and I've seen her on and off for a couple of years dealing with some case or another. She was definitely frayed around the edges."

Susan kept trying to get a handle on it. "Frayed?"

"You know, real jumpy, and not...nice. Sorry to say this, Susan, but, bitchy is the only word that comes to mind. She almost ordered me to the cooler, so I figured, what the heck, it will calm her down to see the body, and then she'll leave."

Carlos sank down to the chair beside the bed, and Susan sat on the end of the mattress. Carlos put his hands over his eyes and rubbed. "Good God, Ken. You are the second person today Lisa has tried to kill."

"Who's the first?"

"Me."

Ken stared at Carlos and then Susan. "Am I hearing this right?"

Susan nodded her head. "We've put a watch over you outside the door. I want you to keep your buzzer handy at all times, Ken. If you see anything suspicious, ring it like it was a church bell."

"I think I just got religion."

"Good. I've got more men to worry about this afternoon than I have in the last three years. This is getting on my nerves."

"Susan. Tell Ken what I told you in the car about my kidnapping."

"Sure, Big Guy." She hunted in her purse and, finding her quarry, tossed him the keys to her car.

"Susan, another thing. Get a warrant out on Lisa Anthony. Something about attempted murder, kidnapping, and whatever else you can dig up. But give me time to get to Grande Glade."

"I'll call it in right now. But, I'm confused; what could she have taken in that plastic bag, Ken? I know she stole some blood samples…"

"Plastic bag?"

Carlos got up to go. "Time's not on our side, you two. I've got to get moving here, before we lose everything. Maybe you could get Lisa on the phone, Susan?"

"And…?"

"Tell her that you need her help at Grande Glade…that she is the only one who can get the real killer of Tremor. Tell her you suspect…mmm…"

"How about the third owner of Tremor, the one no one knows?"

"Yeah. Whatever you think. Just make it sound good, and don't, whatever you do, let on that you have seen me, or suspect her, or, well…you know."

"I know. I'll get her there."

"Thanks, Susan. Three hours. No," he looked at his watch, "let's make it two and a half hours from now."

"What about your truck?"

"Leave it there for now. We don't want her to figure anything out. If she's fraying out as quickly as Ken said, she could bolt and run on us. That wouldn't be good."

"Take care of yourself." Susan couldn't help it; she had to nurture him.

"Bye Buddy," Carlos said as he patted Ken on the shoulder and left.

He heard Ken moan as he turned through the door, "I shouldn't have told her what I was looking for at the lab. It was a stupid mistake to trust her. I know better than that. What was I thinking?"

CHAPTER 33

▼

"Susan, dial the phone for me, would you?" Ken was struggling to sit upright in the hospital bed, but the initial effort seemed to make the room spin and he fell back on the pillow with a groan. He raised an arm hooked to an IV and motioned Susan over to the bed.

"Susan, please, I need the phone."

"What can't wait? You're in no condition to be making phone calls."

Ken was adamant.

"Listen carefully, Susan. The only scientific avenue I have left to follow in this case is the blood work. I had one sample that I saved that I didn't run any tests on. If that sample is missing, we have no proof of what was wrong with Tremor. I hope the sample wasn't in the plastic bag that Lisa carried out of the lab."

"I thought you said that you had decided that the autopsy showed that he died of colic?"

"That was the obvious answer. But I think the question should be: What would cause someone to make it look as if the horse died of colic? I think the answer was in Tremor's blood. It would explain why Dr. Anthony didn't order any initial blood work. I think she knew or suspected something. And, it would explain why she got so frazzled when I told her the body was no longer our focus."

Susan sat down next to the bed and fumbled for her pack of Marlboros, thought better of it with the NO SMOKING sign looming over the oxygen feed, and decided to chew on a pencil instead. "Carlos said something about the groom seeing Lisa give a vaccination, but we're not sure just what she was doing, because the horse's record is missing."

Ken forced himself into a half-sitting position.

"What if she were drawing blood instead of giving a vaccination? Unless you were standing right next to her you would never know the difference. The answer's in the blood. I just FEEL it."

"This is a hundred and eighty degree turn, Ken. You usually don't do this once you've made a judgment. Maybe we should put this conversation off until later. You don't look so good, and I don't think you should get too excited right now. How's your head?"

He gave her a look like she was some kind of idiot, and said patiently, "It hurts." Getting back to his passionate subject, he continued, "When we looked at the gross results from the necropsy, it sure looked like intestinal infarct due to an old strongyles infection. And, there seemed then to be no other logical explanation. Nothing leaped out at me. But, now I'm not so sure any more about my assessment. Now the blood leaps out at me."

"What about the sample?"

"We were holding it until I could figure out what to test for. There are hundreds of tests we could have run, but we only had a few vials to work with. I didn't want to waste it."

Susan dialed the lab number for Ken and placed it by his ear so he could cradle it next to the pillow. Just as she was searching for a piece of gum to replace the pencil, a small commotion erupted in the hallway. The next thing she knew, Charlie's sneaker-clad feet came to a skidding halt at the edge of Ken's bed. He was breathing heavily, and the sound of his husky wheeze tickled something in the back of her mind. Her brief thought was interrupted when the guard burst into the room. Susan waved him off, and he retook his position in a straight-backed chair just outside of the door to Ken's room, but not before shooting a menacing glance at Charlie.

"I was hungry, Suz. Just wanted to get your permission to go to the cafeteria, that's all. Brutus out there didn't like the idea. How about we go get some chow?"

"Charlie, shut up."

Susan turned to Ken, who looked very agitated. "What did you find out?"

"The sample's gone. If she's destroyed it, we have nothing more to go on."

"This what you're worried about?"

Charlie produced a vial of blood with a purple stopper and waved it in front of Susan with a flourish. Susan lunged for it, but Charlie was too quick for her and slipped it back into his pocket. She pounded on his arm, but he wouldn't budge.

Charlie wasn't about to let his moment of glory pass.

"I'm gonna ask Ken about this blood thing if you promise to lay off and stop hitting me, Suz."

"You continue to be a weasel, Charlie. Every time I get ready to trust you, this stuff comes up again. You're like vomit. I get a sour feeling in my stomach every time you deal with this case in any way. I thought Carlos had that vial."

"Yeah. But I palmed it back out of his pocket." With that, he showed Ken the tube.

"That's it! But how did you know we needed it?"

"Yeah, I'd like to know, too," Susan mumbled.

"Well, when the cops stopped Lisa…what a babe, by the way…I moseyed over to say 'hi' and lifted the plastic bag outta the front seat. Piece of cake for a professional. So how much do you think this is worth? I figured it must be important if she pilfered it."

Susan stepped between Charlie and the bed with her arms crossed.

"Turn it over. You are a cheap piece of crap, blackmailing anyone at any time."

"Finders keepers…I got a job to do. You think maybe my clients would be interested in this?"

"I'll tell you who's gonna be interested in it. The federal judge who's gonna give me a warrant for your arrest as an accessory…TURN IT OVER. This is the second time I've had to go through this with you, you jerk." Charlie hesitated and gave the vial to Ken.

"Maybe we can work out a deal later. Say doc, do you think Lisa's Dutch Warmblood mare could have the same thing whatever it is that Tremor might have?"

"Say what? What do you know about a Dutch Warmblood mare?"

Ken was struggling, but definitely interested.

Charlie, obviously the center of attention, puffed out his chest and continued. "In the course of my investigative duties it came to my attention that Dr. Lisa has a very sick horse. She was always out in the paddock talkin' and cooing to it…kept it away from the other horses at her place."

Susan was disgusted but attentive.

"I suppose you were peeking in her windows, too."

"Only when necessary in the course of my investigation."

Susan rolled her eyes. "Of course."

Ken interrupted, "How do you know the horse was a Dutch Warmblood?"

"I was staked out in the bushes and heard her talkin' to that Mexican dude you been hangin' with. What's his name? Juan Carlos?"

"Oh shit!" Ken's head sunk back onto his pillow, and he closed his eyes wearily.

"What's the matter Ken, you look as if you've seen a ghost."

"If we have what I think we have, every horse that has ever been bred to Tremor may have a major reproductive health problem. I should have at least thought of it."

"What in the world are you talking about, Ken?"

"Susan, call the lab for me and have them fax the article about EVA that was in the October issue of the Equine Disease Quarterly. I think you'll find your answer. Then get to Carlos as quickly as you can. If Tremor had EVA and word gets out, his legacy has ended. In fact, he'll be remembered in the most negative of ways."

"What the hell is EVA?" Susan was incredulous.

"Listen. The article will give you the details, since I'm get ting kinda worn out and you've got to go. But in a nutshell, EVA is short for equine viral arteritis. This is a virulent disease that can be spread in horses one of two ways. It can affect the respiratory system or the reproductive system of a horse. Stallions can efficiently pass on this disease through mating with a mare, or…" Ken paused to take a breath. "Or, it can be passed on through the semen during artificial insemination. And, research has shown that insemination is the most important means of persistence and dissemination of the virus in various horse populations."

"You mean in Minnesota?" Susan gasped.

"I mean throughout the entire world, Susan." Ken was grave. "Artificial insemination is a method for dual-hemisphere breeding. If the shedding stallion is not found out, there can be inadvertent introduction of this virus, EVA, into uninfected populations of horses."

"So then, Ken, what is the impact of a stallion having EVA, I mean, besides infecting mares, who then could infect other stallions, I suppose? I still don't get why this impacts our case."

Ken was speaking with difficulty. He had to use his cracked brain, and it was a strain for him. "That's a good question, Susan. There are few recorded outbreaks, this much we know. This could be due to lack of attention by the owner, or the veterinarian, or both. Or the lack of the ability to trace this disease could be due to limitations in available diagnostics, or in our case, confusion with other equine diseases. It takes a very subclinical course. This is a persistent disease. There is a decrease in sperm quality and concentration, especially in the first months after infection. Even after recovery from this disease, carrier stallions continue to shed virus with their semen and will infect 85 to 100 percent of seronegative mares to which they are bred."

Susan was beginning to get the drift of where Ken was going with his thought processes. "And then what happens?"

"Mares abort their foals. There are no healthy offspring. No guarantees for the big stud fee."

Susan whistled through her teeth. "Anything else?" she whispered softly.

"Just an equine epidemic."

Ken had just given Susan what she needed—motives for fraud and motives for murder. The question was, did Carlos know?

CHAPTER 34

▼

It was important to Carlos to be calm, and he was failing miserably at the task. He had no ability to tap into that inner calm space he so often sought—and found. Not now. He wondered if he would ever be able to find that peace again. There had been so many things about this case that had conspired against his tranquility. That concept alone really made him on edge with himself, which compounded his problem even more.

If he could settle down, it would help him get the last pieces of this case together. But then, nothing would bring back Tremor or his boldness and passion for life. Carlos hated to admit, even to himself, that Podsky's death was no loss to him, or in his judgment, the entire horse world. But still, there was no going back on that now, either. Death on earth was really quite final.

It had been a tremendous emotional blow to see Kate and to again feel the impact of her fury and twisted logic. He wondered if he would ever be able to get her to see his side of the story, or if she even wanted to. And, why must he keep trying to get her to understand what he deemed to be of value…his point of view? It was really the final blow to see her pair up with Lisa and find that both women could truly be brutal and evil. It made him ponder on which one of the two did kill Tremor—and perhaps Podsky as well. And then there was Fiona. How did she fit into all of this?

It had begun lightly snowing again, which made Carlos focus on the job of driving to Grande Glade. Susan's car was handling well on the slick pavement of 394, but the junk in the car kept shifting and rolling with each lane change. Again the distraction tested his efforts to keep peaceful. Carlos hated a messy car, a messy house, a messy anything. His life was one of order, at least as much as he could manage. He had to admit the last several days had no particular order. He felt as though he should name this investigation the Chaos Case. Nothing was going as could be expected.

Dusk was descending, and the rush-hour traffic, along with the dusting of snow on the road, created backups and slowdowns. He searched for MPR on the radio and was pleased to hear Mozart's wonderful strains come over the public radio airwaves. The peace that had eluded him seemed to click into his brain, and Carlos was suddenly glad for the traffic, glad for the snow, and glad for the extra time. Mozart really could change the brainwaves, he thought.

As he got further west he headed toward Sally's place. He hadn't even told Susan that he wanted to pick up Britt and take her with him to Grande Glade. He didn't want Charlie to know anything more than he had to, and he felt sure that if Susan was on to his plan, Charlie would be too.

As he neared the back roads, the traffic disappeared. Finding the cutoff in the dark was generally a bit tricky, but tonight it was even more so. Carlos was tired, and he was slightly disoriented in the dark with the swirling snow coming through the beams of his headlights. He would be glad for Britt's second pair of eyes to help him find the back way to Grande Glade.

The light was on in the barn, and like a homing pigeon, Carlos went toward it as the car door slammed behind him. He bent over into the rising wind and put his head down. The door to the barn slid open easily, and he squinted into the light. "Britt? Sally?"

He heard a horse nicker, and went toward the sound. "Britt?"

"Yep. Back here, Carlos."

He followed her voice, and saw her head pop out over the top of his horse's stall. "What is your situation, Britt? In the middle of something?"

"Actually, just getting to know this fine beast of yours, and doing some bond-ing."

"Great. That's heartwarming." He patted Rios on the neck and had a soft look on his face, but there was a bit of an edge to his voice.

In her naive way she looked at Carlos and said, "Oh, I am so glad you are pleased." And of course, she meant it sincerely.

"Could you come with me to Grande Glade? I know…don't give me the argu-ments about not being able to go back there. I need your help. We need to go soon, like in the next ten minutes."

"Well…Carlos, I am afraid to go back there, you're right. Kate is a witch, and well…Raja is so…well…inhospitable and spacey, and well…whatever could I do to be of any use at all?"

"Say yes, and I'll tell you on the way over there. I know this is a bit of a leap for you, but could you do it for Tremor? I think I know how and why he was killed."

"No kidding?"

"No kidding."

"So then my record could be cleared, I mean, no one would suspect me of being a bad groom, or anything?"

"That's right, Britt," he said with assurance, crossing his fingers in his gloves and hoping her faith in him would be justified.

He quickly patted his horse, and said, "You have him looking real good, Britt. Thanks."

She smiled at him and said, "I've got to run up to the house and tell Sally."

"I'll go with you. I have a favor to ask of her."

When they got into the warmth of the kitchen, Carlos sank into one of the familiar chairs. "Sally, I need to borrow an FEI passport from you. Do you have one that is of an ordinary nature? You know, basics kept up, looks fine, and that you don't mind if we use…just for a while?"

"My dear boy. That's not the usual request, is it?"

Teasing her the way he loved to do, he said, "But then I'm not your usual guy, now, am I? In addition, I need to borrow Britt for the night."

Laughing and shaking her head Sally countered, "You just love to keep me guessing, don't you?"

It was true. He could keep her going more than anyone he knew, and she would be continually more patient, and forgiving. "You bring out the best in me, Sally. What can I say? I plead guilty."

Sally told him, "Be good to Britt, now. I'm getting fond of having her around. You did me a favor by bringing her here, Carlos. I had no idea I needed an extra hand until today. Now, I am trying to think of ways to cajole her to stay. So, don't mess around with my newfound help!"

"Listen, Sally. I think it's great that you two are getting along, and I'll let you work out whatever you can with each other. But things are a bit sticky with the case from Grande Glade, and I need Britt to be a live witness and pave the way so we can get this wrapped up. And the passport will be a good ruse to get things out in the open."

"You'll bring it back?"

"Yep. I'll send it home with Britt."

He turned to the young girl, noticing again her wholesomeness and how very innocent she was. "Set to go?"

Nodding her head, she took the passport handed to her by Sally, stuffed it in the inside zippered pocket of her down coat, and followed Carlos out into the gloom.

He gave her the details of the eventful day and watched her lip tremble as he described Kate's and Lisa's treatment of him. She wiped tears from her cheeks when she heard about Ken, and his mention of Tremor in the cooler created full-blown sobbing.

"I'm sorry. I didn't mean to upset you."

"No, it really is quite all right. It's sorta cathartic. I've been holding my anger and sadness back and it just came out."

"You going to be OK?"

She turned to him in the seat and uttered sincerely, "I will be fine. In fact, I am glad you came to get me." There was resolve in her voice and she continued, "What can I do? Better fill me in." With that she wiped her face with her sleeve, and stared straight at the road.

Carlos laid out his plan, and by the time they got to Grande Glade there had been silence for a while. Both were ready for action.

CHAPTER 35

▼

The banshee had begun to howl. Had Carlos paid more attention to the news broadcast on MPR during the ride to Grande Glade, perhaps he would have deferred action to a later time. Slippery roads and a swirl of flakes in the air were a breath of a warning that the beast was beginning to slouch toward Lake Superior from its rebirth in northeastern Nebraska. At this time of year the worst elements of the Jet Stream tended to converge in the northern plains. If Carlos had been more in tune with his environment, he would have felt it coming.

Carlos maneuvered Susan's car to a position at the edge of the woods at the beginning of the curving driveway. He deftly parked so that her vehicle would not be easily seen from the main house. The driveway was too long, and the grove of trees formed a dense thicket. The tree trunks were almost obliterated by scrub undergrowth. It was the kind of dark howling night that is the setting for horror stories. It looked like someone, or something, could come out and drag them both into the woods. Carlos shuddered. He'd had one close call. He didn't need another.

The snowfall was building quickly enough to obscure the view of the main house. The steady howl of the southwest wind forced Carlos and Britt to resort to hand gestures as they put phase one of the plan into action. Britt formed an "OK" with her gloved fingers and headed up the driveway toward the house while Carlos fought his way to the barn through the now drifting snow in the paddock area.

The white ground cover had already obscured the small crater formed by the bomb blast, and Carlos stumbled into the hole, falling hard and twisting his knee in the process. The air was sucked out of him, and he lay in the snow, almost weeping with pain. He wondered abstractly if he had torn a ligament. There was a lump in his throat, and for the second time that day he thought he might puke. Pain always hit him in the gut. He tried to put weight on both legs in order to get out of the deep crater, but found the only way out was to use his hands and undamaged leg to haul himself up. The shooting pains traveled up his leg and centered in the small of his back. He was wet from the fall, and the increasing storm was soaking him further. Carlos realized how tired he was. He wasn't doing well, and he hoped could pull off his part of the plan he and Britt had made.

As he struggled to his feet, he remembered the gun in his glove compartment. But his truck was at Falling Oak Farms, so he pressed on toward the barn entrance. He wasn't dressed for the change in weather, and his jeans served only to transmit the cold and hold it against his bare skin. He limped toward the warmth of the barn. He noticed he had to drag his left leg in order to get it to go along with the rest of his body. Maybe he had done more than just tear a ligament. The nausea would not subside. He was lightheaded.

At last he made it to the barn, but he found it difficult to get in. He couldn't make the latches of the barn door work right, and the wind kept pushing him like a bully. He leaned against the door, and gritting his teeth, grunted as he made an opening and squeezed through.

Closing the door was another struggle. The wind had increased to a strength reminiscent of gales heralding hurricanes in the tropics. When he finally closed the latch, the forces outside let out a piercing wail that seemed to linger for a moment in the barn's rafters until the automatic fans kicked in and the lament retreated. Carlos felt that he had cheated some evil force from entering the structure—and from getting him.

He was wet from the outside, and in a sweat from the strain on the inside. He looked down at his hands and they were shaking. He suspected he was suffering from hypothermia and hypoglycemia. He looked down at his knee and saw blood dripping onto his boot. The leg of his jeans was torn right below the knee. He must have cut himself on some remaining shards from the car that were hiding under the snow cover. He didn't have time to deal with that now.

All the horses were agitated. The gathering forces outside the door had noticeably unnerved the Arabian mare that Carlos had observed in the arena with the governor's daughter just a few days earlier. Her head was erect, and every muscle in her neck was so tense that she looked more like a marble sculpture than a living creature. Carlos wondered if she had seen her young owner since the funeral. The girl's mother was now dead. Was Fiona Andersson's death a simple mistake, a cruel but humorous twist of fate? Or did her death figure into the whole mess that he was trying so desperately to unravel?

Carlos was forced to take another moment to sit on a bale of hay and assess the damage to his knee. He hoped that this would not be one more lost moment of time that he would later come to regret. His leg felt worse rather than better as he stood up to test it. He realized that it was going to be very difficult to bear weight on it any time soon. He muttered a curse as he grabbed a broom that was hanging on the wall to use as a makeshift crutch. A sudden blast of wind against the door caused him to startle, his own neck muscles resembling those of the frightened mare in the stall next to him. The wail began to accelerate again in the rafters and this time was not drowned out by the sound of the fans.

The horses were pacing in their stalls as the storm continued to build. There was more and more snorting, and the Arab mare responded with a high-pitched whinny that only served to agitate the other animals even more. Another whinny followed from a further stall in the adjoining wing. Carlos found his own breath coming in quick starts as he struggled to control his breathing and his focus. And his pain. Whether it was the agony in his leg or the uncontrollable natural forces that were swirling all around him, Carlos knew he was in trouble. He'd been without food or rest for far too long.

Looking up, he realized that he had somehow found his way to Tremor's former stall. He slumped against the open door of the stall and looked at the place in the wall where the front-end loader had pulled out Tremor's body. His hand brushed up against the brass electrical plate on the support beam, and he knew for certain about Tremor's death. What had been an educated guess, even more a suspicion, now crystallized in his psyche as fact. He had bluffed his way with Lisa, trying to get a response. He got such a strong reaction from her, he knew she was guilty of something; he just wasn't sure what. But now, here in the stall, he knew the truth with the same certainty that he knew he was in the middle of a wild winter storm.

It was the most bizarre experience he could remember, and yet he couldn't stop it from happening. He saw through the darkness, and the scene of Tremor's trusting, waiting for treats, flooded him. He could smell the fear beginning to rise in the other horses around him, and felt that same adrenaline surge that Tremor must have felt as the wires were attached to his orifices. Carlos saw the figure going through the motions of death, and the face became so clear he thought for an instant that the image was real. His guess at Lisa Anthony's had been right...dead right. She was dressed in black, and a smooth operator. When he tried to shrug off the vision, he felt shakier than when he had sunk to the ground.

Cradling his head in his hands, he shoved his face toward the floor and took deep breaths. A horse began to beat against the side of its stall, and Carlos's view seemed to take in his present surroundings. Someday, when he had more time, and felt better, he would have to try to figure out what had just happened. But of one thing he was grateful; somehow he had been able to put together the circumstances of Tremor's death.

Maybe, just maybe, if his luck could hold out for a while longer, he could get Lisa to confess. He took her attempt to kill him as a confession. She knew that he knew. But he needed something on paper, something that Susan could use to convict Lisa, something that would put her out of business forever.

He struggled to his feet again and went down the aisle holding onto the sides of the boxes as he went. At the end of the aisle he found the grooming supplies. He grabbed several rags and wrapped one around his still throbbing knee. His first attempt to open the door to the barn failed; it was even harder to open than it had been to close. Had he come through that door just a few moments ago, or much longer? He was sure he had lost some precious time, but was not certain of how much.

He needed to get to the main house and wondered how he could make it. Hoping the wind would be less fierce on the back side of the barn, Carlos decided to take that route. The advantage was clear for him, as the light of the opening door would not attract attention. The disadvantage was it would take him longer to break through the increasingly deep drifts and would tax his draining energies to dangerously low levels.

This door was easier to open, and he slid out the smallest crack and closed it with one hand. He rounded the side of the barn closest to the fenced pasture where he had been hanging on the fence the day he met Britt. Holding on to the rails for support, he moved slowly toward the road. He looked up when he heard a truck door slam. Sonofabitch!

Lisa had driven his Dodge Ram to Grande Glade. That absolutely cut it. He was so mad he started to shake. At least, he attributed his shakes to anger. He didn't want to think that he might be going into shock. That Lisa was a piece of work. When he thought he might jump her and pummel her face in the snow, he saw Susan get out of the passenger side of his truck. He wondered briefly what wild tale Susan had cooked up that not only had drawn Lisa back to Grande Glade, but had convinced Lisa to give Susan a ride as well. He had to admit that it was a perfect way for Susan to keep an eye on Lisa and make sure she arrived according to plan, but he didn't like the idea of Susan riding unprotected in that would-be murderer's car.

No, wait, in HIS car. He felt the anger surge again, but he knew he was too slow to reach Lisa. They were already getting close to the house, while he was still inching his way through the fence drifts. The cold helped numb his leg.

Soon. Damnitalltosonofabitchhell. He would see she paid.

CHAPTER 36

▼

Britt was wet by the time she made it to the front door. This storm was rising fast. The heaviness of the snow caught her off guard, and she was out of breath as she rang the bell. Waiting on the porch, she stomped her feet and got the circulation going in her hands. As she was stomping and flapping her arms, the door opened.

Raja's face mirrored her inner shock. No one disobeyed her when she had given an edict. "What do you think you are doing here, young lady? I did tell you not to show up here again, did I not?"

"Oh, yes, ma'am. You certainly did. I was wondering if we could step inside?"

"And why by the name of the gods, would I want to let you into my home?"

"Because I have something of interest for you, Raja."

Her curiosity got the best of her, and she motioned for Britt to enter. "Make it short," she said curtly.

"Raja, what's gotten into you? You used to be so…well…sweet. Trusting. Has Sasha's death made you completely bitter?"

"I don't believe you came here to find out about my personality, did you?" said Raja, peering over the top of the reading glasses that were still perched on her nose. "I've been trying to go over some papers, and run this business, and I am now very busy. Of course, I was before my dear Sasha died, but, really, this is quite taxing."

"The perhaps we had best sit down," Britt suggested. When they were both settled, she fished into her coat pocket. "What I have here is Tremor's passport. You know, the one you said you knew nothing about?"

Raja's hands began to shake as she reached for it. "Oh. So you had it all along, did you? You little thief."

Britt raised her chin in a courageous gesture, and stared Raja in the eye for a long time as she put the passport back in her pocket and zipped the inner flap.

"You insolent girl!" Raja verbally lashed out at Britt. "Hand it over to me at once."

Britt smiled and folded her arms over her chest. "Are you willing to cooperate with me, just a little bit, Raja? I'd swear you are quickly becoming the little banty rooster that your husband was."

Raja was beginning to tremble in all her jowls. Her hands were flying to her face, and then poking rigidly at her side. Britt could see moist beads on her upper lip. "No one...NO ONE...confronts ME...do...YOU understand that?" She said each word slowly as if she were speaking to someone who was just learning the language.

Britt was beginning to feel more empowered as Raja struggled for control. "Well, now, Raja. Off the record, why are you so upset? It couldn't be my visit, could it?"

Raja slowly shook her head. "You little..."

"No, then. Mmmmm. Could it be the document in my pocket? Now what about that could make you so upset?"

"I want that passport. It's mine."

"Correction. It belongs now to the owners of the dead horse. You know, all his effects, etc., etc.... Perhaps I could make some money with this little piece of...should I say evidence?"

Raja blurted out, "How would you know about that?" Her face was becoming the most marvelous shade of purple, and she was grasping the arms of her chair as if they would keep her from being ejected from it as a jet pilot might from a plummeting craft.

"What I want to know, Raja, is why...honestly...why did you fire me? You have created a very troublesome resume for me now. I would like you to fix that."

"So," the gasping woman said, "this is a little case of blackmail?"

Britt smiled. "It seems you know something of blackmail. Why would that be, Raja?"

"You are a little piece of shit, Britt."

"Well...are you ready to answer my questions? Honestly?"

"It won't matter in the end, you know, Britt. You'll never get far enough from here to use the information. So, sure. I'll tell you what I can."

"Where's Kate?"

Startled, Raja ran her jeweled fingers through her hair. "She left."

"Left where?"

"Back to the riding circuit. Or maybe back to South America. I don't know. She doesn't confide in me. I just know she packed up several hours ago and went to the airport."

"OK. Do you know why she ran so quickly?"

"She always goes like that. It's not unusual for her. She comes like that too. Unexpected. Just shows up and acts all breezy."

"Like you?" Britt asked. Raja gave her a death look.

"All right. Good. You are getting the hang of this, Raja. What's the passport to you?"

"I told you. I'm in charge here. I should keep track of it, is all."

"Oh, oh, oh. I'm disappointed in you, Raja. You were going to try to be honest, but that isn't your style, is it?"

"All my students know me to be very honest. I am guided by The Higher Powers."

"Is that statement supposed to keep you from having to answer the questions?"

"The passport needs to be put to rest with Tremor. Why don't we just give it to Dr. Anthony?"

"Now that's a good idea. Because she will want to know why this passport shows that Tremor had a disease. That is, unless she already knew." This was the question Britt had been leading up to, what she and Carlos had worked out to get Raja to talk. It was a blatant lie, of course. Britt knew that no disease would ever be entered in a passport, but she was pretty sure Raja wouldn't know that fact. What was more important was what the passport didn't show. If Podsky and Lisa weren't giving a vaccination on the day Britt observed them with the syringe, then maybe they were testing for something. Maybe a disease. And maybe Raja would know something about that.

The once purpled face was now an ashen color. Raja seemed to be hyperventilating. "How did you find out? You slut."

Britt opened her eyes wide and gave a shocked look to Raja.

What has happened to the great Queen of Good? You are becoming more like your daughter. I think I am beginning to see where she got some of her character deficits."

"People don't talk to me like this."

Britt, wearing her newfound courage like a shield, said, "Well...they should."

There was the sound of feet stamping on the porch, trying to dislodge snow. As Raja looked toward the door with confusion, Britt said, "Well, now. We'll get the chance to ask Dr. Anthony ourselves just what makes this passport so intriguing."

And with no ceremony or bell-ringing, the door opened, and Susan and Lisa walked in to see a wild-eyed mistress of the house looking for all the world as if she were ready to take on a raging bull in her own bare hands.

Lisa took it all in before she could exhale a greeting. She had gone too far to turn back now. Susan thought she saw it coming, but it was too late. The unspoken communication between Raja and Lisa Anthony was swift and brutal. The pair functioned as one, like a frightened, trapped beast of prey in the initial assault. Out of the corner of her eye, Susan saw the glint of steel from the gun barrel as it grazed her temple and the world went from black to gray and back again. Her second-to-last recollection was being vaguely aware of the screams of the young woman wearing a down parka who was standing with Raja Podsky. Her last recollection was the sound of a gunshot mingled with the tinkling of broken glass.

CHAPTER 37

▼

The commotion inside the big house was not entirely lost to Carlos. It wasn't that he could hear the gunshot above the howl of the wind. Quite simply, the bullet's trajectory took it through the plate glass of the front door, where it ricocheted off the wrought-iron grille until it spent its motion by striking the tree on which Carlos was leaning. He still might not have taken notice had it not buried itself in the bark right next to his ear.

Realizing his disadvantage, Carlos struggled to his pickup in an attempt to even the playing field. His hands were so cold that his fingers were reduced to useless clubs as he tried to force open the glove box that housed his weapon. The keys were gone from the ignition, and he flailed at the stubborn box with his fists in total frustration. His anger was enough to sap the remaining stores of energy in a body that had not been granted food or sleep for interminable hours. He tried to fight the urge; if only he could close his eyes for a minute or two, he would be all right.

That's all he needed…just a few moments to regroup.

Survival instinct and years of military training forced him to try to exit the car and move about, but it was useless. He knew that if he left the relative shelter of the truck cab, the mounting snow would become his shroud. With great effort he closed the door and tried to gain what warmth he could from the windbreak that the vehicle provided. His next best option would be to try to make it the hundred yards or so back to the cocoon of the barn. It would also offer plenty of places to hide while he tried to gain an advantage.

As he slid further into the seat to avoid detection and concentrated on the shortest distance to the barn door, Carlos saw movement between the house and the barn. Two figures were hunched over an object that they were hauling through the snow. Another figure was following and gesturing wildly.

His eyes shifted to the bundle in the snow. He noticed how detached he felt as he observed that it was something wrapped in red; an almost blaze orange red. Then it hit him. Susan! She always wore that ridiculous blaze orange coat when she ventured into the country. Never mind that it wasn't hunting season. She had a pathological fear of being shot. He thought crazily that the coat or her fear hadn't helped her a bit. She probably had been shot already.

The curtain of snow mercifully hid the details from him before he gave in to the storm, the cold, blood loss, and the utter frustration of it all. He passed into a twilight zone of sleep, dream, and hallucination. If Carlos had been awake to see the completion of Raja's hastily arranged plan, the residual images in his dreams would have convinced him that he had certainly gone to Hell.

∗   ∗   ∗   ∗

"Stop whimpering and put some muscle behind it. Or would you rather we left her out in the snow?"

Britt heaved Susan's limp body through the barn door opening as Raja gestured wildly with Lisa Anthony's gun. It was pointed somewhat in her direction. Susan's body felt warm and probably alive, but Britt couldn't be sure. The dead weight was even harder to move because all of Britt's strength and energy seemed to have left her extremities, driven to her gut by the feeling of stark terror she was experiencing.

Lisa Anthony had gone around the corner to the equipment room. The few moments Britt had alone with Raja led Britt to consider making a lunge for the gun. Before she could do so, Lisa came back down the aisle, and Britt's terror turned to total despair as she realized what Lisa was carrying. The sight caused her legs to give way and she fell into a heap next to Susan.

"Get up! Get up!" Raja was screaming now, and Lisa dropped the gasoline can and raced down the aisle to take charge.

"Raja, get control of yourself."

"Get control of myself! Why didn't you tell me Susan Lindstrom was involved in this? She's been persecuting my Sasha for years. I thought he'd taken care of her meddling with his paltry pieces of information, which she sucked up like a vampire."

Lisa looked at Raja with disbelief. "Obviously, his little ploy to pay her off didn't work. She's here, and now we've got to deal with her."

"I'm only going along with you, Lisa, to cover up this Tremor mess. It's all your fault, you know. You and Sasha were so stupid. Oh, I knew about your little trysts, and frankly, I didn't care, not till you ruined the breeding program, you idiots."

Ignoring Raja's outburst, Lisa barked the orders. "Britt, take this tape and secure a piece over our sleeping friend's mouth. Then I want you to tie her up with this baling twine."

Having no choice in the matter, Britt complied, but didn't feel she had to do a thorough job with the baling twine. "Susan, I hope you notice this," she whispered under the howling of the wind.

"Now drag her into the stall and lie down," ordered Lisa, motioning Britt toward a nearby empty stall. "Don't act like you don't have the strength. A strong barn girl like you lifts more in feed bags, I know. Then take the tape and wrap it around your own ankles. Put a piece over your own pretty little mouth and then lie down in the stall."

Britt pressed her face into the dirty shavings as Lisa directed Raja in the fine art of knot tying.

"But they will find them here. Won't it look suspicious?" Raja was pacing and waving her arms.

"All traces of the restraints will be gone. We will be able to give a vivid report of their heroism in the tragic retelling of it all. I know what I'm doing. Do you want to resolve this or not?"

Before closing the stall door, Lisa led the gray Arabian mare from her adjoining stall and locked her in the box with Britt and Susan. "There. They died trying to save the frightened mare. How heroic! How stupid."

The mare stepped carefully over the prone Britt, sniffed, nickered, and took a protective stance as a mother would over her young foal. Inquisitively, she reached over with her nose and nudged the red-orange bundle that was Susan.

With a moaning noise from her throat, Britt produced a low-pitched sound that went unnoticed by Raja and Lisa but seemed to soothe the mare. The mare stood rock-still but kept a wary eye on the two women standing outside the wooden door.

From her position on the stall floor, Britt couldn't see what was happening, but she could smell it. In a way, she was happy, because it could have been worse. This smell gave her a hint of hope.

"It smells funny." Lisa's muffled voice could be heard over the scurrying back and forth through the barn.

"It stinks. Let's get this done and get the hell out of here." Raja sounded totally panicked.

Britt knew that their mistake would give her a few minutes, but that was all. She had told Podsky not to store the fuel oil in the gasoline can. She was thanking her lucky stars that he had ignored her suggestion. The number two oil would burn all right, but it would not be as prone to be explosive. They had a chance to get out of this alive if Lisa and Raja failed to notice the type of fuel in the can.

"Get ready to run when I drop the match. We can go up to the house and call the fire department. It will take them forever to get here through this weather."

Britt heard the sizzle as Lisa struck the match. "It's not burning very fast," Raja's whiny voice was complaining.

"It must be the cold. Don't worry. It'll go."

Footsteps could be heard beating a hasty retreat. A draft of cold, fresh air wafted down the aisle. Britt's senses were heightened with the adrenaline rush of this monstrous situation. She rolled over to Susan and began to moan that sound in the back of her throat again. She tried to wake Susan up, but instead, all she could do was push her against one side of the box and lie in front of her.

Britt could smell the heat rather than feel it. The horses did, too, and were starting down the road to panic. The Arabian was the first to react and began to kick furiously at the outer wall of the stall. Out of all of the horses Lisa could have put in the stall with them, Britt was glad it was this particular mare. Arabians were tough denizens of the desert, and Britt had seen more than one kick its way out of a stall. Their hooves were hard as steel. Britt had seen legs break down from stall kicking before the hooves gave way. The little mare was doing exactly what Britt had prayed she would do. She pressed Susan and herself as far from the working mare as she could, and continued to pray. She wondered where Carlos was. This was far too long for him to have tried to implement their original idea. He was supposed to have slipped in through the kitchen entrance. She hoped he wasn't lost in the storm and circling in the woods. Why couldn't he see the fire?

Britt rolled over onto her back, but the duct tape around her ankles and the baling twine immobilizing her wrists made any other movement impossible. Smoke was beginning to fill the aisle as the fuel oil mixture burned slowly but steadily through the bits of sawdust and straw that littered the aisle. If the flames reached the main sawdust bin…Britt didn't want to think about the results.

The mare continued her frantic kicking, and at least two boards were loose enough that Britt could feel snow blowing through the gap. But unless she could find a way to free her hands, any escape route would be of little use. There were seven other horses in the barn; at least there had been that many yesterday. The frantic screams of the Arab mare alerted the herd before the odor of the smoke reached the far end of the aisle. The combination of the auditory and olfactory warnings increased the anxiety of the other horses to a frantic pitch. Bared teeth chewed at the metal stall doors as ancient instincts of flight took over.

Britt was driven to despair by the screams. She rolled over onto her stomach, her face pressed to the stall mat to avoid the smoke, and began to pray even harder. It was all she could think of to do. "Oh, Christ!"

Someone was cursing. Hands were pulling at the twine around her wrists.

"Mfmmfph," was all Britt could manage to get out. She hoped it approximated Susan's name.

"I know we haven't met, Britt, but we have got to get out of here now. I'm scared shitless, don't like horses much, especially when they are kicking in a closed space that is on fire."

Susan freed Britt's hands and pulled the tape from her feet and then her mouth.

"It worked! I didn't tie you very tight. It worked!" She was childlike in her exclamation.

Susan winced as she rubbed her temple. She had a headache that wouldn't stop pounding inside her brain. "Let's not celebrate just yet; the stall latch is jammed."

Britt turned to look where the little Arab had loosened the boards. She motioned Susan out of the way and lay on her back, giving the loose boards a tremendous kick with her paddock boots as the mare hovered protectively over her. With another kick from Britt, the hole was big enough for them to crawl out, but there was not nearly enough space for the mare, totally crazy with fear. Her legs were bloodied from the hocks down as she continued her frantic bid for an escape, and she was screaming.

Britt rolled Susan out of the opening.

"Get as far from the barn as you can! Find help!"

Before Susan could utter a word, Britt crawled out of the hole and vanished around the corner of the barn. As she approached the door nearest to where the mare was trapped, Britt was faced with a wall of flame that was inching up the weathered boards of the exterior. She leaped through a breach in the flames and forced the adjoining door open. Something felt hot and sticky around her eyes; it felt as though they were blistering, but she knew what she had to do.

A hammer was wedged in the stall latch mechanism. It was easy enough to remove, but there was no halter or lead rope to throw over the head of a mare that was totally berserk. Britt removed her sweatshirt, and making the same low noise that she used earlier, distracted the mare long enough to throw the garment over her head, shielding her eyes from the sight of the flames. The mare was not ready to capitulate. She struck out with both forelegs as she reared, clipping Britt on the shoulder with sharp hooves and drawing blood.

"Come on girl…you'll have to do better than that."

With one athletic leap, Britt was on the mare's back, heels digging into her sides and legs, guiding her forcefully around the flames and through the open door. Sliding off in seconds, Britt slapped the mare on the rump, sending her to the relative safety of the snowdrifts and away from the growing flames in the stable.

Britt felt like she was flying down the aisle. She made it to the far end of the barn and threw open the other doors, dragging a bale of hay to hold them open against the wind. At least the wind was blowing the flames out the other end of the barn aisle. Still, she knew she had very little time left before the fire reached the sawdust storage area. One spark, and an explosion of burning debris would make any rescue impossible.

One by one, she opened the stall doors. The screaming and kicking were getting worse. The horses weren't going to leave without some coaxing, and she could find no lead ropes or halters on the stall doors. She thought about running to the tack room and getting the carbon-dioxide extinguisher that was stored there, but realized that there was no time. A desperate move was all she had left.

The big gelding stabled next to Tremor's former stall was recognized as a leader in the turnout area. If she could just get to him…

The gelding was spinning frantically in his stall, but Britt was able to get an arm over his neck. She hung on with difficulty, her injured shoulder feeling as though it were being ripped from her torso. Somehow, she was able to guide the horse into the aisle, and miraculously, his cries drew the others from their stalls. The relics of their ancestry and the imperative to survive were coming to the fore. The animals would turn to their leader in times of crisis.

Britt tried her best to force the gelding toward the safety of the open door, but the wind and noise from the storm were enough to turn the group toward the feed room and the advancing flames. They were trapped and frozen in panic as the flames reached the sawdust.

CHAPTER 38

▼

"Hey, pardner. Be a good guy, Don Juan. Open the door." Carlos had slumped against the driver's door, his head leaning against the glass. When the door was jerked open, the snapping of his neck and the blast of colder air roused him. He fell into the arms of Charlie Branson.

"What the...?"

"My question exactly. What are you doin' takin' a nap while the joint's burning up?"

"Huh?" Carlos was having trouble focusing. He couldn't orient himself.

"We don't have time to talk now, pardner. What's to be done about the barn? I hear horses going nuts in there."

Carlos looked at his rescuer, and muttered, "Charlie. Help me over there. What are you driving?"

"My car got stuck down the road. The snowplow was coming up the drive and I hitched a ride. He's over there," he said as he pointed toward the road.

"Get him over here. NOW."

Charlie stumbled forward in the snow, and waved a flashlight at the plow. It idled.

Carlos could see Charlie get into the cab. Then, mercy of all mercies, it slowly tracked over to the truck. Charlie got out again, and Carlos staggered over to the door of the plow cab. Charlie pulled him inside.

"We've got to bash down as many walls as we can. As you can. Pronto. Ohmigod. The horses will all get killed," Carlos moaned.

It seemed to take centuries for the plow to lumber over to the barn. As they were making their way across the snowdrifted parking area and the bumpy, mud-holed field, Carlos began to get his wits about him. "Charlie, get on the radio. Get some help out here. Especially police and fire equipment."

Charlie looked at him as if he had left all of his brains in the truck. "You think anybody's moving in this hard-hitting storm? It came up so fast we're all caught with our pants down."

Carlos didn't look at him. With steel in his voice he ordered, "You WILL call. Someone has got to help. We may have more than horses in that barn."

Just then the plow got close to the barn, and in the swirl of snow and blue light a figure in blaze orange could be seen rounding the corner of the building. The wind was whipping hair that seemed to match the coat, and she was waving her arms.

"Charlie. Look. It's Susan!" The driver hesitated. Carlos commanded, "Hit the barn there," and he pointed to the place that had been patched after Tremor's death. "Go, go, GO!"

And in the next instant they were plowing through the side of the barn. There was a roaring sound as the air filled the fire-occupied space, and the screeching sound of metal on metal. The noise was deafening, and no one could talk. "Back up. Back up! Now. Now."

The driver deftly managed to get out of the way, and a horse popped out of the opening.

"Sweet Jesus. It's got a rider on it."

"It's Britt." Carlos was spent again, and relief compounded this.

"Make another hole! Move to the other side of the barn!!"

The driver was beginning to act like he did this all the time. He wheeled the huge vehicle with its three separate blades around the corner and plowed through the side of the barn. The wind did not seem so strong here. Pulling out as fast as he could, the driver left places for more horses to exit. They spewed forth wildly, in a tumble of hooves and golfball-white eyes. There was a primeval sound as the frothed horses found the open space and fresh air.

"Get back. Further. Move this plow! The barn is going to blow!"

Before the vehicle could get more than ten feet, there was an explosion that wracked the air and tore the night sky. A volcano of charred boards, fire, and molten metal had erupted, and they were looking into the maw of Hades.

✳   ✳   ✳   ✳

It took time for their ears to cease ringing and the plow to stop backing up.

The three men were stunned to silence and immobility. Finally Charlie uttered, "Jesus H. Christ." He jumped out of the cab and ran shouting, "Suz, Suz. Where are you?"

Britt came up to the open door and reached for Carlos. She helped to ease him down. It wasn't clear who was hugging whom, but in the end, it was Britt who helped Carlos to walk toward his truck. The wind was still mercilessly whipping the snow into their bodies, stinging their faces as if pricked by a thousand poisoned needles. The sound from the fire, combined with the wind, created the sensation of being in a vast blast furnace. It was impossible to tell the hot from the cold.

Heaving Carlos back into the passenger seat of his Ram, Britt jumped in beside him.

"Here. Eat this." She pulled out a Butterfinger candy bar. She peeled off the wrapper, and broke off a piece and shoved it into his mouth. "Chew, Carlos." Next she took him in her arms, and held him tight. Her shoulder was brutally painful, but all she said was, "I want to warm you up."

Somehow, Carlos had never pictured struggling for survival would be quite like this. He silently chewed. More candy was shoved in his mouth. He could feel the sugar begin to take effect. "Susan? Is she OK?"

"She got out of the barn with me. Well…actually a bit before me. She's fine. Charlie's looking after her."

Britt began to rummage behind the seat of his truck. "Do you keep any water bottles in here? You're dehydrated and need fluids. Your knee looks like it was mauled by a bear."

"No. No water. We'll have to get to the big house. We'll die out in this storm."

"We have a problem. Lisa and Raja are there, and they have a gun they would be more than glad to use."

"I have a gun."

"Where?"

"In the glove compartment." He looked at her and said with feeling, "I like Butterfingers."

"Here. Finish it off. Then you can have the carrot I found in here, too." Britt reached for the glove compartment and found it locked. She looked over at Carlos, who seemed to be getting a more normal shade.

"Lisa's got the keys."

Britt reached into another pocket, and came up with a tweezers. She found a hairpin still in her hair, and miraculously opened the glove compartment by the time the candy bar was gone. Carlos was so relieved he hugged her tightly.

Abruptly, the car door opened and another body shoved in. "My, my, you two are quite the pair, hugging and all that while the barn is burning and the two murderous witches are dancing 'round with glee."

Carlos turned to see Susan. He turned and hugged her, too. "I love to hear that sarcastic voice. I was worried about you."

Susan was speechless. A rare moment. Recovering, she looked at Britt, "Thanks for saving my life in there. You were great. Just great. I really mean it; I don't know how to thank you."

"You would have done it for me…We've got to make plans. Quickly, too," Britt said.

"Where's Charlie?" Carlos asked.

"He went to talk to the plow driver, to remind him to call for help. He had to get his briefcase out of the cab of the plow. He's got a gun in there. Not licensed, I might add. But we thought we could use some help," Susan explained.

The plan they hatched was quick and dirty. Somehow they would have to take charge of the house, disarm the women, and wait until help could arrive. When they were deciding what to do, it all seemed so simple. Implementing it turned out to be another matter.

CHAPTER 39

▼

Nero may have fiddled while Rome burned, but he probably had nothing to do with setting the blaze. He could be forgiven that much. Callousness is not synonymous with murder. The barn was devoured in less than twenty minutes. During that time, the former Bernice Mischke and Dr. Lisa Anthony mistakenly assumed that two human skeletons had been reduced to ashes along with their equine victims.

Luckily for Carlos and his cohorts, the storm obscured the fact that Raja and Lisa had so far not gotten away with murder. In fact, Lisa and Raja could see virtually nothing during the height of the storm and the blaze. They might have been able to see the flashing blue lights of the MNDOT snowplow commandeered by Charlie, had they possessed even a modicum of compassion, or at the very least, curiosity about the fates of their intended victims. As it was, the two women were busy making frantic phone calls to snag a private charter to the Caribbean. They would be long gone, so they thought, by the time the barn fire was discovered.

But they did not reckon on the ferocity of the storm. The loss of electricity was the final blow.

"Shit! Raja! You have a flashlight here somewhere? I can't see my hand in front of my face."

"Look over on the mantle. There should be some candles."

"I found the friggin' candles. You have a match somewhere?" Lisa was about at the end of her rope.

"Oh, dear. Now where would those be?"

"Raja! Do something besides walk around wringing your hands. Someone may have seen the blaze by now, and I for one want out of here. Get on the goddamn phone and find someone to get us the hell out of here!"

"Dear, the portable phone's not working either…try your cell." "It's out in that detective's truck."

"Well, go get it."

"You go get it. I'm not going out in this storm. I can't even see the front steps."

Raja was adamant. "You should have never driven his truck over here. There's no place to hide it. How will I explain how it got here?"

"Forget it. He's been snooping around everywhere. How would you know how or why it got here?"

"He will tell the authorities that you stole it."

"I'm only going to say this once, Raja. So open your ears and listen. Carlos Dega will not be back to bother us again or nose around Tremor's insurance claim. Trust me on this one."

If Raja comprehended the tone of Lisa's statement, she didn't indicate as much. "It's just so messy I had everything under control and now you have gone and complicated things so much and I just don't know how I can live with this untidiness."

"Get a grip, Raja. We just murdered two people and seven or eight very expensive show horses. Your late husband is responsible for this whole mess."

Raja's eyes fairly flashed in the darkness as she whirled on Lisa. "My late husband, as you so delicately put it, was not solely responsible for this mess. I know what was going on between the two of you. Believe me—you weren't the only one. I could kill you for what you both did to Tremor."

Lisa didn't see the gun that was pointed at her midsection. She leaned back, coolly crossing her arms behind her head. "Well, I must say Tremor's death was rather convenient. We were lucky the vet lab didn't have enough to work with. I feel quite good about that. I helped to ensure that the lab didn't have enough to do anymore tests. You know, I am good at managing a crisis, don't you think?"

Raja fairly spit the words. "Lisa, you create crises wherever you go. Tremor's death was a mercy I'm not talking about his death."

"Raja, exactly what are you getting at?" Lisa was pandering to her.

"Your little tryst was one thing, but how could you both be so stupid as to jeopardize Tremor's breeding syndication. Were you both stinking drunk, stoned, or what?"

Raja was gesturing wildly, and that's when Lisa saw the gun. She moved back into the shadows toward the kitchen. One or two steps more, and she would have realized that they had company.

"Raja, calm down and tell me what you are getting at."

"You know exactly what I'm talking about. You couldn't resist breeding that pitiful Dutch Warmblood mare to Tremor on the side, could you? Did Sasha suggest it, or was it your idea? You ruined him and my breeding program. Not to mention a multimillion-dollar syndication."

"Relax, Raja. The insurance will pay for the stud."

"Tremor was going to be my ticket out of here. I was going to cash in on his breeding in a big way so I could leave this place...the cold weather...the whole spa scene...I wanted...I wanted..."

"What did you really want, Raja? You couldn't keep Sasha's interest. Is that what you wanted?" Lisa's voice was fairly dripping with sarcasm.

"No. I HAD Sasha. I had him in the palm of my hand. He was always coming to me to get him out of the scrapes he got himself into. We had a little under-standing. He was totally out of control in the stables, however, and I couldn't make him listen to what to do. He was a stubborn, hardheaded prick. He spent the inheritance. He thought only of himself and his little ego. The horse was all we had that was worth anything at all. It was all Kate and I had left. The bastard!"

Raja's voice got very hard and cold. She spit the words out as if they tasted bit-ter, "He deserved what he got. I am happy do you get it, I am ecstatic, that the little Russian wannabe got what he deserved? What he earned. But the stallion was my purse, and now I have no way out." She was worked up, and anger seethed out of her.

If the lights had been on, Lisa would have looked very confused. She might have had the sense to be a little scared too.

"So you knew about the EVA then?"

"Sasha told me everything. He was dependent on me in a way that you would never understand. But it was your mare that infected Tremor. The spontaneous foal abortions had already started. YOU, you, Lisa, were the real cause behind it. You could have said no to Sasha's little need to dally. You could have kept your middling mare at home. But, oh, no...and once word got around that he was shedding the virus in his semen, everything that we had worked for would be gone. And then there would be the lawsuits." Raja stared hard at Lisa in the dark. Lisa felt the venom at last. With great quiet and emphasis Raja said, "All due to your stupidity and greed."

"It seemed so harmless then, Raja."

"You're a vet, Lisa. You know you never, ever, breed without testing first."

"But it was my little mare…I knew her…" The tables seemed to be turning on Lisa.

"Like hell you did. You see, don't you, that you now are in my way. Instead of helping me, I have nothing. So, I might just as well make sure you don't leave here. Grande Glade will be your final resting place. Sasha got what he deserved. Why shouldn't you?"

"You haven't the guts to do anything about me, and you have no need to, Raja. You have absolutely nothing to gain by getting rid of me."

"You were stupid once, Lisa. You'll be stupid again."

Lisa began to defend herself. It was a quick turn of events. "I was the one to think of putting those women in the barn and burning it down…you'll collect a bundle on the insurance. You'll be all right! I was the one who was strong. You were a blubbering idiot."

"Sasha had borrowed heavily. You have no clue how financially inept he was, Lisa."

Lisa heard the hammer of the gun being clicked back.

"OK, OK. I hear how serious you are. We can work things out." This was a wildcard she hadn't expected. She was the one who should be in control here.

It was then they both heard the front door open, so gently that at first they thought it was the wind pushing it toward the room. Lisa gasped. Raja shouted, "Who's there?"

In the dark, Carlos moaned. His leg was a throbbing mass and the effort to get to the house, even with help, had strained his energy even further. He shut the door. He moaned again. He saw the glint of the gun as the barn fire reflected through the glass. He hoped the others had made it through the kitchen entrance as planned. Raja, rattled, came up to her feet, dropping the cocked gun to her side. Seizing her chance, Lisa jumped up and rushed toward Raja. Unbelievably, at that chaotic moment, the lights came back on, and both Lisa and Raja stared numbly at the moaning "ghost" of Carlos Dega.

"You're dead," Lisa said in a strangled voice.

"I'm an expert at ghosts, Lisa," Raja said, "and this is no dead person." Finding her wits a moment before Lisa, she looked at the younger woman and pointed the gun at her yet again. "I told you that you would make another mistake. Your mistake is standing in my living room."

Carlos kept moving into the room. He limped toward Raja, dragging his leg. He was glazed in the eyes, and sweat glistened off his high cheekbones. There was a chalklike quality to his face. His disheveled appearance made him look even more ghostly—and unpredictable.

It was then that Raja had to make a decision. Which one would she shoot first? Who would she most like to see dead? She motioned to Carlos. "Get over there with Lisa. Sit on the sofa." Carlos just kept gimping his way closer, looking like the walking dead.

Lisa sensed her moment and began to move in Raja's direction. Raja, still pointing the gun at Lisa, closed her finger on the trigger. At the sound of the shot, Carlos leaped the last few steps and struck the gun out of Raja's hand. With Raja's screams, the watchers in the kitchen erupted into the room, racing toward the fray. Britt dove for the gun. Lisa fell flaccid over the coffee table. And Raja went into hysterics. She raged, and cried, and spewed spit over Carlos. Charlie hesitated in the doorway with his gun raised, watching the blood trickling from Lisa's body onto the substantial Oriental rug. All was confusion and mayhem.

Pushing Raja back into her chair, Susan and Britt held her by her arms, pinning her down. Charlie moved toward Lisa, and roughly threw her body back onto the sofa, feeling for a pulse on her neck. Carlos very much wanted her alive. He shouted to Charlie, "What's her situation?"

"Get your fat fingers off my neck, you slob," Lisa spat in Charlie's face.

"Guess that answers your question, pardner. Well, lady you may be a horse doc, but you have no horse sense. You sure as hell screwed up every aspect of your life, and others' too. Some vet you turned out to be."

"Go screw yourself."

Charlie did not let up on her neck. He looked her over and said to Carlos, "It's her leg. Bleedin' like a stuck pig." Throughout all of this, Raja was still screaming and blubbering. She did not appear to be coherent.

Carlos leaned over her, lifted her bodily out of the chair, and looked her in the eye. His voice was as cold as Raja's heart. "Bernice. Snap out of it. NOW This is all part of your show"

The rescuers stared as Raja pulled herself loose, fell back into the chair, and became still as the air. No one moved as each waited to see what would happen next. Carlos was very much in control. "If you move, Bernice, one tiny muscle, you will be very very sorry. I have reached the end of my patience with you." His eyes bored into hers. Everyone could see her move her head, ever so slightly in assent.

"Lisa. You have some serious charges that will be brought up against you."

"You've got nothing on me," she said defiantly. "This is no big deal."

"Oh, I think you and Susan will have a great deal to discuss. The D.A.'s office loves to get you white-collar types. I, for one, will push very hard to make attempted murder, and kidnapping, stick all over you like tattoos. Oh…and murdering horses just got to be another big deal, along with mail fraud for shipping tainted semen. And maybe, just maybe, we'll get very lucky and find you guilty of several counts of mail fraud. Perhaps you even tried to collect on a phony insurance claim through the mail. Whatever I can find, I'll press. I'll dog you every step of the way I promise you, I will be your curse."

Charlie was doing a good job of keeping Lisa from jumping off the sofa to attack Carlos.

Britt had taken the gun and thrown it out into a snow bank, and Susan was writing something into a little book she had. She glanced at her watch.

"We've got a while before the squads can get here."

"Oh. We've got all the rest of the night to wait, if we have to," Carlos said.

Raja spoke, startling everyone, who had dismissed her in their minds. "I'll turn your case around. I'll help you get Lisa and put her away. I'm willing to make a deal. You need me."

"Excuse me?" Susan stammered.

"I have something to offer," she said.

"What could you offer me that I don't already have? I have attempted murder charges. Remember? I was there personally? And what would you want to save yourself from? I mean, what kind of a deal would be worth something to me? Raja, I want to take you down as far as I can." Susan was calm. In fact, Carlos had not seen her that calm…ever.

"I know how Tremor died, and why."

"That's not good enough. We know that, too."

"But I'll testify against Lisa. I'll be a star witness." Straining against Charlie, Lisa made another attempt at a lunge toward her accomplice.

"You just aren't that credible, Raja. Do something better for me," Susan said.

"Give me immunity." Raja was nervous. Her lip trembled. She looked at Lisa and said, "I know who killed Sasha." She was twisting the fabric of her stole.

"Don't start with the hysterics," Carlos interjected.

Lisa spat venom. "You spirit-communing bitch."

Raja stared blankly at Lisa. "I told you there would be more of your mistakes. I told you that you had screwed up, but you wouldn't listen. You underestimated, and undervalued me, Lisa. That is not excusable. I told you that you would get what you deserve. I will just help you get it quicker—and hopefully the punishment will be more harsh with my help."

Looking at Lisa, Susan said, "Come into the kitchen with me, Raja. We'll have a private talk. I'll call the D.A. after we chat and see what can be done."

CHAPTER 40

▼

The storm had died as quickly as it had come, and the day dawned like a jewel in the necklace of Minnesota's winter. Carlos looked at the blue shadows making patterns on the ground, noticing that even the still smoking empty crater that once was the proud cornerstone of Grande Glade was beautiful in its own way. The morning sun contributed to the sensation of happiness, and the muffled sounds in the snow made for a cathedral feeling of reverence. He and Susan were watching Britt trying to coax the remaining horses out of the woods. They still did not have a full head count, and all feared that several beautiful beasts had died in the flames. Still, a feeling of ease could be noticed in the faces of all players, except that of Lisa. She was becoming more bitter with each passing hour.

They all had waited until the plows could clear the roads for the sheriff's department to arrive. Warmth, food, and relief from tension had revived them all so they could be patient for the sun and help.

"There's still a lot of hard work ahead of us," Susan said as she tipped her head up to see Carlos's face.

"Who exactly is the 'us'?" he replied.

"Of course, the D.A.'s office, me, whatever lawyers I can get to work on this. There'll be a long time before this gets to trial…to conviction."

"Oh." He stared at the embers of the barn.

"What did you think I meant?" Susan asked encircling her arm into his.

"I wondered if you were talking about us. You know, you and me."

Susan, tired as she was, laughed. Carlos was uncertain what that meant, but relationships and communication skills were not his strong suit. She could tell he was at a loss.

"I'd rather not do too much talking about us, Mr. Investigator." "Oh." It was all he could manage.

Still smiling, she said, "I was thinking more of action."

Carlos whirled around to face her. "Are you teasing with me?"

"No. But let's get some rest…and then see what happens. I want you to know I am open to…possibilities. I think things have changed for me with you after this case. I wanted you to know that. There are possibilities."

"Maybe being a loner isn't all that I thought or hoped it to be," Carlos thoughtfully said. He pursed his lips as he rummaged his mind.

She was looking at him, waiting.

He glanced at her. She was dishevelled, smudged, and still wearing her hunting jacket. She looked the best he had ever seen her. Susan still smiled, and leading him by the arm, turned him away from the devastation. They viewed the police cars littering the drive, and saw Charlie directing traffic. He was wearing his navy parka and cheap dark stocking cap. His pant legs were haphazardly falling over his old fur-topped boots. He was making sure their two prisoners were well secured and taken downtown. Charlie waved to the two of them as he importantly got into the sheriff's maroon car. They both laughed as the sirens went on. Charlie was in his heaven, and things didn't look too bad for them, either.

EPILOGUE

▼

"Welcome to the Minneapolis, Minnesota, United States Courthouse. The District Attorney's Office solved the Minnesota horse murders as well as a thirty-year-old Florida car bombing…"

Carlos looked up from his newspaper as he sat perched behind the potted plant in the atrium lobby. The gaggle of forty or so tourists was oblivious to his presence as it hung on every word of the tour guide who was shepherding the group toward the public elevators. If Susan was thinking, she would have taken the private elevator; otherwise she would certainly be faced with about a half-hour of questions and autographs. No matter. It gave Carlos more time to read all the summaries of the last month's events. It was hard for him to believe a year had gone by since the whirlwind of deaths, storms, and fire.

Carlos had been busy since those wild February days investigating smaller cases. Of course, each horse death was never small to him, but he had classified those horses that were worth under ten thousand dollars as smaller. There had been difficult deaths to trace, but nothing like the nova of Tremor's case. He shook his head in a gesture of resignation. Horses worth less than ten thousand dollars didn't generate the enthusiasm for investigation by insurance companies. Carlos pitied those "poor" horses that had no one to advocate for them, but the insurance claims people would much rather pay out than go to the trouble or money to hire someone to carry out a proper investigation. At least Tremor's death shattered apart other unsolved cases.

The timing of Tremor's murder coincided with the brutal killings of more than thirty wild horses that were used for target practice in Reno, Nevada, and that fueled a media frenzy that lasted for months. The wild horses died torturous deaths after being shot in the gut or hind legs with high-powered rifles, and being left to suffer in the desert foothills. It was horrific for the veterinarian in Nevada. Yet the massacre brought more national attention to the calloused killing of horses. The nation as a whole was shocked.

The Nevada investigation treated the deaths as if they were human homicides, and therefore, more focus was placed on the case of Raja and Lisa—not only regarding the death of Tremor, but other killings as well. Court TV rolled into town to cover Raja's trial, since her confession to collusion in the murder of Podsky led to the resolution of the circumstances behind the thirty-year-old death of a champion Florida horsewoman. The unsolved details of that case had become a part of mob folklore, ranking with JFK's alleged dalliances with Giancana's mistresses.

Podsky had worked for the intended victim in that case. The young horsewoman just happened to be in the wrong place at the right time, caught in the midst of a blood feud between two prominent brothers. Raja's testimony revealed that the woman had not been the intended victim in the car bombing. She had simply borrowed one of the feuding brother's Cadillacs to run an errand.

Over the years Raja had kept contact with the hit man who had been her young lover at the time of the bombing. When she finally was fed up with Podsky, it was a simple matter to have her old paramour plant a bomb under the hood of Podsky's car. He was willing to try to please his former mistress again, but most especially, he liked the way her money looked. It was quick and dirty to use dynamite, and required no sophistication.

It was that little detail that sold Raja's confession to Susan, allowing Raja to become a protected federal witness. The media had reported all along that the bomber had used plastic explosives. Raja's ex-lover had handled his car bombing the old-fashioned way...with dynamite. No one but the bomber or his accomplices knew that detail.

Raja, it turned out, was a walking encyclopedia of information regarding the horse underworld. Her profession may have been otherworldly, but no one could have guessed that her true ties were with the dark side. Her confessions cleaned up half of the unsolved horse murders that were cluttering Susan's database. Carlos remembered the time the two of them sat at her computer and closed out case after case just by using Raja's information. Carlos kicked himself at having been duped like so many others with Raja's act of complete innocence...no...naivete. No one thought she had much of a brain for anything, much less horse sense.

Unfortunately, the bomber was still unaccounted for, having blended into the seamless underbelly of the horse world's travelling shows and circuses. Raja's daughter, Kate, had vanished by the same route, but the D.A. decided it wasn't worth the time or money to pursue battery and kidnapping charges against her. Flyers were posted in customs booths around the U.S. for them both. It was enough for now.

Horses touched a nerve with everyone, especially if the public perceived torture was involved. The uproar was so great that even Oprah featured interviews on horse issues for the duration of the trial. The news desks on radio and television worked every detail over and over each day. Carlos was pleased to see the continuing horse-consciousness in the media. Perhaps more people would become advocates for the horses…perhaps more people would take better care of their own animals.

The wife of the state's newly elected governor was a local horsewoman like her predecessor, and her sympathies toward horses brought more attention to equine cruelty. The Oprah discussions regarding horses, and interviews with people who had been victims of insurance scams, added more local color. It helped people to grasp the enormity of the horse business and put a face on those who were willing to let people and animals suffer for their own profit. Lisa's and Raja's trials consumed the Star Tribune for months. Local gossip in any restaurant or mall usually drifted toward something equine.

Channel Seven finally completed its exposé on killing horses for the insurance money. Cindi Moreno received kudos for her risky behavior to get the best scoop in town. They even showed her in pictures with Tremor, in happier days. Ironically Tremor hadn't been killed for the insurance money, as everyone had initially suspected. Of course, Carlos and Susan had come to that conclusion before everyone else, having realized that his death was a financial millstone; he was woefully underinsured for the depth of his loss. The lack of insurance fraud motivation to Tremor's killing almost blew the lead elements of the TV story, but there was enough that came out in the trial to show that horse insurance scams were a lucrative industry.

Lloyd's of London did pay out the full policy to Tremor's owners, since there was no foul play on their part. Carlos was glad to see that Raja did not collect on the barn fire. Having witnesses to the act of arson pulled the plug on any question of accidental fire. Part of him still grieved for the three horses that were killed, as well as for the surviving ones, which had suffered irreversible psychic trauma.

Murdering a horse wasn't a federal crime, but it damn well should be, Carlos thought as he read another story. However, Susan was able to use the RICO laws to get Raja and Lisa on racketeering, mail fraud, and kidnapping charges. Carlos had been astonished to discover that Lisa and Kate had driven him across the state line to Wisconsin while he was in the car trunk. It was a bonus for making a stronger case against Lisa, however. Lisa was also charged with three counts of attempted murder.

Raja's murder charge was reduced in return for information she provided on the Florida horse mafia, although everyone doubted that the witness protection program would do her much good. The mafia had a way of taking care of people whose loyalty faltered. In the end, it would be difficult, if not impossible, for Raja to save her own skin. Surprisingly, Carlos had no feelings about this, knowing that in the end justice had triumphed. Raja would have to live, and perhaps die, according to the laws she had set in motion. He was beginning to understand that he could try his best to bring justice to bear in cases he was involved in, but in the larger scheme of things, justice took care of itself. He would continue to do his best and let the rest unfold. He found a certain internal peace with this thought.

The American Horse Show Association stripped Raja and Kate, in absentia, of all rights and privileges. The two women were identified as having participated in a plan or conspiracy to commit acts of cruelty and abuse to a horse. The Association, in its dour lack of hyperbole, accused the trio of "unsportsmanlike conduct," since it was likely that electrocution would cause pain and suffering to a horse. The exact citation read that "evidence presented at the hearings established that death by electrocution causes pain to the horse." Carlos mused about how anti-climactic that statement was, considering all he had been through trying to get the horse killer…and considering what T emor had suffered.

Randolph Decker, the silent partner in Tremor's ownership, had finally been located on an archaeological dig in Israel. He had had little contact with the outside world for weeks. When he found out that he was part owner of a famous horse, and a dead one at that, he was horrified. He preferred keeping an obscure profile, not wanting to advertise his millions of dollars or the investments his advisors made for him. Susan's people had tracked him through his corporation, which held the title to the Florida houseboat that served as his U.S. residence. Decker issued a statement expressing his condolences to those who had suffered in the circumstances surrounding T emor's death, and disappeared again.

Charlie Branson's prominent appearances on the Oprah segments earned him some connections in Hollywood. He ultimately gave up his career as a local private eye to host an L.A.-based talk show on home security. It pleased Carlos, because he was getting pretty fed up with Charlie's calls to his new "pardner" soliciting more work. L.A. was the perfect place for him to move, and the consummate venue for his inflated sense of importance.

The unfortunate death of Fiona Andersson, late wife of the previous governor, was officially ruled an accident. Carlos thought of how long he and Susan had puzzled over her bizarre electrocution, trying to nail down a reason why someone—anyone—might want her dead. It was with great reluctance, and some dissatisfaction, that they had to remind themselves that sometimes what looks suspiciously like an accident really is just an accident. Carlos noted with some pleasure, though, that Raja faced a civil suit from Fiona's children and husband for negligence after the federal trial wrapped. It was evident Raja would have to sell the house and land at Grande Glade in order to pay for her trial costs and the judgment the Anderssons were sure to receive. The spa was already in receivership.

According to the article Carlos was reading, Lisa not only would face sentencing for kidnapping and attempted murder on top of the RICO indictments, but her veterinary license had been permanently revoked by the state licensing board. But, of course, he already knew that had happened. His inside sources were always helpful. Meanwhile, the developers had begun to devour Falling Oak Farms. It was the only way Lisa could fund her legal expenses. Carlos regretted the demise of such a beautiful facility and surrounding land.

That meant Sally's barn was the only facility left in the river valley. How long she could survive before zoning changes brought commercial interests to the corridor was anyone's guess. Carlos hoped a good long time. Meanwhile, Carlos knew her business was thriving with Britt's help. They had added fifteen new stalls as word spread about Britt's heroism in the barn fire. That, combined with Sally's down-to-earth honesty and low-key approach, drew a lot of horse owners to Sally's horse haven.

Ken recovered nicely from his injuries and was hired by the Equine Disease Quarterly to edit an issue devoted entirely to equine viral arteritis. Lloyd's of London, which published the journal, wanted to make a point about the rationale for greater control of EVA. By using data banks going back as far as 1984, Ken was able to establish the importance of the carrier stallion in the spread of EVA.

That may have been Tremor's greatest legacy, Carlos thought. His case brought worldwide attention to the fact that seropositive stallions shed EVA constantly in their semen and transmit it whether they breed by natural or artificial means. What a shame that such a trusting, marvelous stallion had contracted the virus from Lisa's Dutch Warmblood. It was such a mindless, stupid waste. But this case was rife with seemingly pointless actions that resulted in unaccountable loss.

What especially galled Carlos was that with some careful management, disclosures, and the use of immunized mares, Tremor might have been able to continue his breeding. He might have even been one of those lucky stallions that spontaneously stopped shedding the virus. Who could tell? No one, of course, would ever know now. Lisa and Podsky had panicked. Carlos kept coming back to the fact that this disease could have been managed. If only...how did that saying go...if wishes were horses, beggars would ride. Carlos had a lot of horses he wished he still could ride.

Even after all these months, Carlos was not certain he could grasp the malignant effect all this craziness had had on all these people. Death, scheming, loss of land and facility all for greed and the massaging of little self-important human egos. Thinking of the positive aspects buoyed him, however, and he concentrated on those. Horses were being noticed and viewed differently Britt and Sally were successful beyond their wildest dreams. His knee, after surgery, had healed nicely. He was running and riding again. The greatest positive aspect was his ability to give up certain aspects of being a loner...with pleasure. In fact, a great deal of pleasure.

Looking up again, Carlos saw that the tourists and their guide had just disappeared into one bank of elevators. Another door opened, and Susan hopped out on one foot, trying to put on her stiletto heels as she walked across the granite floor. Carlos beamed. His dark handsome face glowed with an inner light. His tall frame unfolded as he stood up and opened his arms wide. Susan came directly into them. They stood together in the cold granite lobby of the Federal Building, exuding warmth. People looked and smiled as they passed.

At last the two of them turned toward the doors. Rios was waiting for them.

978-0-595-38299-6
0-595-38299-1

Made in the USA
Lexington, KY
08 April 2013